Spiritual Warfare

in the

New Covenant

T M Leszko

Merging Streams Media

mergingstreamsmedia.com

Spiritual Warfare in the New Covenant

www.mergingstreamsmedia.com

ISBN: 978-0-9959520-2-7 softcover book

ISBN: 978-0-9959520-3-4 electronic book

DEDICATION

To my Lord and Savior Jesus Christ; the most faithful friend anyone could ever hope to know.

Once again, I want to extend my sincerest thanks to Ruth, Nicole and Jon. Your help in every phase of this project was greatly appreciated.

Table of Contents

Foreword

At the Wiedrick home, our family has the joy of watching a 53 inch, large screen, rear projection TV. Since it is 15 years old, the picture quality is relatively poor, and it could be officially considered an antique!

Occasionally, maybe at a friend's house, I have the opportunity to watch a brand new, state of the art, flat screen, HD television whose picture is so sharp and crystal clear that it is breathtaking!

Sometimes, it's like that with our theology. Without realizing it, we can have an outdated, fuzzy view on a given topic, which years ago may have been "cutting edge" but now is drastically in need of updating and fine-tuning.

In his well-written book, *Spiritual Warfare in the New Covenant*, T M Leszko takes us on a journey through the Bible, bringing balance and clarity to this very important subject.

In a very practical, yet, scholarly way, T M leads us through a systematic exploration of spiritual warfare from its earliest history in Genesis, through to its fuller New Testament expression, right up to and including the book of Revelation.

Along the way, he addresses some of the excesses and imbalances that have been a part of the spiritual warfare movement. While exposing some of the extreme (and possibly dangerous) positions we've seen, he also brings into the foreground some of the more neglected aspects of this topic.

What is the Old Testament precedent for spiritual warfare? How has that changed in the New Testament? How does spiritual warfare relate to the Great Commission? How do I practically walk out a balanced expression of spiritual warfare as a New Testament believer?

These are some of the topics that are covered from chapter to chapter. I especially recommend the section on "The Armor of God," which is one of the most well-researched and excellent treatments of this subject I have ever read!

As brothers-in-law, over the years, Terry and I have had many discussions, debates, and disagreements concerning theology. As Bible teachers, ours is truly a relationship where "iron sharpens iron." Sometimes, we would end our conversations by simply agreeing to disagree.

But in this book, I have to say I am in full agreement with every premise he brings forward.

If you are serious about coming into greater alignment with the Word of God in this area, I would challenge you to read this book! I believe you will agree with me that
T M Leszko scores a victory!

Dennis Wiedrick

Wiedrick & Associates Apostolic Ministries

1Contend, Lord, with those who contend with me; fight against those who fight against me. 2Take up shield and armor; arise and come to my aid.

3Brandish spear and javelin3 Or and block the way against those who pursue me. Say to me, "I am your salvation." Psalms 35:1-3

Mighty Fortress is our God (3rd stanza)

And though this world, with devils filled,
Should threaten to undo us,
We will not fear, for God hath willed
His truth to triumph through us:
The Prince of Darkness grim,
We tremble not for him;
His rage we can endure,
For lo! his doom is sure,
One little word shall fell him (Martin Luther).

Introduction

This book is not what is typically expected from readers on the subject of spiritual warfare. As a backdrop to the subject matter, I have taken the approach of providing a historical narrative as told in the Bible. The chronological use of biblical history is for the purpose of showing the spiritual realm and the ongoing war between the kingdom of God and the kingdom of darkness. That timeline will be separated into three stages or eras. It will take us from Genesis to Revelation and bring us to our present day. We will examine how mankind is affected by the warfare in the heavenly places as Paul described it and how that world translates into the natural realm. The first stage is the world out of covenant with its Creator. We will look to Scripture to reveal what was happening in heaven, on the earth, and the transitional spiritual realm known as the heavenly places. We will then move on to the Old Covenant era and use this same format to track Israel as a nation and the spiritual dynamics that came into play during that era under the Law of Moses leading up to the coming of the

Messiah. All roads past, present, and future go through Jesus, and it will be at this crossroad of human history that everything will change. We will focus on what Jesus accomplished for us through the cross and what His victory means for us in the New Covenant. Those new realities are brought to bear on the spiritual realm and we will learn how everything was forever changed by King Jesus.

Within that backdrop, we will then look at the differences of how warfare was conducted in the realm of the spirit during those three stages of mankind. The New Covenant is the world that we as believers live in; therefore, it will be through the teachings of our Lord Jesus and the apostolic writings that we will establish our foundation of understanding.

In our mind's eye, we see the images of war in all its violence and bloodshed with horrific losses to man and machine. But is that how war appears in the realm of the spirit? Contrary to those images, the scriptures will show us a completely different type of war that occurs in the spirit and that knowledge will be important for us, in the here and now. We will examine and track the enemy's tactics throughout the ages with the purpose of making the believer aware of how the demonic realm operates. Those revealed tactics, enable us not to be ignorant of his plans and schemes and help to prevent us from being ensnared by his devices. We will then discuss the weapons and armor of our warfare and how we engage the enemy on the ground of the Lord's choosing.

In each stage, we will see the dynamics of the spiritual realm and how the landscape of spiritual warfare is affected on the earth and with mankind. If history is not your thing, I ask that you persevere through the early chapters because they will prove to be an important backdrop of understanding as we move into the New Covenant. I have also purposely added complete scripture passages as opposed to just adding the verse that I want to highlight. I have done this so the context of the subject matter is clearly visible to the reader. This may seem like laborious reading to some, but it is necessary because so many Christians today are confused about the differences between the two covenants and how they are affected by them. Once we are firmly entrenched in the New Covenant, we will review the teachings of Jesus on the subject and look carefully at how He modeled warfare for us. I trust that it will lead us to know how masterfully the Lord Jesus brought forth His redemptive victory and the restoration of all that God had originally intended for mankind.

In breaking down biblical history into three eras, we can examine more accurately what is taking place during each time period. It will reveal to us the distinct differences between the two covenants and how the spiritual realm is affected by the terms of those legal agreements. All of this is done for the purpose of helping you, the reader, to be more effective in your warfare through prayer and your testimony of Jesus to the world.

The military has a name for bombs that do not explode when fired. The term they use is, "unexploded ordinance" or UXO, for short. I think it can be safe to say that at times, the church has experienced an unexploded ordinance problem (UXO) as it relates to spiritual authority. Our prayer and intercession have often times produced fruit that was far less than what was believed for. We seem to be firing one dud after another and wonder why and who is to blame for this lack of explosive power.

We have failed to realize that this comes from trying to live under two covenants at the same time. A common belief is that a person's works of uprightness or the lack thereof, are the reasons those shells do not explode. Those beliefs are based on an Old Covenant thinking of what righteousness is and how it is attained. In the New Covenant, it is based solely on the fact that we are the righteousness of God in Christ Jesus, which is founded on grace through faith. Satan will always keep you under accusation to weaken your confidence in God and that is like emptying your shell of its explosive power. You cannot put an Old Covenant firing mechanism on a New Covenant shell that is designed for a precision-guided weapon and expect New Covenant results. They may have similarities in appearance but their capabilities are as extreme as night and day.

When you understand who you are in Christ and what has been given to you through Him, you will find yourself properly armed for battle with His state of the art weapons. My hope is that this book will serve in training you to learn how to use those weapons and understand the tactics of spiritual war so that you can wage a good warfare and see your day of victory in Him.

> *Timothy, my son, I am giving you this command in keeping with the prophecies once made about you, so that by recalling them you may fight the battle well* (1Timothy 1:18).

Chapter 1

WORDS

Words. Not just any words — believed words. Not just any believed words but believed words, which become the core thought process in a person's life that leads to and produces action. You may be saying to yourself, "I thought this is a book about spiritual warfare?" Be assured — it is just that. We will see throughout this book that the projectiles fired from the weapons of our warfare are these most powerful, believed words.

I would like to show you a different perspective as we peer behind the veil of the symbolic clash of swords and look directly at what is actually taking place in the realm of the spirit. The weaponry depicted in scripture gives us a picture of the tools of warfare. But what is really happening behind the imagery? If we were looking at the time displayed on a Swiss watch and I opened its clock face, it would reveal all of the inner moving pieces. We would see an assortment of levers, gears, and springs that make up over 100 working parts. We marvel at the craftsmanship and design when we see that so much can be fitted into such a small space of a wristwatch and we never give it a second thought.

What if we were to look behind the veil of our humanity and gaze into the realm of the soul and spirit? Similarly, if we looked behind that clock face to see our inner being and the things that make us tick, what would we see? It too would reveal a host of working and living parts but I submit to you that those gears and working parts are made up of an entire life of believed words. Words that you have believed about yourself and believed words that have come from every facet of your life's experience. Words that your parents have said about you, words from family, friends, and enemies. Taught words from schoolteachers and professors, religious leaders, pastors, and other authority figures in your life. Written words, lyrics from music, words from movies, social media, and news media, they all play a part in shaping our thoughts creating within us our held beliefs.

Those believed words whether they are good or bad become a part of the unseen inner workings of our lives. Just like those watch parts, they set in motion the watch and direct its function. Similarly, James wrote in his epistle that words act like the rudder of a ship steering the course of our lives. For this reason, believed words carry so much importance for the believer in every area of life and are key battlegrounds in our spiritual warfare. Whoever wins over an area of belief will define who they are and direct their paths to future victories or defeats.

When we put bits into the mouths of the horses to make them obey us, we can guide the whole animal. Consider ships as well. Although they are so large and are driven by strong winds, they are steered by a very small rudder wherever the pilot is inclined. In the same way, the tongue is a small part of the body, but it boasts of great things. Consider how small a spark sets a great forest on fire (James 3:3-5).

The good man brings good things out of the good treasure of his heart, and the evil man brings evil things out of the evil treasure of his heart. For out of the overflow of the heart, the mouth speaks (Luke 6:45).

When those beliefs are articulated in the words that we speak, they release a creative force in our lives and like the internal parts of that watch, it goes to work fulfilling its designed function. (We will go into greater detail on this subject in later chapters of this book).

So, what would we see if we looked beyond the surface of the imagery of spiritual battle? Would we really see a clash of swords by spiritual beings fighting in an armed conflict? I am certain that we all readily accept that Jesus did not actually have a physical two-edged sword in His mouth. There is no doubt that we view this as symbolic imagery indicating the authority and power of His words. Furthermore, spirit beings such as angels and demons are not wielding swords at each other as if somehow, they can create wounds in one another or kill one another. The real weapons of war in the realm of the spirit as manifested in the image of the sword in the mouth of our Lord or held in the hand of angels, reveal to us that the weapons of war in spiritual battles are words and the authority backing those words.

"Words. Not just any kind of words — believed words."

Edward Bulwer-Lytton in 1839 coined the phrase: "*The pen is mightier than the sword.*" He wrote those famous words to imply that thoughts and ideas were greater than physical strength and battle. Was he correct? Or would it be more correct to say, "*Believed words and ideas are mightier than the sword*" or that "*Believed words are in fact, the sword*"? The pen is a mere conveyance to put into words what one believes. The sword in the Lord's mouth conveys this same thought. It is at this very point of believed words that the entire created world exists after being spoken into being by Jesus. Not only was creation brought about by words spoken by God, but also, the universe is held together by the word of His power.

> *On many past occasions and in many different ways, God spoke to our fathers through the prophets. But in these last days He has spoken to us by His Son, whom He appointed heir of all things, and through whom He made the universe.*
>
> *The Son is the radiance of God's glory and the exact representation of His nature, upholding all things by His powerful word* (Hebrews 1:1-3a).

As believers, we recognize that the unseen is responsible for all that is seen; furthermore, it is the unseen that holds everything in place. We know that this is none other than the Lord Jesus, but to the world of science and physics, the question of what holds atoms together remains an ongoing mystery. I am going to take you on a brief side road from this subject of spiritual warfare, and I assure you, it will all make sense in the end.

The world of physics was forever changed by the theories of Albert Einstein and Niels Bohr. Their research on the subject of Quantum Theory and their debates with one another in the 1930's created a revolution of understanding in the field known as Quantum Mechanics.

Let me share a few of their quotes with you on the subject: *"Reality is merely an illusion, albeit a very persistent one"* (Albert Einstein).

"Everything we call real is made of things that cannot be regarded as real" (Niels Bohr).

"Once you can accept the universe as matter expanding into nothing that is something, wearing stripes with plaid comes easy" (Albert Einstein).

"If quantum mechanics hasn't profoundly shocked you, you haven't understood it yet" (Niels Bohr).

"Time is an illusion" (Albert Einstein).

Quantum theory is the theoretical basis of modern physics that explains the nature and behavior of matter and energy on the atomic and subatomic level. The nature and behavior of matter and energy at that level is sometimes referred to as quantum physics and quantum mechanics.

The debate was simple and mind-blowing in complexity at the same time. At its base was their theory that everything that is visible comes from the invisible atomic and subatomic level. So a question raised would be, "Is the moon still a moon when it is no longer seen?" Or is it simply a mass of atomic particles that comes into focus when viewed through the lens of the eye?

I know, I know, it's beginning to sound like the philosophical question of "if a tree falls in the forest..." But this question was so important because atoms, at their core structure, do not want to stay together and so, what is holding them in place? Furthermore, the debate brought to the forefront the unseen world as the true power or force behind the seen or created world.

Einstein thought that Bohr's theory was an impossibility because there had to be substance to that perceived world. The moon had to tangibly exist; it could not simply appear as substance when looked upon, but he had no answer as to what holds the atoms together. You may be surprised to know that in the decades that followed to this present time, Niles Bohr's theory is holding up under both experimental lab trials and academic scrutiny, while Einstein's arguments against Bohr's theories have not been able to prove themselves out over time on this issue. The scientific studies of recent decades have to their astonishment validated many aspects of Bohr's interpretation of Quantum Mechanics, which is called the Copenhagen Interpretation. His theories are still the most widely taught on this subject in our universities. It was mind-boggling to those atomic scientists using Bohr's theories because it made no sense; yet, it worked. A phrase coined by David Merman, "shut up and calculate" became the slogan of the era and the research continued. It was from that determined mindset that we are now witnessing technological developments and advancements at an unprecedented rate in our history. If Quantum Physics would give Jesus His due, we would then see that Einstein's assertions were correct, atomic matter does become a solid because it is Jesus who holds it all together.

Also along this train of thought, we find that the world of mathematics comes into play validating the theories of Quantum Mechanics. In a recent PBS documentary that is part of the *Nova* series, a physics professor from MIT brought forth the theory that all creation equates to mathematic sequence and formula. In the episode titled, "Is God a Mathematician," he likens the universe to a video game. The sophistication of a game's movement, color, reaction to command and choice are all controlled by its programmed numerical sequence and equations. In other words, if you looked behind the video's image, it would reveal a mass of numbers, numeric codes, and mathematical equations creating the experience that you, the player are creating by directing the game with its keypad or joystick.

We could discuss at length how the Italian mathematician named Leonardo Fibonacci developed a numerical sequence that ties the created universe together to a perfect order. From things in the heavens to things on earth and in the sea, from galaxies to flower petals and seashells all hold within it a perfect numerical sequence. That is the brilliance and the genius of our God and no detail is too small or insignificant and in His eyes — neither are you. If these things are created for our pleasure, how much more important is the smallest detail and need in your life to God. You were in His heart when He made these things and gave them as a love gift designed for you. So to answer the astrophysicist Mario Livio, who titled his book, *Is God a Mathematician?* I can answer him with an emphatic "Yes!"

The world of science is all about language; computer software is a language; mathematics is a language, and physics has a language of its own. It was Galileo Galilei who stated, *"Nature is a book written in the language of mathematics."* In fact, all of the sciences carry with them an interpretive language. The same can be said in the spiritual realm of the kingdom of God. There is a prophetic language of dreams and visions as well as a scriptural language of truth, history, parables, allegory, and symbolism. The scriptures provide for us the core interpretive language for all of these languages that are given by the Spirit of God.

For instance, if the book of Revelation was written in our day, we might see a weaponized laser that is represented in the Lord's mouth, instead of a sword. The symbolism creates a language of expressive thought that says more in its imagery than many written paragraphs. The world of physics and mathematics has been used to develop and create the most fearful weapons the world has ever known, leading Einstein to say,

"The release of atomic power has changed everything except our way of thinking ... the solution to this problem lies in the heart of mankind. If only I had known, I should have become a watchmaker. (1945)" - Albert Einstein

The Lord has made it clear to us through His imagery that His words, backed by His authority are truly the most powerful force in the universe. He has given us His words to use as a force for good in the world and not evil.

Einstein helped to decrypt the language of atomic power and by doing so, he inadvertently helped to unleash a world of weaponry that could destroy all life on the planet. Little do the Quantum physicists and mathematicians realize that the road they are traveling on will eventually lead them (whether they like it or not) right into the path of Jesus. God created the sciences. God created mathematics and all its complexities. Math is not the creation of man; it was merely discovered by man but was in place from the beginning of creation. Something more powerful exists for those who are new creations in Christ because the God who holds all power and authority dwells in us. His heart is to make your words manifest His power when you act upon His Word and are led by His Spirit.

> *Truly, truly, I tell you, whoever believes in Me*
> *will also do the works that I am doing. He will*
> *do even greater things than these, because I*
> *am going to the* Father (John 14:12).

It can be argued that God has used His created sciences to be the conveyance for His creative release through words. The world of Quantum Mechanics might also just be the vehicle to explain the inner workings of how miracles occur. On the other hand, the science of Mathematics and Physics may well learn that this is nothing more than another law of the universe that is part of God's creative order yet undiscovered.

We relate to things in terms of our language when we imagine how God spoke during the six creation days. I feel quite assured to say that when Jesus spoke those words at creation, He did not speak English. Neither was it Hebrew, Aramaic, Greek, Latin or any language that was the result of what took place at the tower of Babel. It might have been that first language that was broken up at Babel, which probably would have been the language that Adam originally spoke and, therefore, it was a language from heaven. I wonder if on the day of Pentecost as described in the book of Acts if the language of heaven, otherwise known as speaking in tongues, was the restoration of that first language that was spoken in the garden of Eden. Remember, it was not just the Galileans speaking earthly languages on that day, for we are told that it was with tongues of men and angels.

Here is something else to ponder: did Jesus use the language of Mathematics and Physics as the language of creation? God created the sciences, did He not? I remember as a teenager reading about a poll that was taken on university campuses, which asked the question, "Does God understand radar?" The answer was overwhelmingly, no. This was as absurd to me then as it is now, that the God who created all things, supposedly did not understand the sciences, but instead, He operates from some supernatural magic up His sleeve to do miracles and science is beyond Him. A poll such as this reveals what an ignorant perception the world holds in their understanding and theology about the intelligence of God.

So why is this important to this discussion on spiritual warfare? The reason is this: everything in war and peace will find its root in believed and spoken words. It is from this foundational base of believed words that power is released to set in motion the creative forces that can affect the earth, or on a personal level, affect your life. When God spoke the created order into being, He spoke from a posture of believed words. He had no doubt that what He said would come to pass. In like manner, what we believe is released through what we speak and those believed words will find themselves aligning with either God or the Devil. Like a magnet, those believed words will join or align themselves with spiritual power. Each believed word is like an atom that comes together with other atoms of believed words and eventually, they will manifest into reality in the natural realm.

Your dreams and goals are important to God. He is good to all even to those who do not know Him. When the apostle Paul spoke in Lystra, he alerted the people to the fact that it is God, who is the source of all blessings,

> *In past generations, He let all nations go their own way. Yet He has not left Himself without testimony to His goodness: He gives you rain from heaven and fruitful seasons, filling your hearts with food and gladness* (Acts 14:16, 17).

Just as God is watching over His word to bring it to fulfillment, it is because of His kindness and mercy that He seeks to bring to completion the good, faith-filled words that people speak over their own lives. Yes, even those who do not know Him are not far from His gracious lovingkindness as Paul said. For it is a testimony to all people of the goodness of God.

There is yet one more language that will make up another important key in the realm of spiritual warfare; some call it "legalese." I was surprised when I began to look closely into the Hebrew and Greek words relating to the scriptures that focused on warfare that there was an undeniable legal language inferred. Translated words into English were more often than not, words that carried a strong legal emphasis. These are not the everyday words used by Jews or Greeks to convey their thoughts; they were words that carried in them legal implication as words that are used in courtroom arguments and trials. This legal language will reveal itself through the scriptures as the authorization to use force and make a legal declaration of war by both kingdoms. God is a God who makes covenant, which is at its core understanding, a legal treatise.

In warfare, whoever controls the high ground controls the field of battle. In terms of spiritual warfare, what you believe and speak forth from a right legal standing, determines which kingdom controls that high ground.

It is for that reason that we will begin this study in the book of Genesis and follow it through to Revelation using biblical history as the timeline. Through the three stages of civilization, we will see the shift of powers in their rise and fall. We will see how mankind faced their world through the lens of both the seen and unseen. We will then cover what it means for us who live in the New Covenant, bringing us to a present and future peace, leading to a world without war.

Chapter 2

IN THE BEGINNING...

In the beginning was the Word, and the Word was with God, and the Word was God. He was with God in the beginning. Through Him all things were made, and without Him nothing was made that has been made. In Him was life, and that life was the light of men. The Light shines in the darkness, and the darkness has not overcome it (John 1:1-5).

"If we were to look beyond the veil of all things, we would see that its DNA is comprised of words from the very one who is the Living Word."

The Son is the image of the invisible God, the firstborn over all creation. For in Him all things were created, things in heaven and on earth, visible and invisible, whether thrones or dominions or rulers or authorities. All things were created through Him and for Him. He is before all things, and in Him all things hold together (Colossians 1:15-17).

As we explore the subject matter of this book, no words will prove to be more important to the act of spiritual warfare than those that are found in John's opening remarks of his gospel. Those words are, in fact, the battle plan of the kingdom of God, and they will reveal to us the essence of God's truth on this subject.

This book is about words that are infused by the power of God, spoken with the authority of God, which release the light of His glory that expels the darkness. Jesus is the Word; it is by the words He spoke that all things came into existence. Astronomy declares that the universe is still expanding. As Christians, we know that it continues to do so because of the words of God's unceasing creative power. If we peel back the veneer of all creation, if we were to look beyond the veil of all things, we would see that its DNA is comprised of words from the very One who is the Living Word.

When the symbolic imagery of all spiritual warfare is removed, we see that the sword coming out of the mouth of Jesus is, in fact, — His words. Our conquering hero, Jesus Christ the Righteous and the weapon He wields are none other than His spoken words, coming from the One who is the Living Word of God. His light expels the darkness and so our warfare will be summed up in making Him known and bringing the lost into that light. Evangelism is what every believer is called to do. It is our rallying call and our marching orders.

The First Man

When you think about it, the first man, Adam, was created in the image of God. He initially knew no sin and walked in perfect union with God. In his DNA was the same nature of his Father: no impure thoughts, no idle words; he was perfect and without sin. He had unbroken fellowship with God and would speak to Him from the inner man of his heart. He also talked to God face to face as they walked together in the cool of the day.

Adam was given authority by God over a planet to enjoy and steward on God's behalf; all of this began on a tract of land in Eden. The Lord would have backed man's authority with His mighty power if it was ever called upon and needed. Adam was using 100% of his mental capacity because there was no corruption degrading his mental faculties. Anything he said to God's creation, whether animal, mineral or vegetable responded to the creative authority and power given to him by God. If you pause and think about Jesus, whom Paul calls the last Adam, you will see someone who has complete authority over all of creation. The earthly life of Jesus as a man is a window into what Adam's world was like before he gave place to sin and transferred authority and rule to Satan.

So let's review what happened, what went wrong, and God's action plan to make it right. These lessons are for our instruction; for mankind's heritage was never meant to be absent of the honor, privilege, and birthright of being a child of God.

The Other in the Beginning...

I suppose if we are going to start somewhere, we may as well begin with the book of Genesis and the opening salvos of this war of the ages.

> *In the beginning God created the heavens and the earth. 2Now the earth was formless and empty, darkness was over the surface of the deep, and the Spirit of God was hovering over the waters* (Genesis 1:1, 2).

From the opening sentences, I would suggest to you that there is a vast eon of time between Genesis 1:1 and Genesis 1:2. I say this because of the description used that finds the earth in a state of being without form and empty or void. This is a Hebrew idiom and its phrase *tohubohu* translates as chaos, disorder, confusion, desolation or emptiness. In Paul's first letter to the Corinthians, we learn that God is not the author or originator of confusion or disorder and so we must conclude that this was not God's original state of creation. It was from that place that we find a planet that was in darkness and confusion and that we see God begin to bring His creative order into play and it begins with light.

It is here that the Gospel of John introduces that light as a person and that person is Jesus. The Lord is the Light and from Him comes all created light sources. It was through His words that creation took place and a planet was brought into creative order. He would then create man in His image and make him a ruler over this planet and over all of God's creation. This planet called Earth would become the contested ground and mankind would be the contested people.

So, if we assume that the earth, beautiful in its origin came to a catastrophic end and was left in utter desolation, then what could have happened? While these questions may never be fully understood by us here on the earth, we certainly are given the knowledge of who is at fault; it is our adversary. In examining the scriptural passages that reference Satan, they offer us some clues as to what happened.

Satan Cast Out of Heaven and Thrown Down to Earth

How you have fallen from heaven, morning star, son of the dawn!

You have been cast down to the earth, you who once laid low the nations! 13You said in your heart, "I will ascend to the heavens;

I will raise my throne above the stars of God; I will sit enthroned on the mount of assembly, on the utmost heights of Mount Zaphon. 14I will ascend above the tops of the clouds; I will make myself like the Most High." 15But you are brought down to the realm of the dead, to the depths of the pit (Isaiah 14:12-15).

Isaiah foretold the destruction of Babylon in Chapter 14 of his prophetic book and promised that Israel would be delivered from the clutches of this empire. They are told that they will one day see and mock this evil enemy when the future time of their defeat comes. Embedded in this passage as part of that taunting, is the picture of Babylon being likened to the casting down of Satan or Lucifer (the morning star) as he was once known before his fall.

It is a description of the utter pride of an empire and its ruler, which will mirror the prideful fall of Babylon's true spiritual ruler. Satan's desire was to have his own kingdom and make it as great as God's. He would form his kingdom to be like God's and, in fact, he would be the anti-God. In the New Testament, we read of the term "antichrist," and its definition carries the thought of one who sets himself up alongside the real Christ to oppose Him. You can see that the origin of Satan's plan is first revealed through this passage of scripture and will be a running trait of all that the Devil tries to reproduce. In the blindness of his pride, he failed to see that the power and splendor of his authority were given by God and could be removed by God should He choose to do so. Satan's corruption was exposed; he and every angel that chose to follow him were thrown out of heaven and were subsequently cast down to the earth. The Hebrew word *gada* that is translated for "cast down" paints a picture of a tree being chopped down; there is no talk of a war or even so much as a battle. It was merely a swift and sudden eviction.

To expand further on Satan's fall, the prophet Ezekiel delivers a similar word against an earthly king who unveils the true source of power within the city-state known as Tyre.

> *The word of the Lord came to me: 12"Son of*
> *man, take up a lament concerning the king of*
> *Tyre and say to him: 'This is what the*

Sovereign Lord says: 'You were the seal of perfection, full of wisdom and perfect in beauty. 13You were in Eden, the garden of God; every precious stone adorned you: carnelian, chrysolite and emerald, topaz, onyx and jasper,

lapis lazuli, turquoise and beryl. Your settings and mountings were made of gold; on the day you were created they were prepared.

14You were anointed as a guardian cherub, for so I ordained you.

You were on the holy mount of God; you walked among the fiery stones.

15You were blameless in your ways from the day you were created

till wickedness was found in you. 16Through your widespread trade

you were filled with violence, and you sinned. So I drove you in disgrace from the mount of God, and I expelled you, guardian cherub, from among the fiery stones. 17Your heart became proud on account of your beauty, and you corrupted your wisdom because of your splendor.

So I threw you to the earth (Ezekiel 28:11-17).

This passage describes Satan as being perfect or blameless before his fall. He is adorned with something that resembles an ephod except, it holds only nine stones instead of twelve.

From this ephod-like adornment, music comes forth. The word translated as "settings" is the Hebrew word *toph* that literally translates as a tambourine or timbrel. The throne room has in its description angels with trumpets, the twenty-four elders, and saints with harps and then we read of Lucifer being adorned with a percussive instrument. It certainly gives a picture of a musical spectacle with various colored gemstones reflecting the glory of God. There is a sentence used twice in this passage, which says: "You walked among the fiery stones." It creates the picture of something like the mother of all light shows. This is the picture of the throne of God as described in Revelation, Chapter 4.

> *At once I was in the Spirit, and I saw a throne standing in heaven, with someone seated on it. The One seated there looked like jasper and carnelian, and a rainbow gleaming like an emerald encircled the throne. Surrounding the throne were twenty-four other thrones, and on these thrones sat twenty-four elders clothed in white garments, with golden crowns on their heads. From the throne came flashes of lightning, and rumblings, and rolls of thunder. Before the throne burned seven torches of fire. This is the sevenfold Spirit of God. And before the throne was something like a sea of glass, as clear as crystal. In the center, around the throne, were four living creatures, covered with eyes in front and back* (Revelation 4:2-6).

For a moment, picture the scene in your mind's eye. The radiant glory of our God who is seated on the throne has the appearance of the colors jasper and ruby. Jasper can be orange, red or even shades of yellow. Ruby is an intense red in color. Our God is pictured like a fire radiating from His throne. Daniel in his vision of the throne of God sees a similar picture,

> As I looked, "thrones were set in place, and the Ancient of Days took his seat. His clothing was as white as snow; the hair of his head was white like wool. His throne was flaming with fire, and its wheels were all ablaze (Daniel 7:9).

A rainbow encircles this seat of all rule and power, and it is like an emerald as it glistens in the intense light of His glory. The crowns of gold are shimmering and the crystal glass is reflecting a prism-like splendor amidst the lightning and thunder of the presence of God. The seven torches blazing symbolize the awesome perfection of the Holy Spirit. Heaven's throne is a sight that has no words suitable to describe it. With colors defying description, it is no wonder the twenty-four elders cast their crowns before our Majesty in worship and adoration. Our God is an awesome God; He is awesome in His splendor!

This is what Lucifer witnessed as he served before the throne of God and was called the guardian cherub. *Strong's Concordance* reveals that the Hebrew word for guardian is *sakak*, which literally translates as "cover or overshadow." When I think about Satan's role in the throne room as a covering angel, it immediately takes my mind to the Ark of the Covenant. The scriptures teach us that the contents of Israel's tabernacle in the wilderness are a symbolic shadow of what is in place in heaven. Over the mercy seat of the Ark, which symbolizes God's throne, are two kneeling cherubim. They are facing each other, covering the throne with their wing tips touching and their heads are bowed in worship as they look upon the mercy seat, which symbolizes the true heart of God's rule.

1Hear us, Shepherd of Israel, you who lead Joseph like a flock. You who sit enthroned between the cherubim, shine forth (Psalms 80:1).

Lucifer would have been one of those two angels that covered the throne of God. Ezekiel's description in this passage certainly makes this argument and if that was so, then who was the other angel? The book of Daniel describes Michael the archangel as a ruling angel or prince angel. The Greek word describing "archangel" as written in the New Testament reveals that the root of this word is the Greek word *archos*. It is from this word that we get the word "arch," which is used to describe a canopy or a spanning over something or someone. The two angels' wings form an arch over the mercy seat, so it would certainly make one wonder if Michael the archangel was that other angel. No other angel is described in scripture that carries the same weight of authority that Lucifer once had. Furthermore, Michael is listed as the guardian of Israel in the book of Daniel.

> *At that time Michael, the great prince who protects your people, will arise. There will be a time of distress such as has not happened from the beginning of nations until then. But at that time your people—everyone whose name is found written in the book—will be delivered* (Daniel 12:1).

36

The book of Daniel lists Michael as just one in the rank of princes (Daniel 10:13) or archangels, but his authority is without question; it is of the highest order. My last comment before we return to the matter at hand is this: in the throne room described by John in his revelation, he gives no indication that angels are still covering the throne. Was that because the role of the covering cherub was removed as a result of Lucifer's fall or was he simply relating the view from his vantage point? In the sixth chapter of Isaiah, we read that seraphim angels hover over the throne room calling out to one another saying, *"Holy, Holy, Holy is the Lord Almighty, the whole earth is full of His glory"* as a thunderous ovation of praise in this awe- inspiring scene. The fact that David wrote in the Psalms describing the covering cherubs, prove in my mind that this is still the case. When we get to heaven, all of these wonderings and questions will be clearly revealed; for we will see it in its entire glorious splendor, first hand.

Nine precious stones in a setting of gold adorned Lucifer. In that brilliant light of the throne room, he too would have radiated the glory of God. He was created with a beauty and splendor and wisdom as one befitting his service before the Almighty God. All of it was stripped away and he was cast out of heaven. No longer a light bearer, now a fallen Satan whose name means adversary. He would forever be known as the enemy of God. It is staggering to the mind that Lucifer would have risked and lost all of this by being consumed with pride. It should serve as a warning to all of us how deceitfully intoxicating pride can be. We should be alert to it and live out our lives in humility before God.

This fallen angel would coerce and deceive a myriad of angels to join him in the belief that an alternate kingdom could be established. Satan believed it could be equal in its glory and like God's kingdom once it was formed. Teachings that present Satan as a conspirator trying to overthrow God in a war of rebellion do so with a complete lack of understanding of the All Mightiness of God. If the Devil had a million angels, the Lord could have created a hundred million more angels. There was no war, the Devil and those that followed him were cast down immediately in their treachery. This teaching of a war was taken from a verse in Revelation 12 and from that verse this doctrine has emerged. It is taken out of context and fails to recognize that in that verse, it is God who goes on the offensive through the ministry of Jesus as the proper stated context. (I offer a complete review of Revelation 12 in Chapter 11 of this book.)

Thrown out of heaven, Satan and the fallen angels with him are now left with the stark reality that they are without the presence of God and no longer able to experience God's glory. They are reduced to being fallen devils. Their dwelling is a realm of darkness, and they are destined for all eternity to a judgment in the lake of fire. In the rage of their misfortune, Satan seeks to destroy the earth and everything that was created for God's pleasure and those loved by Him. Was it that rage against early planet Earth that resulted in its utter ruins of darkness and left it immersed underwater? Again, one day, we will all know with certainty what the events that followed Satan's fateful fall were. In the meantime, we must deal with the fact that he is our adversary while we are here on the earth and not be ignorant of his schemes.

Chapter 3

THE CREATION OF MAN

B efore we enter this discussion on the creation of man, I want to clearly state that the story of Adam and Eve is neither a parable, an allegory, symbolic, a myth nor is it poetic license. They were real people and Adam was the first man. Jesus spoke of him as a real person and Paul the apostle stated that Adam was the first man in 1 Corinthians 15. In fact, Paul called Jesus the last Adam who reclaimed all that was lost by the first Adam. If Adam was merely a symbolic figure representing the sin of man then Jesus could have merely died symbolically to redeem man and complete the allegory. He could have spared Himself the horrible suffering and torture that He had to endure in the flesh. This, of course, was not the case, for Jesus did come in the flesh, He suffered, died and rose from the dead on the third day. I can assure you that Adam is grateful that He did.

A New Age of Enmity Begins

Therefore, in picking up where we left off, we see that Satan has now been cast out of heaven with his demonic minions that chose to believe his lies. His grand scheme to have a kingdom and his desire to be like God has one key flaw: he as an angelic being (albeit a fallen one) and is incapable of creating any form of beings entirely on his own. However, he can affect and subvert what has been created by God. In fact, the only uniquely creative claim he can make is that he is the father of lies. His kingdom is made up of beings that were created by God and are now fallen demonic spirits. His only prospect is to live out his delusional scheme in trying to mimic the kingdom of God. To do this, he must try to subvert more of God's creation and bring them under his rule. As Satan witnesses God's creative power at work on the earth during those six days of creation, he sees before him a new opportunity.

The third verse of the first chapter of Genesis continues with the description of that initial week of creation. Adam will be the first created son for earth's new start, and he will find himself immediately in the crosshairs of Satan. Adam was created a man fully developed physically and mentally, a perfect man — spirit, soul, and body. He was not an infantile mind needing to be nurtured like a child, but rather when God's life was breathed into him on the day of his creation he was a highly intelligent being. He was complete in knowledge of all things that were good without any defilement of knowledge from the perspective of evil. God had made the earth for mankind and presented it as a gift to Adam to be the steward of it in all its beauty and splendor. Satan has witnessed what God has created for man and he wants it for himself. He witnesses the relationship God has with man and he also covets that for himself. He will try once again to gain a kingdom and be worshiped. With that in mind, he plots to deceive and enslave Adam and in so doing, usurp God's authority and become the god of this world. The earth remains the Lord's; the minerals and resources of the planet are still God's assets; even the animals and livestock are the possessions of the God of Heaven.

By causing Adam to sin, Satan will break the relationship between man and God and create the same spiritual death he experienced when he rebelled against God. Furthermore, he will use the same temptations that brought about his own demise.

The Bloodless Coup

1Now the serpent was more crafty than any of the wild animals the Lord God had made. He said to the woman, "Did God really say, 'You must not eat from any tree in the garden'?"

2The woman said to the serpent, "We may eat fruit from the trees in the garden, 3but God did say, 'You must not eat fruit from the tree that is in the middle of the garden, and you must not touch it, or you will die.' "

4"You will not certainly die," the serpent said to the woman. 5"For God knows that when you eat from it your eyes will be opened, and you will be like God, knowing good and evil."

6When the woman saw that the fruit of the tree was good for food and pleasing to the eye, and also desirable for gaining wisdom, she took some and ate it. She also gave some to her husband, who was with her, and he ate it. 7Then the eyes of both of them were opened, and they realized they were naked; so they sewed fig leaves together and made coverings for themselves (Genesis 3:1-7).

Satan's strategy to subjugate mankind is found in this passage of scripture. He ushered in the defeat of mankind and enslaved humanity through this simple ploy. You will notice that is was not through combat that Satan succeeded in conquering man; it was through words. It is these same tactics he still uses to his advantage this very day.

3But I am afraid that as the serpent deceived Eve by his cunning, your thoughts will be led astray from a sincere and pure devotion to Christ (2 Corinthians 11:3).

Adam's fall and the surrender of his rule on the earth remind me of the fall of the monstrous Crusader fortification in Syria that took place during the siege by the Mameluke Empire of Egypt in 1271 AD.

The Crusader castle, Crac des Chevaliers was considered to be an impregnable fortress. However, it fell, not through battle to the sieging army of the Mameluke's from Egypt, but rather, by deception and lies. In those days before gunpowder was widespread in its use, a long drawn out siege would have been the only way possible to take down a heavily defended position such as this castle. The Mameluke Sultan Babyars had a document created and forged its writing to appear that it was from the Hospitalier Knight's commander with orders calling for the Knights to surrender the garrison. The document of lies was believed and the Crusaders and the inhabitants of the castle surrendered. Crac des Chevaliers remains intact to this day and has been a contested fortress even in modern war. The Syrian government forces and ISIS have battled over the control of this fortress because of its strategic location in the land. It stands to this day as a reminder of how cunning and deceit are the least costly weapons in the arsenal of war. Once again, believed words, albeit complete lies can change the perspective from strength to weakness and faith to fear in mere moments.

Satan had deceived man into entering the code, triggering the nuclear option, and wiping out humanity as it was to be originally known.

When Adam and Eve fell, they died spiritually and were the first converts of a fallen race called mankind with Satan as their ruler. Often, in Islam's wars, if you were defeated, your option was forced conversion or death. At the fall of man, you were dead, and you automatically became a convert to a false god and false religion that left mankind as a conscript in a continual state of war against the Most High God.

The Root of all Personal Attacks in Spiritual Warfare

"You will notice that is was not through combat that Satan succeeded in conquering man; it was through words."

The first tactic of deception that the Devil used against Eve was to come to her in an unthreatening manner. Satan has embodied an animal that was familiar to both Adam and Eve. In fact, Adam probably had already named this serpent in the same manner as he did with God for all of creation.

Here is something to ponder: at this point in time, Adam and Eve are without sin, in complete fellowship with God, and in tune with all of His creation. Also at this point in history, they are able to communicate in every way with creation just as God is able to communicate with His creation. Was dialogue possible with all of the animal kingdom in verbal or non-verbal communication? I believe so. That would mean it would not have shocked Eve that she was speaking to or with one of God's creation. The picture that I am trying to convey is not the verbal communication that you may have with your dog, and the non-verbal signals returned by your pet. Rather, it is God's sophisticated way of communicating in a non-verbal manner that can enter the non-verbal communicative world of the animal kingdom. Today, we know so little about how the animals are able to communicate one with another, but I believe Adam and Eve intuitively knew exactly how it took place and it was a part of how they executed their authority on the earth.

I want to use an example of what I am referring to that may help to explain the point I am trying to make. Scientists have titled a study called the "Hundredth Monkey Effect," a phenomenon that explains the theory of learned knowledge through a species. In 1952, scientists on the Japanese island of Koshima were conducting a study of the Macaque monkeys that were indigenous to the region. The scientists recorded in one of their observances that a monkey learned to wash sweet potatoes before eating them. Gradually, this new behavior spread through the younger generation of monkeys who were copying the pattern they learned through observation and repetition. The researchers concluded through their study, that once a critical number of monkeys were reached with this newly learned knowledge, i.e. the hundredth monkey, it seemed to be an acquired knowledge by all.

This learned behavior instantly and miraculously spread immediately through the entire community. Furthermore, they noted that this knowledge traveled across the sea to the monkeys on nearby islands. My point to all of this is just as God is able to communicate with every species in His creation, that ability was also once a part of man's ability. I relate this piece of information to you to show that we have so little understanding of the animal kingdom's ability to communicate to one another. Yet, intuitive communication seems to be part of their repertoire. God, who gave creation this ability, also gave it to Adam and Eve to communicate with them as part of their authority to rule. Adam and Eve were not simpletons in knowledge and understanding, but rather, sophisticated created beings by God. If what I am presenting to you is a plausible scenario, you can then see that the whole experience of Eve speaking with a creature would have been nothing out of the norm; no more so than it would have been for God to communicate with his creation.

Consider this as well: in the book of Revelation, we see again that picture of the throne of God. No one is able to open the scroll until Jesus comes forward as the Lamb of God and opens the seals that locked the scroll. At that point where Jesus opens all of the seals, all of creation in heaven and on earth, in the sea, and under the earth, all worship together in unison. Somehow, and in each way, they conduct their communication as it comes up as a perfect and harmonious tribute of praise to the Lord Jesus.

> *Then I looked, and I heard the voices of many angels and living creatures and elders encircling the throne, and their number was myriads of myriads and thousands of thousands. In a loud voice they said:*
>
> *"Worthy is the Lamb who was slain, to receive power and riches and wisdom and strength and honor and glory and blessing!"*
>
> *And I heard every creature in heaven, and on earth, and under the earth, and in the sea, and all that is in them, saying:*
>
> *"To Him who sits on the throne, and to the Lamb, be praise and honor and glory and power forever and ever"* (Revelation 5:11-13).

I shall be quite curious to learn one day what the sound of praise coming from a worm should sound like. But whatever that might be, it is a clear and distinguishable communication to God. So if a worm has a voice, so too does a serpent and Satan will use that voice as a part of his plan.

Baited Words, Set the Trap

As we continue in the Genesis story, we read how the Devil covertly sets his trap with something that is familiar and unthreatening and then makes his next move. Satan now deploys his second tactic, which is to create uncertainty about what you know and believe to be true. He catches Eve in an overstatement about the repercussions of eating the illegal fruit. Eve was not even created when God warned Adam not to eat of the tree that was located in the center of the garden. Satan had told Eve that by eating that fruit she would be like God, knowing both good and evil. Everything that she and Adam had received from God had come from the Father's pure and good knowledge. It would be through an act of disobedience that man would acquire the knowledge of evil. So where did she get the notion that it was illegal to even touch the fruit? Adam had probably added that part to God's warning and told her with the intent that it would be best to just stay clear of that fruit tree altogether.

Not to eat the fruit of this one tree was the only rule God made for their lives in the garden of Eden. The fruit of that tree was not a magical piece of fruit that contained some superior form of knowledge; rather, it is what it symbolized by eating it. The knowledge of evil would come through disobeying God's command. This command not to eat of that fruit was the only authoritative line that differentiated God's authority from mankind. Furthermore, Satan would have known that Adam and Eve's understanding of death would be extremely limited, for the simple fact that no one had ever died before — either spiritually or physically for that matter. By exploiting their lack of experiential knowledge as to what kind of death God was addressing as an immediate effect, he could deceptively state that death would not be the result. In bringing forth some confusion as to the facts, he then goes in for the kill by appealing to Eve's own physical senses. We should also take note of the fact that deceit and lying would also have been a completely foreign concept to Adam and Eve's reasoning. They may have been forewarned who Satan was, but may not have been alert to his ability to embody a creature made by God.

The Lust of the Flesh, Lust of the Eyes and the Pride of Life

In verse 6, we read that as Eve looked upon the fruit, she saw that it was good for food. The enticement that her flesh could be satisfied by this most appealing fruit, revealed that the "lust of the eyes" and the "lust of the flesh" were at work. Then by eating this forbidden fruit, she could attain a new level of wisdom and be like God. In this deception, she found herself giving in to the "pride of life." She simply did not understand that God had no intention of depriving them of any knowledge; the issue was from which perspective that knowledge would come. By being deceived to disobey God's only rule of law, they would come to the knowledge of good and evil experientially from the standpoint of being fallen. A monumental paradigm shift would take place, and their worldview would come through sin rather than continuing in the knowledge as learned from God. Their eyes were opened, but what they would now see was a world from the viewpoint of their fallen state. This proved to be all Satan would need to depose this couple and enslave them to a new world order. In bringing Adam and Eve into sin and separation from God, he has also taken from them their rule over the earth. They would be removed from the garden of God and have to face a world that is poisoned by the presence of its new ruler.

The apostle John from his epistle would later warn the believers of the new faith to be on guard for Satan's time-proven devices of deception.

> *Do not love the world or anything in the world. If anyone loves the world, the love of the Father is not in him. For all that is in the world—the desires of the flesh, the desires of the eyes, and the pride of life—is not from the Father but from the world. The world is passing away along with its desires, but whoever does the will of God remains forever* (1 John 2:15-17).

The Greek word *epithumia* that is translated into the English word "lust" carries within its meaning a passion, inordinate desire, and longing for someone or something. This strong pressure of want added to the pride of possessing things or status in this world are the tools Satan uses to bring a person to the precipice of sin. How did he know this? This is how Lucifer, who was a perfectly created angelic being would fall, and he knew that Adam and Eve could fall in the same way. It is also worth noting that after Jesus concluded His fast of forty days and was at His weakest physical point, being hungry, that Satan came and tempted Him. He made his move on the Lord using the same forms of temptation that he used on Eve. The lust of the flesh, the lust of the eyes and the pride of life in all its various forms and enticements, are the enemy's "go to" option against humanity every time.

Cause and Effect: the Immediate Fall of Man

Cause and effect is a relationship between events or things, where one is the result of the other or others. This is a combination of action and reaction.

8Then the man and his wife heard the sound of the Lord God as he was walking in the garden in the cool of the day, and they hid from the Lord God among the trees of the garden. 9But the Lord God called to the man, "Where are you?"

10He answered, "I heard you in the garden, and I was afraid because I was naked; so I hid."

11And he said, "Who told you that you were naked? Have you eaten from the tree that I commanded you not to eat from?"

12The man said, "The woman you put here with me—she gave me some fruit from the tree, and I ate it."

13Then the Lord God said to the woman, "What is this you have done?"

> *The woman said, "The serpent deceived me,*
> *and I ate"* (Genesis 3:8-13).

The Lord now appears as He has always done in the past. God, who is all-knowing, is also, always faithful. Some paint the picture of a God in disgust rebuking them in His anger, but I see a different picture. I see God in a sorrowful resignation saying, "What have you done?" For He knows that what has happened is going to spiral out of control so terribly for those He loves.

We need to recognize what is going on here; Adam and Eve knew they were fallen and in judgment before God had even spoken one word to them. The glory that had clothed them immediately departed from them and they saw themselves as naked and in shame. They are hiding from God in fear and would not even come out of hiding when God called out to them. They didn't need to be judged by God because their sin took care of that in and of itself. It triggered a firestorm of degradation to all of creation on the earth. Everything has changed and Adam knows it. What is worse, he blames God and Eve for what has happened to him. God had forewarned them but He didn't need to pronounce judgment on them because that took effect on its own. He did, however, reveal to them what their actions had caused and what it would mean for them in the future.

There is no fear in love, but perfect love drives out fear, because fear involves punishment. The one who fears has not been perfected in love (1 John 4:18)

51

Adam and Eve were perfect and had no experiential knowledge of fear or shame; they lived in a realm of God's love. The moment they fell, the fear of judgment took hold and was embedded in their psyches. It would transform the DNA of all mankind. It is not the reverential awe of God kind of fear, but a dread of being in judgment that will lead to death. The demons know this fear, first hand. Every time they came into contact with Jesus they were terrified that their time might be up. Fear is now the anti-type to what faith is. A new conduit to power is now released at the fall of mankind; unfortunately, it is a release of the worst kind. At the sub-conscious level of humanity dwells the thoughts that your time to receive your just desserts is at hand. That belief sets off a firestorm of mental images and beliefs that something bad is coming your way, culminating in death. Satan has been given a new weapon in his arsenal to steal, kill, and destroy. Fear will be as a homing beacon that draws a person like a magnet into the sphere of demonic power to bring to reality those darkest thoughts.

If all this was not bad enough, they then lived with the fact that they were in the domain of Satan and under his rule. Lucifer was perfect in creation as were Adam and Eve. They all had manifested and radiated the glory of God in their perfection until sin was found in them. At the point of that committed sin, their universes came apart at the seams; everything without a further word being spoken, immediately unraveled. Some people argue, "How could such a loving God be so harsh?" "Where is this great mercy that He is supposed to have?"

The scripture says that all things are held together by the word (holy, perfect and true word) of His power (Hebrews

1:3). What would be the outcome of every atomic particle that makes up the world that is seen if that power was broken or degraded because there was no longer any eternal absolute truth to God's words? If God were to compromise His absolute word and truth in any form, or in any way, would the entire universe unravel? There would be no longer any integrity within that power to hold together the atomic and sub-atomic world.

Even ancient kingdoms held decrees and laws that were issued as unbreakable and unchanging. Darius the king of the Medo-Persian Empire could not even change his own edicts as Daniel Chapter 6 reveals. Darius was deceived by his royal council, who out of envy advised the king to enact a law they knew could destroy Daniel's life by his certain violation of that law. Darius deeply regretted his own law, which was at the expense of his friend but could do nothing to change it.

> *Now, Your Majesty, issue the decree and put it in writing so that it cannot be altered—in accordance with the law of the Medes and Persians, which cannot be repealed." So King Darius put the decree in writing* (Daniel 6:8, 9)

> *The king answered, "The decree stands—in accordance with the law of the Medes and Persians, which cannot be repealed"* (Daniel 6: 12b)

In the book of Esther, we read of a similar decree that was issued by Xerxes the ruler of the Persian Empire. A law was passed that all of the Jews in the 127 provinces within the kingdom were to be killed on the 13th day of the 12th month. Haman's wicked plot was exposed but the decree could not be changed. Esther pleaded with the king to spare the Jewish exiles, and he issued a new decree that allowed all of the Jews to defend themselves and entirely destroy their enemies. A law could not be changed but a new law of self-defense was mandated that prevented the genocide that was plotted against the Jews. If the world held decrees with this kind of reverence, how much more so does God watch over His word?

The world of physics continues to reveal what are to them, new laws that govern the universe. These laws are in point of fact, not new. What are being discovered are laws that have always been in place since the foundation of the world. Those laws are unchanging unless superseded by a higher law. The highest law is what God says about Himself and that is – He is unchanging and cannot lie. The unchangeableness of His perfect word is found in the DNA of everything that was created and established before time and creation began. Would God bear the same fate as Lucifer, Adam, and Eve if He were to compromise His very nature? Would it be suicide to the order of the universe and the unraveling of all creation? Thankfully, it is impossible for God to lie (Hebrews 6:18). Therefore, this could never happen, but it does reveal there are far more complex issues with other far-reaching ramifications than just making it about a singular perception of the absence of love.

It was because of God's love that He put the rescue plan of redemption in place. For all that befell Adam and Eve, God did not leave them without hope. In the form of a prophecy, He promised that Satan will be defeated and through mankind, a future redeemer would come.

So the Lord God said to the serpent, "Because you have done this,

"Cursed are you above all livestock and all wild animals! You will crawl on your belly and you will eat dust all the days of your life. 15And I will put enmity between you and the woman, and between your offspring and hers; he will crush your head, and you will strike his heel" (Genesis 3:14, 15).

This marks the first prophetic promise of Jesus and the war against Satan. Adam and Eve must exit the garden of God and struggle to live in a world absent of the relationship they once had with Him. The glory of God that once covered them as a garment is gone. They now live with a nakedness that is a reminder of the glory that is now departed. Satan will waste little time in establishing his rule over mankind and now presides as the god of this world.

There is a difference between the world and the earth in our understanding of scripture. The earth represents the physical realm; the world represents a sphere of influence that can be either spiritual or physical in application. As I stated earlier, the earth is the Lord's and all of its assets within it.

To the woman he said, "I will make your pains in childbearing very severe; with painful labor you will give birth to children. Your desire will be for your husband, and he will rule over you."17 To Adam he said, "Because you listened to your wife and ate fruit from the tree about which I commanded you, 'You must not eat from it,' "Cursed is the ground because of you;

> *through painful toil you will eat food from it*
>
> *all the days of your life. 18 It will produce thorns and thistles for you, and you will eat the plants of the field. 19 By the sweat of your brow you will eat your food until you return to the ground, since from it you were taken; for dust you are and to dust you will return"* (Genesis 3:16-19).

The earth, which was a gift, would now become toil and an ongoing challenge. What was once a perfect partnership between Adam and Eve will now be the struggle of the stronger dominating the weaker. Their children, who were to be the greatest of blessings, will now be birthed in pain caused by the corrupted seed of man. The spiritual death that immediately transpired at the point of their sin will, one day, culminate in their physical death as man will return to the dust of the earth from which he was formed.

> *Adam named his wife Eve, because she would become the mother of all the living. 21 The Lord God made garments of skin for Adam and his wife and clothed them. 22 And the Lord God said, "The man has now become like one of us, knowing good and evil. He must not be allowed to reach out his hand and take also from the tree of life and eat, and live forever." 23 So the Lord God banished him from the Garden of Eden to work the ground from which he had been taken. 24 After he drove the man out, he placed on the east side of the Garden of Eden cherubim and a flaming sword flashing back*

and forth to guard the way to the tree of life
(Genesis 3:20-24).

What we need to realize is that there are no idle verses in the book of Genesis. Over two thousand years of biblical history is covered in this first book of the Bible. More than one-third of the entire Jewish calendar is recorded in the first 50 chapters of this book. Every bit of information offered is critical knowledge for the reader. So it is with that understanding that we read that the Lord has clothed Adam and Eve with animal skins to provide a temporal covering for their bodies. The life of an animal was taken for this to happen. The scripture teaches us that life (blood) must be exchanged for life (blood). The blood of an animal was a temporary exchange awaiting the one who will make an offering for sin once and for all.

According to the Law, in fact, nearly everything must be purified with blood, and without the shedding of blood there is no forgiveness (Hebrews 9:22).

It should be noted that in the entire region known as the Fertile Crescent, sacrificial offerings would be a part of their practice in these ancient civilizations. From Egypt to the nation states that surround the Mediterranean Sea, throughout the Middle East and on to the borders of the Indus Valley, archaeological evidence supports this reality. Early man learned it from someone and that person was Adam. He would have learned this from God as indicated by the fact that animal skins are provided for Adam and Eve as clothing. It would have been far less complicated to simply instruct them to weave leaves and use other vegetation for this provision of clothing but that was not the case. For that reason, whenever you read in Genesis of a covenant or treaty being made, it was cut or enacted with the shedding of blood.

As we continue, notice the language that is used when God speaks about the terrible plight that has befallen man. God addresses Himself in the plural. We see even at the very beginning of the beginnings the understanding that God is one, but that He is also what we know to be the Triune God. Man has come to knowledge, albeit completely the wrong way. He has come to the knowledge of evil by being a partaker of it and now should he eat of the tree of life, he will be an eternally fallen creation as well as all of their future offspring. That cannot happen and before Adam and Eve leave the garden, an angel is placed to defend access to the tree of life. It makes one wonder why that tree's fruit was never eaten. Was it that unappealing to the eye? Now, that tree would have to be removed from the earth awaiting a new day of hope for mankind. That tree will be seen once again in the book of Revelation and is highlighted in the last chapter of the Bible.

> Then the angel showed me a river of the water of life, as clear as crystal, flowing from the throne of God and of the Lamb, down the middle of the main street of the city. On either side of the river stood a tree of life, producing twelve kinds of fruit and yielding a fresh crop for each month. And the leaves of the tree are for the healing of the nations (Revelation 22:1, 2).

What may interest you to know about this tree is how it literally translates from the Greek word that John used to describe it. The Greek word that is the normal or generic description of a tree is the word, *dendron*. The Greek word used to describe the word "tree" in Revelation is the Greek word *xulon*. Here is the definition of the word that John used to describe this tree, the tree of life:

Strong's Concordance

xulon: **wood**

Original Word: ξύλον, ου, τό
Part of Speech: Noun, Neuter
Transliteration: *xulon*
Phonetic Spelling: (xoo'-lon)
Short Definition: a staff, cross, anything made of wood
Definition: anything made of wood, a piece of wood, a club, staff; the trunk of a tree, used to support the cross-bar of a cross in crucifixion.

The tree that lines the streets of New Jerusalem is none other than a symbolic picture of the cross of Christ that provides healing to all mankind. For every moment of every day, all year long, forever in Christ is the picture of salvation offered for all mankind. Symbolically, its leaves are for our healing regardless of the affliction and for our every need. The fruit of salvation is in a continuous state of being ready to be harvested, all we have to do is freely come, taste, and see that the Lord is good.

> *But to all who did receive Him, to those who believed in His name, He gave the right to become children of God—children born not of blood, nor of the will of the flesh, nor of the will of man, but born of God* (John 1:12, 13).

Jesus is the last Adam. He is the rescue plan from the Father to restore mankind to our original birthright. I cannot help but to stop and worship the Lord when I read this. He is altogether lovely; there is no spot in Him. He is beautiful beyond all comprehension. It's hard to write a book that walks through a historical timeline when you already know who has won, and you cannot contain the thankful joy to our mighty conqueror, Jesus Christ the Righteous.

The Results of the Fall

If we look at what has happened through a modern lens we might call the fall of mankind, "The First War of Subversion." It was a propaganda war engineered by a covert operative, which led to a bloodless coup and the surrender and enslavement of mankind to a foreign army.

The atmosphere of the earth and mankind were poisoned with ungodly fear; this gave Satan the weapon and shield to preserve his empire. Godly belief would lie in ruins for more than a hundred and twenty years until the birth of Seth. What began as a bloodless coup would now be marked by bloodshed at every turn as Satan makes cruel and ruthless sport over the beloved creation of God.

Seth also had a son, and he named him Enosh.

At that time people began to call on the name of the Lord (Genesis 4:26).

The Lord is now on the outside of His own creation, but God will not give up on being reunited with His beloved children. Satan knows this and will do everything within his power to solidify his defenses of fortress earth and ensure the stability of his empire.

Chapter 4

LIFE UNDER THE NEW REGIME

Rapidly, the earth enters into decay and in its new volatility, it is crying out to be rescued from its enslavement. Climate change is in full effect with famines, floods, and other extreme conditions, now regularly affecting the area known as the Fertile Crescent. As a matter of course, it is also taking place throughout the entire planet. The earth cries out in volcanic eruptions as if the planet is vomiting at the thought of its new ruler.

The creation waits in eager expectation for the revelation of the sons of God. For the creation was subjected to futility, not by its own will, but because of the one who subjected it, in hope that the creation itself will be set free from its bondage to decay and brought into the glorious freedom of the children of God.

We know that the whole creation has been groaning together in the pains of childbirth until the present time (Romans 8:19-22).

The World without Covenant

After Adam and Eve left the garden of Eden, they also left their relationship with God. It was only after the birth of Seth's son Enosh, which was more than one hundred and thirty years later that people began to seek the Lord again.

A population explosion is underway. People at this time are still living long into their hundreds with families becoming clans within a biblical generation. The effect of sin in degenerating the human body is still at this point only just beginning to shorten a person's longevity. With every new generation of humanity the lifespan shortens and by the time we reach the days of Noah, living to a ripe old age of 120 is considered to be a long life. This is a far cry from what God had planned for man, for man was never meant to die. Death was the result of Adam's sin and was part of the judgment of humanity; now, humanity just accepts death as a part of life.

Physical death has come to all mankind as the result of the fall and is the last enemy to be destroyed by Jesus our mighty conqueror.

Sin has exploded as a plague uncontrolled and the violence of man is unrestrained. Evil has taken hold of hearts and minds and whatever sin can be imagined, is a sin committed because the people have no moral restraint. The passions of mankind are inflamed for everything temporal and very few seek after God.

The Sons of God and the Daughters of Men

In Genesis the sixth chapter, we read about the wickedness of mankind that leads to the devastating flood of early civilization. The scripture makes mention of the sons of God and their cohabitation with the daughters of men. Who were these sons of God? In the chronology of Jesus' ancestry in Luke's gospel, Adam is listed as a son of God. In what is considered the oldest book of the Bible, the book of Job, fallen angels are listed as sons of God. In fact, the word "sons" has been translated at some point to represent all of creation in one form or another. What is described in Genesis is what appears to be the final straw leading to the great flood. These giant men called the Nephilim held rank and renown amongst the people and were taking as wives the women of humanity.

> *When human beings began to increase in number on the earth and daughters were born to them, the sons of God saw that the daughters of humans were beautiful, and they married any of them they chose. Then*

the Lord said, "My Spirit will not contend with humans forever, for they are mortal; their days will be a hundred and twenty years."

The Nephilim were on the earth in those days—and also afterward—when the sons of God went to the daughters of humans and had children by them. They were the heroes of old, men of renown.

The Lord saw how great the wickedness of the human race had become on the earth, and that every inclination of the thoughts of the human heart was only evil all the time. The Lord regretted that he had made human beings on the earth, and his heart was deeply troubled (Genesis 6:1-6).

This NIV translation says, "They were heroes of old, men of renown." The Hebrew words used in that phrase imply an antiquity to these ancient ones. You can read commentary after commentary on what these verses mean and from scholars and non-scholars alike, but in the end, one is left mostly to speculate who these Nephilim were.

I was going to avoid this passage except for one thought that seemed to keep repeating through my mind. Satan has successfully poisoned the bloodline of humanity by drawing man into sin; yet, God has given a covenant promise that He will overcome this dilemma with a promised deliverer. The Devil knows that God cannot lie, so what could be his next step to stop this threat to his empire? If somehow he could alter mankind from being in the image of God into some other created being, would that not thwart God's plan to deliver humanity? This is the only reason I have even made comment on this controversial passage. I have read commentaries from some that suggest these are the fallen angelic beings that took to living as earthbound beings — I agree. But I must confess, I have not read any commentaries, which suggest that Satan's plan was to affect the human biological order by creating a race of half-bred humans. The purpose of this sabotage of the biological order was to nullify and destroy God's plan of redemption for mankind. It will be from this paradigm that I am presenting to you a possible scenario that led to the great flood. There is a curious verse from the book of Jude that may shed some light on this discussion.

> *Beloved, although I made every effort to write you about the salvation we share, I felt it necessary to write and urge you to contend earnestly for the faith entrusted once for all to the saints. For certain men have crept in among you unnoticed—ungodly ones who were designated long ago for condemnation. They turn the grace of our God into a license for immorality, and they deny our only Master and Lord, Jesus Christ.*
>
> *Although you are fully aware of this, I want to remind you that after Jesus had delivered His people out of the land of Egypt, He destroyed those who did not believe. **And the angels who did not stay within their own domain, but abandoned their proper dwelling,** He keeps under darkness, in eternal chains for judgment on that great day* (Jude 3-6).

Notice the context of Jude's letter as he addresses the sexual immorality and perversion that was being introduced to the church. Jude likens this to the angels that left their position of authority and are now bound with chains in darkness awaiting the final judgment. We know that Satan and his demons are roaming the earth seeking whom they may devour to this very day, so who are these fallen spirits that Jude is referring to? Are these the fallen spirits that took to living on the earth and taking wives for themselves from the children of men? Again, I draw you to the context of the passage from Jude's letter that a perversion of God's order is being introduced, which he likens to the action of those fallen devils he is describing.

Another question to ask is: what could have been going on that was so evil that God regrets the day He made man and brings upon the earth a flood to cleanse the earth of every living being? The days of Noah do not seem to be that different from the current human conditions of our day. Jesus was the prophesied answer to Adam regarding the fallen state of mankind, so why the drastic reset? It gives credence that something more diabolical had come into play, which required a purging of the planet. The effects of this perversion must have become so widespread that if it were not stopped, what we understand as humanity could well have been completely erased over time.

It is for that reason that I offer that the plan of Satan was to contaminate humanity with a half human, half fallen being and thereby pollute God's creation of man. In this new state, man is no longer made in the image of God. Clearly, when angels take on the form of humanity, we read in scripture that they can rest, eat, and drink as any human could. So is it that far out to believe that they could perform other human functions when they transition from the spiritual realm to the natural world? Was this act so evil that God had no choice but to destroy the world by a flood or else risk the success of Satan's plan? Did He then cast those fallen angels who offered themselves to Satan's plot into a prison of utter darkness being bound in chains after the flood awaiting their final Judgment?

Again, let me reiterate, the discussion of angels leaving their first estate of being spirits and then becoming a type of physical creation is not a new theory or premise. I just simply know of no commentary that places the context of this thought in the way that I have presented it to you as being the reason for the purging flood. That being said, I again must say that with so little cross-referencing of scripture available to us on this subject, we must hold this in the category of "could be, possibly or you're nuts" as all valid opinions. I think what we can all agree on is that the enemy will stop at nothing to destroy everything God loves and the destiny He has for us all.

Regardless of what was the build-up to the events that led to that cataclysmic flood, it worked as a reset button for mankind, but only for a short while. I cannot imagine the grief of heart that our God experienced as He made the decision to flood the earth. The Father, Son, and Holy Spirit did what must have been their very last option to preserve humanity. Some, once again argue how can a loving God do such a seemingly terrible act to His own creation? They ask this without having any understanding of the larger picture and its ramifications in this war of the ages. I can only wonder of the great conflict of soul that President Truman underwent when he made the decision to drop the atomic bombs on Nagasaki and Hiroshima. The U.S. military planners made the assessment that the invasion of Japan could be at a cost of over 1 million American casualties and that the war may continue beyond 1946. The decision to drop the atomic bomb potentially saved the lives of millions of Japanese and Americans had the war continued to an eventual invasion of Japan.

It is decisions such as these that bring the words of William Shakespeare to life from his play King Henry the VIII, "Heavy is the head that wears the crown." Decisions of life and death are the most grievous weight that any ruler must bear, how much more so would it be to our Heavenly Father.

Babel

I would be remiss if I failed to comment on the events after the flood that led man to unify under Satan's mandate and the building of a tower. By modern standards, this would hardly have been an impressive structure, although I'm sure it was in their day. It's not that the building was significant; it was their unity to fulfill Satan's vision. As we read earlier, Satan wanted to have his kingdom ascend to be like the Most High God and he had people who were of one mind with that purpose.

> Now the whole world had one language and a common speech. As people moved eastward, they found a plain in Shinar.
>
> They said to each other, "Come, let's make bricks and bake them thoroughly." They used

brick instead of stone, and tar for mortar. Then they said, "Come, let us build ourselves a city, with a tower that reaches to the heavens, so that we may make a name for ourselves; otherwise we will be scattered over the face of the whole earth" (Genesis 11:1-4).

The people partnered in Satan's plan and from their united words, they knowingly or unknowingly worked together to fulfill the evil vision. They were going to build a tower and ascend into the heavens, but God denied their wrongly placed intentions and dismantled their wrongly placed unity.

But the Lord came down to see the city and the tower the people were building. The Lord said, "If as one people speaking the same language they have begun to do this, then nothing they plan to do will be impossible for them. Come, let us go down and confuse their language so they will not understand each other."

So the Lord scattered them from there over all the earth, and they stopped building the city. That is why it was called Babel because there the Lord confused the language of the whole world. From there the Lord scattered them over the face of the whole heart (Genesis 11:5-9).

God makes a powerful statement in this passage that nothing is impossible to a people who are united in a vision. Take a moment to consider that there is no distinction in those words between a good motive and an evil one, except that unity can achieve the impossible.

71

It is interesting that Satan uses words to create his world and uses man to do it. Man is made in the image of God, and He has endowed mankind with the innate ability to create. Satan cannot create his world without man; he needs what has been made inherent in man to bring to pass his purposes on the earth. Believed words that are acted upon, make up the essence or root of faith. In this passage, God recognizes the evil intent and scatters their speech creating an untold number of new languages. The people band together under one of those new languages and each of these new tribes set off looking for a new place to settle and dwell.

This brief passage from the book of Genesis is packed with so much spiritual truth to help us contend with the powers of darkness. The demonic realm needs our words and our belief to bring forth its purposes on the earth. We should guard our speech carefully and not enter any agreement with the Devil. If we do this, we will negate his ability to operate freely in our lives.

Satan has tried to destroy mankind by using the womb to birth a defiled humanity. The flood was used as the preventive measure to ensure humankind. Now, Satan shifts his plans to that of using the heart of a person or people as the womb whereby he can impregnate it with his words. Those words will form beliefs that will create the offspring of his fallen vision. Our minds and hearts act as an incubator to develop those beliefs into a manifested form of action on the earth.

> *We all stumble in many ways. If anyone is never at fault in what he says, he is a perfect man, able to control his whole body.*

When we put bits into the mouths of the horses to make them obey us, we can guide the whole animal. Consider ships as well. Although they are so large and are driven by strong winds, they are steered by a very small rudder wherever the pilot is inclined.

In the same way, the tongue is a small part of the body, but it boasts of great things. Consider how small a spark sets a great forest on fire. The tongue also is a fire, a world of wickedness among the parts of the body. It pollutes the whole person, sets the course of his life on fire, and is itself set on fire by hell (James 3:2-6).

The book of James paints a clear picture of how words used wrongly bring forth an onset of the destructive force of hell. The Internet and social media show us how words, whether they are truth or lies, can remain in some form ever existing on the World Wide Web. The effects of those words can be devastating to individuals, corporate entities, and groups. Propaganda in the form of lies is one thing, but indoctrination into a form of held beliefs will move evil to a completely different level.

At Babel, we see that Satan's plans are being cast down and he along with them. His plunge to the earth will be a picture that will often be repeated in scripture. Every time he thinks that he has gained some form of ascendency, he finds himself being thrown down to the earth. He is plagued by the very curse that he uses against man – *"Pride goes before a fall."*

Satan Consolidates His Power through Propaganda

The first two thousand years of the biblical timeline reveal to us that early civilization is in a struggle for survival from the elements and from their fellow man. During this time, few people will call on the one true God. Humanity will instead follow after false gods; they will see the creation of new gods and worship them to Satan's great pleasure. What I find interesting is when you study the beliefs and religions of early civilization; it seems to play out two ways. The first type is one of appeasement to an angry deity and the subsequent offerings to quench its wrath. In return for man's offering and obeisance, that individual receives a measure of favor and protection.

This to me is the ultimate slander campaign of Satan against the God of Heaven. It paints God to be a harsh vindictive God who requires constant appeasement to avoid judgment. Adam lived 930 years, which would have brought him close to or being a witness to the days of the Nephilim. Adam and Eve would have told their sons and daughters about the God of Heaven, but now that belief has been morphed into a lie that makes man the victim at the hands of a merciless and angry God. The real truth is that this is the picture of how Satan operates in his rule over mankind. He then shifts any and all perceived blame and redirects them to God. This is done to further incite enmity and mistrust against God and cause man to trust himself above all else, which works perfectly in Satan's favor. The prince of the power of the air, to this very day, is still using this same propaganda of lies. The voice of God had become all but a faint memory of what was once true and now this anti-type of God is the model for most religious beliefs. Sadly, this kind of thinking can even be found in the Christianity practiced by many, even in our day.

The second type of deity relationship with man would be something similar to that which is seen in the gods and goddesses of ancient Greece and Rome. It was unthinkable to an ancient Greek or Roman person that you could have a personal relationship with a god. These gods have little interest in the daily affairs of man and offerings and worship are to garner favor and keep them from meddling in the lives of man. They were often perceived as treating mankind as a sport and would take pleasure in messing with their lives similar to the way a cat plays with a caught mouse until it finally dies. This also is a mirror to Satan's rule and authority structure as he uses his hierarchy of ruling spirits to wreak havoc on humanity. So much of the observation of early civilization is this picture of rule under the new regime of darkness and has nothing at all to do with the God of all creation. This is all part of Satan's propaganda war to make sure that in the minds of men that any thought of returning to God is the greatest of all mistakes. Satan for all intent and purposes is quite content to move covertly in his rule and deflect all his due blame on the images of god that he has masterminded.

The manner in which he governs all the kingdoms of the world paints the clearest picture of his tyrannical rule. Kingdoms are waging war against kingdoms with the common person as the usual fodder. Satan operates his rule as a competition amongst his ruling class of fallen spirits. It is a disorder to maintain order that keeps all of his minions of spirit and humanity on a razor's edge. There is never any real peace; it is always a state of competition for survival. Satan maintains his rule through merciless power and every fallen spirit is united with him because of their fear of him.

The pressures of a dog eat dog existence that is void of true peace and joy drive a person to live a life of self-preservation. The world today models this lifestyle and rule in all its forms. It is not just a picture of a militaristic rule but is readily seen in government, finance, business, education and the entertainment medium in all its forms. Further to these things, it is pervasive in religion and is never more personal than when families are reduced to a house of individuals all seeking their own agendas regardless of the cost to the family as a whole.

Satan relishes this environment of unceasing tension and lack of security. This environment, absent of any real peace, always leaves him in a position of strength and control. This is the world that man lives in and from this reality of life, man still dreams to be restored to a life that was once his in Eden.

Chapter 5

THE BOOK OF JOB

INTRODUCES SATAN AS THE ACCUSER

The book of Job is believed to be the oldest book of the Bible and it is said by some scholars to pre-date Abraham. It is listed as one the poetic books of the Old Testament placed alongside, Psalms, Proverbs, Ecclesiastes, and the Song of Solomon. We learn from other passages in scripture that Job was a real man even though the events of his life are placed in an allegorical setting. It is done in this manner to show how the unseen world affects the seen world and is an influence in every area of a person's life. This unfolding drama gives us an early glimpse of the workings of Satan on the earth.

6And the day is, that sons of God come in to station themselves by Jehovah, and there doth come also the Adversary in their midst.

7And Jehovah saith unto the Adversary, 'Whence comest thou?' And the Adversary answereth Jehovah and saith, 'From going to and fro in the land, and from walking up and down on it.'

8And Jehovah saith unto the Adversary, 'Hast thou set thy heart against My servant Job because there is none like him in the land, a man perfect and upright, fearing God, and turning aside from evil?'

9And the Adversary answereth Jehovah and saith, 'For nought is Job fearing God?

10Hast not Thou made a hedge for him, and for his house, and for all that he hath--round about?

11The work of his hands Thou hast blessed, and his substance hath spread in the land, and yet, put forth, I pray Thee, Thy hand, and strike against anything that he hath--if not: to Thy face he doth bless Thee!'

12And Jehovah saith unto the Adversary, 'Lo, all that he hath [is] in thy hand, only unto him put not forth thy hand.' And the Adversary goeth out from the presence of Jehovah (Job 1:6-12, Young's Literal Translation)

I have used *Young's Literal Translation* for this passage because it helps to reveal the content with more clarity when it is seen in its literal form. You will note immediately that any reference that does not speak specifically of Jehovah (YHVH) is simply translated as God (*Elohim*). This is important because any time you see this word used (*Elohim*) it is a generic term and can also be used to describe God, gods, angels, demonic spirits, humans, rulers or judges. The narrative in this passage is speaking about a confrontation in the spiritual realm that pits demons led by Satan to stand before Heaven railing accusations against mankind to his Creator. Satan's particular focus is on a man named Job. It is to be noted that *Yahweh (YHVH)* and its translation into English as Jehovah is a distinct affirmation of the God of Heaven and *Elohim* is the generic term in this passage for God as laid out in the earlier clarification.

From this opening chapter, we learn that Satan is searching the earth for someone to prey upon. He has found a man named Job, and he has set his sights on his destruction. He cannot get to him because God has placed a hedge of protection and safety around him. He knows that through Job's stated fears, he has found a legal right to get to Job. He then stands off against God, railing his accusations against Job and claiming his right to him. He demands in the heavenly places his legal right of access to Job with the intent of gaining access to his family as well.

From the writings of the apostle Peter, we are given an image that is suitable for the description used in the book of Job.

> *Be sober-minded and alert. Your adversary the*
> *devil prowls around like a roaring lion, seeking*

someone to devour (1 Peter 5:8).

Should there be any doubt as to who bears responsibility for mankind's woes, John quotes Jesus to make perfectly clear the difference between the two kingdoms.

> *The thief comes only to steal and kill and destroy. I have come that they may have life, and have it in all its fullness* (John 10:10).

Through Adam's fall, the authority of rule over the earth was ceded to Satan. He is now, as Paul would write, *"the god of this age"* and as far as the Devil is concerned, any worship of the God of Heaven is illegal. Job is found to be a seeker of the God of Heaven and the Devil wants to sift this man's life as wheat. We will see a similar scenario unfold just hours before Jesus would be arrested. The Lord will warn Peter that Satan is demanding access to him,

> *Simon, Simon, Satan has asked to sift each of you like wheat. But I have prayed for you, Simon, that your faith will not fail. And when you have turned back, strengthen your brothers* (Luke 22:31, 32).

In Job's case, the entry point was fear. In Peter's case, one can surmise that it was due to pride. In the days leading up to the Passover and even as the disciples were partaking of that last supper, the gospels record their debate as to who was the greatest among them. In Proverbs 16:18, we are warned that *"Pride precedes destruction; an arrogant spirit appears before a fall."* If one is looking for a probable cause this could well be it.

Young men, in the same way, submit yourselves to your elders. And all of you, clothe yourselves with humility toward one another, because,

"God opposes the proud, but gives grace to the humble."

Humble yourselves, therefore, under God's mighty hand, so that in due time He may exalt you. 7 Cast all your anxiety on Him, because He cares for you (1 Peter 5:5-7).

I want you to file in your mind that both Job and Peter's sifting by Satan, take place before the New Covenant is enacted. This will prove to be an important key for our understanding in the later chapters of this book.

I believe the imagery given by many translations is completely off course. The implication that Satan would be able to enter heaven's gates and come before God's holy throne is a misguided notion. They are not speaking to one another in a way like a rebellious child would give flippant answers to a father. The Devil and his demons have been out on the earth going to and fro gathering accusations against humanity in order to justify their actions against man. Furthermore, Satan was cast out of heaven. There is no sin in heaven; if he were allowed entry, then sin would be found in heaven. Be assured of one thing, this dialogue is not taking place in heaven. It is taking place in the spiritual realm but not at the location known as the Third Heaven where God dwells. Some have implied that Satan has come into the courtroom of heaven; this is an overreach of the description of this passage. While it is true that Satan is using his legal claim against a person's rights, they are not meeting with God in a courtroom. Improperly translated Hebrew words by some translators have created these errant images in our thinking.

Take for instance the word "presence" that is translated from the Hebrew word *panim* or *paneh*, which translates as "face or faces." The word "presence" creates a soft or amenable image in our minds similar to that of a loyal subject going before a king. *Young's Literal Translation* of the Bible uses the word "station," which adds more illumination to the context to face or facing. This word is sometimes used to indicate two foes standing off against one another as if they were about to engage in battle. Here are some examples of how this word *panim* or *paneh* are used with a hostile implication,

> *When the Philistines heard that David had been anointed king over all Israel, they went up in **full force** to search for him, but David heard about it and went out to **meet** them* (1 Chronicles 14:8).

The word "meet" is the same Hebrew word that is translated as "face."

> *Then Amaziah sent messengers to Jehoash son of Jehoahaz, the son of Jehu, king of Israel, with the challenge: "Come, let us **face** each other in battle"* (2 Kings 14:8).

These two examples ("meet" and "face") are also from the same Hebrew word *panim* or *paneh* and give no vague interpretation as to what is being implied. The imagery from the book of Job, which depicts Satan and his demonic forces arrayed before the Lord should not be treated any differently. It also reminds me of the passage in 2 Kings 18 when the armies of Sennacherib king of Assyria stood outside of the walls of Jerusalem as his emissaries read out his accusations and threats against Israel. There was dialogue, but in no way was it a friendly exchange of words.

This is not a cordial visit, nor is it merely a hostile lawyer appearing before a judge. It is an army of satanic forces arrayed before God hurling accusations outside of heaven's gates by demonic hosts against the people of the earth. We, through this story, are listening in on one of those exchanges as Satan, who is not omnipresent, tries to have God bring judgment upon a man by lifting the protective hedge. Furthermore, Satan is a liar; why would God have any interest in having any exchange with someone known as the "father of lies" and "the accuser of the brethren." Is there any knowledge that Satan knows that is beyond that of an omniscient God? You also have to note this in your mind that Satan, because of his former position, knows that God is omniscient, more so than anyone else.

As he rails against man to God, he also rails those same accusations at mankind on a personal level. Accusation leads to condemnation, and it is through this imprisonment of the soul that Satan keeps a person living in defeat. If we let those words echo continually in our minds and believe them, those beliefs will enslave us. Receiving condemnation from the Devil via his accusations is tantamount to being injected with poison. Receiving conviction from the Holy Spirit and turning our hearts toward God is tantamount to being injected with an antidote for that poison and the sin that opened the door in the first place.

The key to growing spiritually is to quickly move from the condemnation of sin to the full acceptance of the grace of God through Christ. If you have walked with the Lord for any length of time, you must have surely noticed by now a spiritual dynamic that takes place after you have sinned and asked for His forgiveness. The Lord responds to you with great grace that immediately manifests in your life. Is this done to shame us because of that committed sin? Absolutely not! The Lord does this as a demonstration of His lovingkindness because He wants us to quickly get back into the walk, in order that the Devil gains no place or ground into our lives. When you were learning to ride a bike or a horse and you fell off, you were told to get back up and get on it quickly. In doing so, you prevent fear from taking hold and setting you back from learning how to ride.

> The Law was given so that the trespass would increase; but where sin increased, grace increased all the more, so that, just as sin reigned in death, so also grace might reign through righteousness, to bring eternal life through Jesus Christ our Lord (Romans 5:20, 21).

The rabbit trail that Satan wants to lead a believer on is one that begins with condemnation and makes you want to hide in fear as Adam and Eve did. You then play out all the religious angles of your self-proclaimed judgment and perceived necessary penances. As days pass, you begin to feel a bit of confidence and you start to approach God as a lowly worm. All of this leads to a great loss of time in your relationship with God as another week goes by. Once you finally feel that you are at peace with God, you might have sinned again and the cycle of guilt and shame is repeated. This is why it is of absolute importance when you sin that you run to God immediately and reaffirm yourself to Him and in the righteousness of Christ.

You do this by declaring to the father that your righteousness is only through Christ and not of your own works or piety. This shows a level of maturity in that you regard the truth of the gospel of Jesus Christ as greater than your own feelings of guilt and remorse. This is how to maintain every day as a day of fellowship in Christ and live daily with Him. Those who understand what I am saying about Satan's rabbit trails will affirm that virtually six out of every seven days gets lost from your communion with God in that mental snare. To live out your walk in this way will make you ineffective as a soldier in the army of God. The remorse and guilt game offered by the Devil is a cunning and sly lie cloaked in a garment of religious piety, which the Devil is more than happy to have you wear. Satan loves religion. That cloak he offers seems to weigh a thousand pounds, and it will make you unable to move in the freedom whereby Christ has set you free.

Do not play the religious game of condemning yourself thinking that this somehow pleases God. IT DOES NOT. Acknowledge the finished work of the cross and reaffirm that truth by entering the throne room with thankful worship for His great grace. This destroys the work of Satan before his poison can work in you.

Receiving condemnation from the Devil via his accusations is tantamount to being injected with poison. Receiving conviction from the Holy Spirit and turning our hearts toward God is tantamount to being injected with an antidote for that poison and for the sin that opened the door in the first place.

Another implied thought by some is that God is trying to have Satan consider Job as a candidate to be attacked. This could not be further from the truth, as Job 1:8 in its literal form confirms that this passage does not make that implication.

God is responding to Satan's accusations with his assessment of Job. You will notice by the following statement that God makes that He is speaking in defense of Job. He is refuting the Devil's accusations, which were not recorded but are stated in the past tense. Satan wanted to have God judge Job as guilty; instead, God calls him blameless and upright.

> 3And Jehovah saith unto the Adversary, `Hast thou set thy heart unto My servant Job because there is none like him in the land, a man perfect and upright, fearing God and turning aside from evil? and still he is keeping hold on his integrity, and thou dost move Me against him to swallow him up for nought!'
>
> 4And the Adversary answereth Jehovah and

saith, `A skin for a skin, and all that a man hath he doth give for his life.

5Yet, put forth, I pray Thee, Thy hand, and strike unto his bone and unto his flesh--if not: unto Thy face he doth bless Thee!'

6And Jehovah saith unto the Adversary, `Lo, he [is] in thy hand; only his life take care of ' (Job 2:3-6, Young's Literal Translation).

Some translations read, "very well then" in the sixth verse as if to imply an agreement by God to Satan's accusation. This phrase does not exist in the text and is added as a liberty taken by the translators. What God did acknowledge was that the enemy did have a door into Job's life to attack him; it was the door called "fear."

In the first chapter of the book of Job, we read that Job would continually offer sacrifices on behalf of his children out of fear that they might have sinned against God. He would later say,

> *What I feared has come upon me; what I dreaded has happened to me* (Job 3:25).

This reveals that fear is one of the most powerful poison arrows in the arsenal of darkness.

In closing out this discussion of the book of Job, we need to remember that it was written as a poetic allegory of a real event. It is unwise to form a biblical doctrine from it, but instead, the use of its metaphors should be a complement to all of the scriptures that clearly lay out our understanding of the spiritual realm. I too am considering this as I write, and I do understand the term, "poetic license." However, poetic license should not deviate from our basic core knowledge of scripture, and I see no need for some of the translators' liberties that are taken in the book of Job.

Another point that is important to note is that this is a period of human history that is even before the implementation of the Old Covenant and the safety, which was provided through adherence to the Law of Moses. After Jesus enters humanity and offers Himself up for mankind, the realm of the spirit as it relates to man would be completely changed forever through our Lord's glorification.

The book of Job gives us a glimpse into demonic activity in the spiritual realm and Satan's desire to try to turn God's heart against man. What is astonishing to me as I read this book is that from the moment Job's friends appear on the scene in Chapter 3 and on through to Chapter 37, which is before God begins to speak for Himself, there is no discussion whatsoever that Satan is to blame at any time. God is accredited as the one who is pouring out His judgment on Job. According to Job's friends, it is Job's committed offenses and in their judgment, he is too proud and sinful to acknowledge his evils and repent. It seems that little has changed in man's understanding and council to those who are in trouble as this perception continues to this very day.

At the center of the book in Chapter 21, Job basically says, "Hey, wait a minute, if what you all are accusing me of is the reason for my plight, how is it that bad people get away with murder?"

> *Why do the wicked live on, growing old and increasing in power?*

They see their children established around them, their offspring before their eyes. Their homes are safe and free from fear; the rod of God is not on them. Their bulls never fail to breed; their cows calve and do not miscarry. They send forth their children as a flock; their little ones dance about. They sing to the music of timbrel and lyre; they make merry to the sound of the pipe. They spend their years in prosperity and go down to the grave in peace. Yet they say to God, 'Leave us alone! We have no desire to know your ways. Who is the Almighty, that we should serve him? What would we gain by praying to him?' (Job 21:7-15).

Job asks the question, but he is still not wise enough to discern the work of the Devil. Unfortunately, he is not aware of the first two chapters of his own biography. What we see is the development of Satan's strategy whereby he hides in stealth in order to inflict maximum damage and operate in the shadows. Just as he did in Eden, he remains covert in his evil works and is a spin-doctor directing the blame at God. He is a propaganda genius that uses his own repertoire of created gods in which he deceives man into their worship as a way to further foster the mistrust toward heaven. It is the ultimate blame shift. Satan creates untrustworthy deities to embed into the human psyche never to fully place your trust in any god. Meanwhile, he promotes the idea that he (Satan) doesn't exist. That strategy is the essence of the perfect crime; someone else has to be blamed because you don't exist.

Furthermore, the demonic realm focuses its attention on anyone who is experiencing an awakening in his heart to the one true God. Those forces of darkness go searching for anything that they can use against those people to accuse and justify their legal right to plunder dear souls. If it were not for God's hedge of protection on these individuals, no one would be spared; it truly is a vulnerable era for humanity. This will begin to change with a man called Abram and his life will mark a turning point for the future of mankind. God will make a covenant with this man that through his lineage, a Redeemer will be born who will bless all the nations of the earth.

Your descendants will take possession of the cities of their enemies, 18and through your offspring all nations on earth will be blessed, because you have obeyed me (Genesis 18:18).

Chapter 6

THE END OF AN AGE DRAWS NEAR

Abraham and the Promise of a New Day

Abraham and Job are thought to be near contemporaries in the biblical timeline. They each lived approximately 500 years or more before the birth of Moses and the advent of the Old Covenant. Both came from lands east of what is now modern Israel. Job came from an area in or near what is now Jordan and Abraham was a Chaldean from what is now southern Turkey or Iraq. Both men were found to be seekers of the God of Heaven and shunned the worship of the idols of the region. Both experienced the favor of God in their lives, amassed great wealth and had large prospering families. But for all of the comparisons to their lives, there is a dramatic shift in the way each walked out his beliefs.

As we read earlier in regard to Job, he would always offer sacrifices to God after family gatherings and celebrations out of fear that maybe a family member had sinned. Later, he would lament at his devastating turn of events that what he dreaded and feared had come upon him. He had a worldview whereby he believed that God was just waiting for someone to do something wrong and would act swiftly against the offender in judgment. Do you really think that a peace offering from this held belief would have been a sacrifice that God would have felt honored with? That kind of offering was the perception of those who worshiped the idols of their day and is how they made offerings to their gods. Job was probably not conscious of the fact that by doing so, he was dishonoring God with his offering of fear. Job was treating God in a manner familiar to all of the other gods that were worshipped in his day. He was inadvertently lumping the God of Heaven with those that were made of wood, stone, and metal. You will notice if you study the life of Abraham that he never makes an altar of offering out of fear or appeasement; it is always out of worship and thanksgiving.

When you look at the life of Abraham, you see a life marked by his faith and an unshakeable trust in the goodness of God. No matter what Abraham was asked by God to do, he obeyed. He acted upon God's words to him believing that God would not fail him. Even when he was asked to offer up his son as a sacrifice, he did not shrink from obeying that unimaginable request. Instead, he believed God could not lie; God had made promises concerning Isaac and would, therefore, raise him back to life.

By faith Abraham, when he was tested, offered up Isaac on the altar. He who had received the promises was ready to offer his one and only son, even though God had said to him, "Through Isaac your offspring will be reckoned." Abraham reasoned that God could raise the dead, and in a sense, he did receive Isaac back from death (Hebrews 11:17-19).

Abraham's life is a life marked by faith. His unshakable resolve that God would not break his covenant with him is the example for every believer to follow. Abraham would have enjoyed that same hedge of protection that Job had. He and his family, and all who were with him, his livestock and possessions were surrounded by the grace and favor of God. Abraham faced numerous serious challenges but never experienced the absence of that hedge because he never moved from a posture of faith to fear. He held within his heart that God was looking out for his wellbeing at all times and in all circumstances. By trusting in God's goodness, he never gave the enemy any major entrance into his life.

The point I am making through this comparison is to show that faith and fear are two equally similar conduits that seek a power source. Through Adam's fall, fear emerged as a new entity and Satan now had a conduit to mankind. Faith was God's conduit, which connected man to His power. But now, the anti-conduit of fear would connect to Satan's power and seek to interrupt God's flow of power. A heart that lays its confidence and trust in God will leave no place for fear to take residence. You may be aware of fear being just outside the door, but you never give it the right to access your life. When fear and faith are at work in us at the same time, it is like an improperly wired circuit that causes our lights to flicker and be subject to power outages. Faith and fear are ever in conflict with each other; therefore, we need to heed the words of James and guard our hearts and minds:

> *If any of you lacks wisdom, he should ask God, who gives generously to all without finding fault, and it will be given to him. But he must ask in faith, without doubting, because he who doubts is like a wave of the sea, blown and tossed by the wind. That man should not expect to receive anything from the Lord. He is a double-minded man, unstable in all his ways* (James 1:5-8).

Up to this point, we have been focusing on and learning of Satan's strategies and weapons. The early history of mankind gives a clear picture of his enticements and his use of fear to ensnare people and hold them in bondage. We also see through the biblical timeline of events, the formation and rule of the kingdom of darkness on the earth and in the heavenly realm. It is as though the Old Testament is giving us a bird's-eye view of what is going on whereas; when we arrive at the New Testament, we will see everything as it is, up close and personal.

A faith-filled life in God will absorb and neutralize every fiery weapon of fear that seeks to lay siege to and pierce your soul.

In Abraham, we not only see a person through whom the Messiah will come via his physical bloodline; we also see that

94

it is through his faith that the spiritual bloodline will come for all mankind. You would think that with the knowledge of all that is promised through Abraham's seed that a huge target would be on Abraham and his family by the forces of evil. No doubt, they were public enemy number one on Satan's list of threats to his empire. Yet, Abraham just continued to grow stronger in the land. He never experienced Job's trials and his prosperity and stature in the land of Canaan never abated. A faith-filled life in God will absorb and neutralize every fiery weapon of fear that seeks to lay siege to and pierce your soul.

God was not vague with Abraham and through a dream, he will address the next four hundred years of history concerning his descendants.

> *12As the sun was setting, Abram fell into a deep sleep, and a thick and dreadful darkness came over him. 13Then the Lord said to him, "Know for certain that for four hundred years your descendants will be strangers in a country not their own and that they will be enslaved and mistreated there. 14But I will punish the nation they serve as slaves, and afterward they will come out with great possessions. 15You, however, will go to your ancestors in peace and be buried at a good old age. 16In the fourth generation your descendants will come back here, for the sin of the Amorites has not yet reached its full measure"* (Genesis 15:12-16).

There are a couple of points I want to draw to your attention from this passage, which I believe are important to the study of spiritual warfare. A prophetic dream has come to Abraham revealing four generations amounting to four hundred years. Biblical generations are very fluid in their duration and meaning especially as it relates to early civilization. As the sin took its toll on man's life expectancy rates, the generations became shorter in duration as the years went on.

God has alerted Abraham that his descendants will be enslaved, freed from that slavery and leave with the wealth of the nation that enslaved them. You may have noticed that at no time is Egypt named as that nation. Why did God refrain from telling Abraham that it is in Egypt that all of this would occur? Remember, that it was not too long ago during the days when he was called Abram that he moved to Egypt during a time of famine. He knew Pharaoh. They met over the issue of Sarah being a candidate for his harem, and he treated Abraham with great favor thinking he was Sarah's brother. Would he have tried to intercede for his descendants in the flesh (literally and carnally) to enact some future protection for his descendants? Sometimes, by having too much familiarity and knowledge of a situation, we can color the will of God with our perspectives and our opinions. This invariably leads to presumption and even interference in our intercession.

The second point I want to make is that of timing. We read in verse sixteen of this passage that there was a correlation of timing in relation to God's dealings with the Amorites. We have a tendency to jump to conclusions when God's timing does not meet our expectations of what we believe should be the timeline. This more often than not leads navel-gazing and questions that create doubt and uncertainty. When you begin to entertain the varying degrees of self-doubt, you will find yourself inundated with well-meaning counselors and their opinions.

The enemy loves introspection; it is there that seeds of doubt can germinate and grow into weeds that will contend with the life of the plant you are growing by faith. You also can be certain that he will be sure to send some of his own council your way to throw you completely off course. Unfortunately, that may even come from a most trusted source just as Jesus experienced from Peter who was one of the Lord's closest friends. Jesus had just praised Peter for the revelation he had received that Jesus was the Christ. A mere four verses later, Jesus is rebuking Satan in Peter for trying to talk the Lord out of His impending death. Peter went from the penthouse to the outhouse in about the time it would take to fall down a flight of stairs.

> *Then He began to teach them that the Son of Man must suffer many things and be rejected by the elders, chief priests, and scribes, and that He must be killed and after three days rise again. He spoke this message quite frankly, and Peter took Him aside and began to rebuke Him.*

> *Turning and looking at His disciples, Jesus rebuked Peter and said, "Get behind Me, Satan! For you do not have in mind the things of God, but the things of men"* (Mark 8:31-33).

Satan's goal is to draw us from God's interests and set our minds to our self-interest and preservation. Jesus rebuked Peter for being used by the enemy to attempt to shift the Lord's focus onto His own wellbeing instead of the will of God. The enemy will seek to do the same with us and will act

97

covertly in trying to set our minds on our interests. The Devil knows that a person's self-interest will find an indirect path to collusion with him if it is in conflict with the will of God for his/her life.

When we allow our focus to shift from God's purposes during times of introspection, it literally opens up an avenue that the enemy can use to exploit us. As intercessors, we need to have a bird's-eye view as those who are seated in heavenly places in Christ and not as those who live in the small world of our fishbowl. We need to see the view from God's perspective, not merely from the current crisis. If you do this, the clouds will break, and you will begin to see what the Father sees. From His vantage point, you may see that timing delays were critical to shift the field of battle to your favor. Abraham was not shaken by delays and neither should we misread delays as automatically missing God's timing and will.

The Rise of Nations and Emerging Empires

Over that next period of 400 years, settled communities grow into city-states, and city-states become nations. As the nations grow in strength economically and militarily, the emergence of empires begins to take shape. Egypt will be one of the early great empires of the world and through the providence of God, it will act almost as a guardian for this fledgling young clan of 70 persons who will settle there. Israel will grow into a nation on foreign soil and when that favor lifts, it signals the time to move. A spiritual allegory takes place, as it was Joseph who took Mary and Jesus to Egypt to preserve the family almost two thousand years or so, later. Even in the smallest of details, Jesus retraces every step that Israel took in order to bring the fulfillment of Israel's destiny in Him.

Wherever peoples gather in communities, Satan responds by setting up his authority structure over that region. Those ruling spirits will then extend their rule through the carnal appetite of the populace giving each region an identifying trait that ties it to that ruling power. It's like a dog marking its territory; unfortunately, the ones being marked are people. Even in our day, we can enter a city or locale and pick up the vibe of the region. It will manifest in the speech and manner of the people revealing their customs through their actions.

Just as we have seen in the two scriptural passages about Satan, his story is embedded in the two nations that were being addressed in the prophecies of Isaiah and Ezekiel. This is done to give us an understanding of who the real rulers of the kingdoms of the world were in the early history of man. Having said that, there are a remarkable number of interactions by God to the kings of the earth through dreams, visions, and encounters with Him. Satan may be the ruler of this age but all the while, the voice of God is building on the earth and the Lord is going directly to those who govern the people.

Summary of the Age without Covenant

Through the first section of this book, we have looked at the workings of the spiritual realm and how mankind was affected by the fall. As it relates to spiritual warfare, the picture for humanity is one of one defeat after another, whereby things seemed to only get worse, not better. If I were to recount to you something similar in the history of warfare, I would liken it to Nazi Germany from 1938 to the summer of 1940. It seemed that the Nazi war machine was unstoppable with nation after nation being brought to enslavement under the blood-red banner of the swastika. At this stage of the war, the prospects for any success looked bleak. Britain was trying to take some solace in the fact that 300,000 soldiers were rescued at Dunkirk and made it back to England. This led a somber Winston Churchill to reply, "Wars are not won by evacuation." In the months that followed, a change of fortune would mark a turning point in the war that would eventually lead to Nazi Germany's unconditional surrender. In like manner, as we close out the age before covenant, God is about to make a significant move on the earth.

The fall of Adam ushered in an era of death and destruction for mankind and servitude to the personification of evil. Over these first two thousand years, Satan has revealed a lot of his tactics through this age, which are as follows:

1. He remains covert and hides in familiarity.

2. He seeks to exploit the weakness of our knowledge of God.

3. He lies to create mistrust towards God through his propaganda.

4. He uses the lust of the flesh to exploit human weaknesses.

5. He uses the lust of the eyes to create and incite misdirected desires.

6. He uses the pride of life to ensure a fall.

7. He uses fear as an entry point into people's lives.

8. He uses false beliefs sown into the heart to move a person to a wrong action.

9. He needs man to release his creative power in order for Satan's power to flow.

10. He uses accusations to create a legal judgment against man.

11. He uses those accusations and condemnation to enslave humanity.

12. He seeks to create a continual atmosphere of stress to deprive any real rest.

13. He will rob, kill, and destroy his victims at the end of their usefulness.

We have learned that he projects his rule through the kings of the earth and his schemes and attacks make their way down to the common person. The ruling principalities and powers then carry out Satan's mandate and directives in the following manner:

1. To maintain his kingdom as a covert shadow kingdom until it gains ascendancy to rival God's.

2. Execute and maintain a continual propaganda campaign of mistrust, accusations, and hate against the God of Heaven.

3. Create alternate gods of worship and false religions that promise gratification, provision, and protection. These gods are easily offended and are always poised to invoke judgment and wrath.

4. Principalities and powers endeavor to create a continual hostile world void of peace and always edging towards war.

5. Ruling spirits are to contend with the conscience of humanity resisting all that is good and creating an appetite for all that is evil.

6. Principalities and powers are to guard their domains against outbreaks of righteousness and resist angelic actions and incursions by the God of Heaven.

This age of the world without covenant marks a low point in the relationship between God and man. During this period of time, only a small part of humanity will experience friendship with God. It certainly is a far cry from what Adam and Eve experienced in the garden of Eden. God created man in His image, and He endowed Adam with His very nature for the purpose of friendship and having a family to share in His love. So much time has elapsed that one would wonder if it would be too late for mankind. This could be so except for the fact that God knew what He placed in the DNA of man and that humanity would eventually seek for more than what was being offered by Satan. By the time Moses makes his appearance in scripture, approximately 2500 years would have elapsed on the Jewish calendar.

Chapter 7

MOSES AND THE TURNING POINT FOR HUMANITY

Israel will spend approximately its first 275 years living in Egypt with some of the best pastureland of Egypt in the Goshen region. The scriptures speak of the people as being oppressed during their stay in Egypt. They would have been a discriminated minority because Egyptians considered sheep and shepherding as an abominable livestock and trade. Israel had grown and multiplied into nation status during this period of growth and prosperity. For this people, all they have ever known is the land of Egypt is its Egyptian culture, its lifestyle, and its gods.

There is no written history of the Israelites at this time; for it would be Moses who would record the first five books of the Bible, and he was not yet born. For the most part, they have assimilated into the Egyptian way of life. According to Psalms 106, even as the children of Israel would make their way to the Land of Promise, they would continue to worship the Canaanite and Egyptian gods. It was an age where polytheism was the norm and Yahweh would not be accorded the sole worship as being the one true God of Israel. The book of Acts would also record their wilderness years in this manner:

> *This is the same Moses who told the Israelites, 'God will raise up for you a prophet like me from among your own brothers.' He was in the assembly in the wilderness with the angel who spoke to him on Mount Sinai, and with our fathers. And he received living words to pass on to us.*

> *But our fathers refused to obey him. Instead, they rejected him and in their hearts turned back to Egypt. They said to Aaron, 'Make us gods who will go before us! As for this Moses who led us out of Egypt, we do not know what has happened to him.'*

> *At that time they made a calf and offered a sacrifice to the idol, rejoicing in the works of their hands. But God turned away from them and gave them over to the worship of the heavenly bodies, as it is written in the book of the prophets:*

> *'Did you offer Me slain beasts and sacrifices forty years in the wilderness, O house of Israel?*

> *You took along the tent of Moloch and the star of your god Rephan, the idols you made to*

worship. Therefore I will carry you away beyond Babylon' (Acts 7:37-43).

Egypt was defeated in war by a nation east of what is modern Israel called the Hyksos. Now, a new Pharaoh came to power and that nation had no historic relationship to Joseph or the children of Israel. The Hyksos dynasty brought Egypt under foreign rule and the Hyksos deemed this nation within the nation as a potential threat. Israel was enslaved as a people and through their suffering, they would cry out to the God of their forefathers.

Moses

It would appear that during that period of time, the hedge of protection had been lifted and Israel would suffer under Satan's oppression. The powers of darkness would be quite aware that mankind's deliverer would come through Israel and they may have been aware of Israel's blessing and prophecy over his son Judah. God's timetable was aligned in relation to all of His other dealings with the nations that would be players in Israel's return to the Promised Land. Do you recall the earlier quote from Genesis 15:16 where God tells Abraham that before Israel would return to the land Canaan, the sins of the Amorites would have to reach their full measure? That time had finally come, and it would be through a man named Moses, who was carefully prepared to lead this people out of Egypt.

Once again, we see another allegorical parallel in play that would relate to the life of Jesus. Pharaoh ordered the destruction of all males in Israel as a way for him to control the population of the Jewish nation. Spiritually, we can see behind the veil of history that it was Satan trying to prevent the birth of the Messiah. This scenario will play out again some 1500 years later as Satan learns that the Messiah had been born. He then uses King Herod to destroy all the male children 2 ½ years of age and younger in Bethlehem.

Moses would be spared the death by drowning and would be adopted into Pharaoh's own household. That is what you call a turning of the tables in the life of Moses whereby, it will be Pharaoh who will become the physical hedge of protection for Moses. This young man will have his own mother as his nanny who will keep him tied to his people and their heritage. At the same time, he will be schooled and trained as a future heir to the Egyptian throne. He will be required to master their religion, sciences, military, and governance should the transfer of power ever be accorded to him. All of this knowledge will play a role in this future leader of God's appointed nation.

> By faith Moses, when he was grown, refused to be called the son of Pharaoh's daughter. He chose to suffer oppression with God's people rather than to experience the fleeting enjoyment of sin. He valued disgrace for Christ above the treasures of Egypt, for he was looking ahead to his reward.
>
> By faith Moses left Egypt, not fearing the king's anger; he persevered because he saw Him who is invisible. By faith he kept the Passover and the sprinkling of blood, so that the destroyer of the firstborn would not touch Israel's own firstborn (Hebrews 11:24-28).

God will judge the Egyptians by judging the god's they worship. Every one of the 10 plagues correlates to a particular god of Egypt. I see little need to spend any depth of time on the events of the Exodus because they are well documented and understood.

Hapi the Nile god and Ra the sun god have been humiliated by the judgments against them by Yahweh, the God of Israel. The Egyptian people witness this first hand and they turn in favor towards the Israelites and venerate their God. Israel would leave for the Land of Promise with the wealth of Egypt as their repayment for more than 100 years of slavery. Egypt has been left in partial ruin and its armies will have to conquer new nations to replenish their slave labor workforce to continue their massive building projects.

The Long Awaited Invasion by the Kingdom of Heaven Has Begun

The war of independence from Egypt had been won without Israel having to wield a single sword in defense or anger. God had fought the battle for them without a single loss of life or casualty. In fact, they left Egypt, young and old without a single feeble one among them. Once again, we see a war being fought without the weapons of man, but rather, the decrees of God as spoken through His prophet. This warfare would again repeat itself at the battle of the Red Sea, with Egypt suffering another dramatic defeat.

Israel is now free of her oppressors and a people estimated to be more than a million are moving through the wilderness of Sinai as they make their return to the land promised to Abraham. One can only imagine the panic that was taking place in the war room of darkness as they witness the God of Heaven miraculously protecting Israel from the armies of Egypt. Michael, the archangel who is called the guardian of Israel leads the nation in safety to the place where God has chosen to make covenant with man and initiate the process to take back His rightful place with mankind on the earth.

To the kingdom of darkness, this must have been like the allied landings in Normandy France on D-Day, June 6, 1944. The enemy knew the invasion was coming but was unsure of exactly where or when it would take place. Now, the tide has turned and what Satan has feared has come upon him.

God Offers Covenant to Israel at Mount Sinai

On the first day of the third month after the Israelites left Egypt—on that very day—they came to the Desert of Sinai. After they set out from Rephidim, they entered the Desert of Sinai, and Israel camped there in the desert in front of the mountain.

*Then Moses went up to God, and the Lord called to him from the mountain and said, "This is what you are to say to the descendants of Jacob and what you are to tell the people of Israel: 'You yourselves have seen what I did to Egypt, and how I carried you on eagles' wings and brought you to myself. Now if you obey me fully and keep my covenant, then out of all nations you will be my treasured possession. **Although the whole earth is mine, you will be for me a kingdom of*** *priests and a holy nation.' These are the words you are to speak to the Israelites."*

So Moses went back and summoned the elders of the people and set before them all the words the Lord had commanded him to speak. The people all responded together, "We will do everything the Lord has said." So Moses brought their answer back to the Lord (Exodus 19:1-8).

Within this passage is the offer of the ages given by God. Israel was to be set apart as a nation and everyone would be as a priest before Him. Every person would have the privilege of coming directly before God without the need for an institution or person serving as the intermediary. Moses would essentially find himself needing to be reassigned to a new job description.

God wanted the restoration of the relationship that He had with Adam in the garden of Eden. Few on the earth at that time enjoyed what could be called a friendship with God. For most of humanity, those who even gave any consideration to the God of Heaven offered an acknowledged reverence from afar. The idea that God could bless you, protect you and prosper you was not an unfamiliar one in the minds of men. But to have friendship with God, well that was a completely different story?

We need to remember that at this time, there are no scriptures; there are no commandments, no laws, no statutes and essentially no religion of their own in Israel. Israel was told to celebrate the Passover each year as a remembrance of their deliverance from Egypt, but apart from that, there is little else about the events that led to the Exodus. The only prophetic words about the future Messiah at that time are that they now know He will come through the tribe of Judah. David, Isaiah, Zechariah and all of the other prophets who foretold the coming of the Lord and how and what He would suffer, have not even been born; therefore, their prophecies at this time, do not exist. The only indication of confrontation between the Redeemer of mankind and Satan is what God told Adam and Eve in Eden. Messiah's heel would be bruised as He uses it to crush Satan's head. The crushed head symbolizes the end of Satan's rule and the bruised heel of the Lord is not the picture of the horrible suffering that would later be foretold by the prophets. It makes one wonder if Israel had accepted the covenant as originally offered by God if the suffering of the nation and its Messiah would have been greatly lessened or not have happened at all?

More questions can be asked as these thoughts are pondered. What would a nation of priests look like and how would they minister to a lost world that does not know the one true God? All of history would have to be re-written and with what we now know concerning the New Covenant, (which is what God wanted in the first place) would it have been brought forward and implemented, right at that time? We will not learn the answers to these questions because the people, after first agreeing to God's offer, had a complete change of mind.

> *On the morning of the third day there was*
> *thunder and lightning, with a thick cloud over*
> *the mountain, and a very loud trumpet blast.*
> *Everyone in the camp trembled. Then Moses*
> *led the people out of the camp to meet with*

God, and they stood at the foot of the mountain. Mount Sinai was covered with smoke, because the Lord descended on it in fire. The smoke billowed up from it like smoke from a furnace, and the whole mountain trembled violently. As the sound of the trumpet grew louder and louder, Moses spoke and the voice of God answered him.

The Lord descended to the top of Mount Sinai and called Moses to the top of the mountain (Exodus 19:16-20).

In the midst of this awesome and terrifying display of the presence of God, the voice of God resounds like thunder as He declares to all of the people, the Ten Commandments. They were getting their first taste of what being a priesthood nation could entail as they heard directly from God.

When the people saw the thunder and lightning and heard the trumpet and saw the mountain in smoke, they trembled with fear. They stayed at a distance and said to Moses, "Speak to us yourself and we will listen. But do not have God speak to us or we will die." *Moses said to the people, "Do not be afraid. God has come to test you, so that the fear of God will be with you to keep you from sinning"* (Exodus 20:18-20).

The children of Israel did not realize what the cost of rejecting God's offer would mean as a people. They had heard the audible voice of God speak His commandments. If they had agreed to know Him intimately they could have known

111

and understood a love that would make one never want to violate their neighbor in any way. The laws of God would have been placed in their hearts and there would have been no need for them to be written in stone. As a result of their rejection of such intimacy, they and the world would see a setback to the plan of God that would add almost 1500 years before that offer would again be given to man. Jesus will fulfill this desire of the Father for a nation of priests, and it will now come through the spiritual seed of Abraham comprised of Jews and Gentiles who enter in by faith, through Jesus.

The people have requested that Moses be their spokesperson to God and God's voice to them. They will do what God requires from them and will obey the rules as set forth by Moses. The people did not want to be that close to God and preferred to be given rules and ordinances. That was precisely what they received in return from the Lord. One might make the comment that maybe God came on a little too strong in revealing who He was at Mt. Sinai. But we must remember that the children of Israel had witnessed His mighty acts and extraordinary supernatural events in their deliverance from the Egyptians. Furthermore, they had witnessed an unprecedented display of His awesome power at the Red Sea, so this was not some new experience they were unprepared to deal with or see.

Over the next three chapters, from Exodus 20 and on through to Chapter 23, Moses would receive a long list of rules and ordinances and that was only the beginning. From the remaining chapters of Exodus and on through Leviticus, Numbers, and Deuteronomy the people now had a comprehensive list of rules and requirements called the Law of Moses. The Ten Commandments that were audibly heard by all could have seen its fulfillment through God's love out of a living relationship with Him; it will now be laws etched in stone. That symbolic rigidity is exactly the impression that was to be understood by the nation. Now, God tells Moses what the covenant will require of both parties as they move to ratify the pact between God and man.

> *See, I am sending an angel ahead of you to guard you along the way and to bring you to the place I have prepared. Pay attention to him and listen to what he says. Do not rebel against him; he will not forgive your rebellion,* since my Name is in him. If you listen carefully to what he says and do all that I say, I will be an enemy to your enemies and will oppose those who oppose you. My angel will go ahead of you and bring you into the land of the Amorites, Hittites, Perizzites, Canaanites, Hivites and Jebusites, and I will wipe them out. Do not bow down before their gods or worship them or follow their practices. You must demolish them and break their sacred stones to pieces. Worship the Lord your God, and his blessing will be on your food and water. I will take away sickness from among you, and none will miscarry or be barren in your land. I will give you a full life span.
>
> "I will send my terror ahead of you and throw into confusion every nation you encounter. I will make all your enemies turn their backs and run. I will send the hornet ahead of you to

drive the Hivites, Canaanites and Hittites out of your way. But I will not drive them out in a single year, because the land would become desolate and the wild animals too numerous for you. Little by little I will drive them out before you, until you have increased enough to take possession of the land.

"I will establish your borders from the Red Sea to the Mediterranean Sea, and from the desert to the Euphrates River. I will give into your hands the people who live in the land, and you will drive them out before you. Do not make a covenant with them or with their gods. Do not let them live in your land or they will cause you to sin against me, because the worship of their gods will certainly be a snare to you" (Exodus 23:20-33).

God has laid out His commitment to the children of Israel. It is a promise of blessing, provision, safety, health, healing and a home. You may have noticed that this sounds very familiar to what we are promised in the New Covenant. The word "salvation" is from the Greek word *soteria* and is as follows:

Strong's Concordance

sótéria: deliverance, salvation

Original Word: σωτηρία, ας, □
Part of Speech: Noun, Feminine
Transliteration: *sótéria*
Phonetic Spelling: (so-tay-ree'-ah)
Short Definition: deliverance, salvation
Definition: welfare, prosperity, deliverance, preservation, salvation, safety.

The difference between the covenants is that under the Law of Moses each person will bear the judgment of his/her sin and that sin can be applied to the generations that follow. In the New Covenant, Jesus takes upon Himself the sins of the world and ends the judgment through His sinless life and the blood of His cross. Now, notice the first part of this passage is describing the angel that God would place over the nation to bring them to the Land of Promise. As previously mentioned, this guardian cherub is none other than Michael the Archangel as told by the prophet Daniel. You will notice that he has significant authority and will not compromise in any way his assignment from God. Israel is told to listen carefully to what they are told by the angel because he will be merciless towards any rebellion against God. We will see this scenario play out several times as Israel settles in the land of Canaan.

The people wanted rules; rules create laws and the violation of laws brings forth judgment. The template of the Old Covenant is now in place and will soon be set in stone. As with every covenant in the ancient world, it is sealed by shed blood. Moses prepares the altar for sacrifice and then gathers

115

together all of the elders of Israel to come before the Lord for the cutting of the covenant and the customary covenant meal.

> *When Moses went and told the people all the Lord's words and laws, they responded with one voice, "Everything the Lord has said we will do." Moses then wrote down everything the Lord had said.*
>
> *He got up early the next morning and built an altar at the foot of the mountain and set up twelve stone pillars representing the twelve tribes of Israel. Then he sent young Israelite men, and they offered burnt offerings and sacrificed young bulls as fellowship offerings to the Lord. Moses took half of the blood and put it in bowls, and the other half he splashed against the altar. Then he took the Book of the Covenant and read it to the people. They responded, "We will do everything the Lord has said; we will obey."*
>
> *Moses then took the blood, sprinkled it on the people and said, "This is the blood of the covenant that the Lord has made with you in accordance with all these words."*
>
> ***Moses and Aaron, Nadab and Abihu, and the seventy elders of Israel went up and saw the God of Israel. Under his feet was something like a pavement made of lapis lazuli, as bright blue as the sky.*** *But God did not raise his hand against these leaders of the Israelites; they saw God, and they ate and*

drank.

The Lord said to Moses, "Come up to me on the mountain and stay here, and I will give you the tablets of stone with the law and commandments I have written for their instruction" (Exodus 24:3-12).

As the elders and leaders of Israel come before the Lord for this most holy event, there is something that seems to get lost in telling of this story. In verse 10, we are told that the entire gathering witnessed the God of Israel standing on a ramp that was descending to the earth and it looked as though it was made of Lapis Lazuli. This brilliant blue gemstone is deeper in color than that of a sapphire. If you can imagine the death mask of King Tut and those brilliant stones of blue that were set in it, you can form the picture in your mind of this ramp, which appeared as the Lord stood upon it.

The color blue is the symbolic color of revelation and the prophetic. At that moment of history, nothing would have been required further in order to fulfill the prophetic promises of the coming Redeemer. This could only have been Jesus standing on that blue ramp a short distance from the earth in His glorification. This gives us an indication as to how close the Lord was to making His appearance on the earth. Israel chose an intermediary to be a spokesperson for them instead of being a priesthood nation where all could communicate directly, hear from God, and receive His instruction. They were offered the highest privilege that could have been given to anyone from God, which was the restored relationship that God and Adam shared. Israel's fearful refusal meant the world would have to wait until

Jesus makes that step off that celestial blue ramp through the womb of a woman and accept the Father's offer on behalf of mankind.

Israel saw the presence of God as being terrifying and frightful and would say no to God's covenant offer to them to be a priesthood nation.

Jesus would enter the world, stand on mankind's behalf and say yes to that same offer. Through the new birth, He would create a nation of kings and priests unto God.

Approximately 1500 years would elapse before the Lord Jesus would stand on behalf of mankind. Israel has suffered greatly as a nation during that time and now, so will the Messiah. The prophecies of David, Isaiah and others speak of a Messiah who will suffer and bear the full weight of the sin of mankind. When Jesus was in the garden of Gethsemane praying and seeing what would shortly happen to Him, at that moment, He could have said no. The plan of man's redemption would have been over and 12 legions of angels would have ended the entire ordeal. In the first century, a Roman legion numbered 10 Cohorts, which was 5,000 men. Jesus speaks to their understanding and tells them that He could have dispatched 60,000 angels to depart this earth and let it remain under judgment. In 2 Samuel 24, we read of David's sin and subsequent judgment that cost Israel 70,000 lives at the hand of a single angel. If we use that instance as a number to indicate what 60,000 angels could do in carrying out judgment, the number would equate to 4.2 billion people. 1st-century estimates of the earth's population are placed at 300 million persons; in other words, the population could have been erased some 14 times over.

There are an untold number of "what ifs" if Israel would have said yes to the covenant as first offered by God. Was this a glimpse of how close Jesus was to entering the world as Messiah in their day at Mt. Sinai?

There is a picture in my mind that is somehow reminiscent of a sci-fi movie from the fifties, "The Day the Earth Stood Still." In the closing scene, the man from another planet is standing on the ramp of his spaceship. He had come to warn the inhabitants of the earth to change their ways or face destruction. They do not listen at that time, but there is some hope given that a future generation may show a willingness to change. It makes you wonder if the writer of the script from that movie had taken it from this passage of scripture.

And so, the earth will have to wait for another day for the appearing of the Messiah and must persevere in hope for the promise of that future day.

Ramifications to the Spiritual Realm through the Enacted Covenant

The day the covenant was ratified between children of Israel and Yahweh, over 1 million people transferred out of the clutches and rule of the kingdom of darkness. The Law of Moses was weak in that it could not prevent a person from sinning, but it did give every person a temporary recourse to deal with his or her sins. When the accuser would come against them demanding judgment, the sacrificial offerings of the Law of Moses would be their defense. In the previous age, a person was always vulnerable to have his or her life sifted as wheat and under constant threat of reprisal.

The Old Covenant will act as a tourniquet to stop the bleeding of humanity until the New Covenant can deal with the wound of sin and completely heal it through Christ.

> *Therefore, just as sin entered the world through one man, and death through sin, so also death was passed on to all men, because all sinned. For sin was in the world before the Law was given; but sin is not taken into account when there is no law.* **Nevertheless, death reigned from Adam until Moses,** *even over those who did not sin in the way that Adam transgressed. He is a pattern of the one to come.*

> *But the gift is not like the trespass. For if the many died by the trespass of the one man, how much more did God's grace and the gift that came by the grace of the one man, Jesus Christ, abound to the many! Again, the gift is not like the result of the one man's sin: The judgment that followed one sin brought condemnation, but the gift that followed many trespasses brought justification.* **For if, by the trespass of the one man, death reigned through that one man, how much more will those who receive an abundance of grace and of the gift of righteousness reign in life through the one man, Jesus Christ!** (Romans 5:12-17).

Satan has suffered a setback but it is by no means a defeat. Israel's change of heart has given him a reprieve of time to come up with a counter strategy against the covenant made between God and the children of Israel. He will use his previous tactics of success but will do so on a much larger scale. It will be business as usual as it relates to his spiritual rule over all the other peoples and nations of the earth. An entire nation is now in a covenant relationship with the Almighty God and what the ramifications of this new development will mean for the planet, remains somewhat of a mystery to the powers of darkness.

Chapter 8

_____

THE AGE OF THE FIRST COVENANT

The Law is only a shadow of the good things to come, not the realities themselves. It can never, by the same sacrifices offered year after year, make perfect those who draw near to worship. If it could, would not the offerings have ceased? For the worshipers would have been cleansed once for all and would no longer feel the guilt of their sins.

Instead, those sacrifices are an annual reminder of sins, because it is impossible for the blood of bulls and of goats to take away sins. Therefore, when Christ came into the world, He said:

"Sacrifice and offering You did not desire, but a body You prepared for me.

In burnt offerings and sin offerings You took no delight.

Then I said, 'Here I am, it is written about Me in the scroll: I have come to do Your will, O God.'"

In the passage above He says, "Sacrifices and offerings, burnt offerings and sin offerings You did not desire, nor did You delight in them" (although they are required by the Law).

Then He adds, "Here I am, I have come to do Your will." **He takes away the first to establish the second. And by that will, we have been sanctified through the sacrifice of the body of Jesus Christ once for all** (Hebrews 10:1-10).

Israel had made its choice. A covenant was then ratified and put in place. As the writer of Hebrews so eloquently explained, this first covenant is but a shadow of what God had originally intended. A shadow is but a dark outline that is cast only after the light has touched the real image. The New Covenant was the real deal plan of God that was rejected and was brought down to a mere shadow of the glory that God had intended. God would not be satisfied with this first covenant and will one day make His original offer to humanity and see its fulfillment through Jesus the Christ of God.

Therefore there is now no condemnation for those who are in Christ Jesus. For in Christ Jesus the law of the Spirit of life has set you free from the law of sin and death. **For what the Law was powerless to do in that it was weakened by the flesh, God did by sending His own Son in the likeness of sinful man, as** *an offering for sin. He thus condemned sin in the flesh, so that the righteous standard of the Law might be fulfilled in us, who do not live according to the flesh but according to the Spirit* (Romans 8:1-4).

Now if perfection could have been attained through the Levitical priesthood (upon which basis the people received the Law), why was there still a need for another priest to appear—one in the order of Melchizedek and not in the order of Aaron? *For when the priesthood is changed, the Law must be changed as well. He of whom these things are said belonged to a different tribe, from which no one has ever served at the altar. For it is clear that our Lord descended from Judah, a tribe as to which Moses said nothing about priests.*

And this point is even more clear if another priest like Melchizedek appears, one who has become a priest not by a law of succession, but by the power of an indestructible life. For it is testified:

"You are a priest forever in the order of Melchizedek."

So the former commandment is set aside because it was weak and useless (for the Law made nothing perfect), and a better hope is introduced, by which we draw near to God.

125

*And none of this happened without an oath.
For others became priests without an oath, but
Jesus became a priest with an oath by the One
who said to Him:*

*"The Lord has sworn and will not change His
mind, 'You are a priest forever.'"*

**Because of this oath, Jesus has become the
guarantee of a better covenant** (Hebrews
7:11-22).

Despite the inherent weaknesses of the Law of Moses, the
Old Covenant will give man a legal recourse against the
accusations of Satan and the demands for punishment. The
Day of Atonement will be the yearly "catch-all" for sin and
you could also go immediately to the temple and make an
offering for more specific offenses that may arise. These
offerings would provide the legal shield that would be able to
withstand the enemy's fiery projectiles. The vulnerability of
this kind of hedge of protection is that it would be based
entirely on man fulfilling to the letter, the requirements of
the covenant.

This proved to be an impossible task to do and it makes you
wonder what the children of Israel were thinking when they
said to Moses that he should hear from God, find out the
rules, and they would obey them. This was not the covenant
that God wanted to make and the elders of Israel should have
realized that they were incapable (as any people would) of
following the rules to the exact letter.

Ramifications to the Realm of the Spirit by the Old Covenant

I wish that I could record some dramatic changes that scripture reveals took place in the heavenly places when the first covenant was enacted. This would not be the case beyond anything that I have previously stated. Demonic principalities and powers carry on their dominion throughout the earth with very little impact on their operative rule. The only significant change is that they must now contend with angelic authority as it relates to the nation of Israel. In fact, as populations increase and empires rise to power, man's inhumanity to man worsens with every generation. To further add to the scope of this perspective, we need to see this covenant through the lens of all humanity. Population estimates for the entire world place the number in excess of 100 million persons in and around 1500 BC. Israel's population as we discussed earlier, places the population at around 1 million or more, which amounts to approximately 1% of the earth's population.

Jesus spoke of a parable of the good shepherd leaving his 99 sheep to seek out his one lost sheep. Imagine the reversal of those numbers. He has 99 lost sheep and has recovered just one lamb up to that point in history. I think you can see that the period before covenant and the first covenant created only a slight impact on the kingdom of darkness and mankind's enslavement to sin.

Israel, on the other hand, would have the opportunity to live under an open heaven if they would remain faithful to the covenant and their God. Unfortunately, the desire to be like the other nations that surround them proved to be too much of an enticement. They do not want God as their King; they want to have a king who is like all of the other kingdoms of the world. The seductive worship of the gods of the region also proves to be a continual stumbling block for them. Any revival in the land will barely last that generation before Israel would go off chasing some other god. The appetite of the lusts of the eyes and the lusts of the flesh is never satisfied. The pride of life will ever drive them to be as or better than their neighboring nations.

Satan exploited the weakness of this agreement for the simple reason that these holy laws, (which are truly beautiful in origin), could not be fulfilled by fallen mankind. No matter how devout or determined man thought he could be, his fallen DNA would at some point fail him, time and again.

God certainly knew that this would be the case, but unfortunately, Israel would have to come to that same knowledge the hard way. Over the course of Israel's history, the nation experiences a pattern of rising by the favor of God, falling into sin and being ransacked by her enemies. They then cry out to God in desperation and repentance. God is always faithful to honor His commitment to the covenant and His people and once again, He comes as their deliverer. Once safety and calm are restored, the cycle repeats itself and continues to be the case, over and over again. This pattern is not just Israel's story; this will be true for anyone who believes they can find their justification through works of righteousness in his or her strength. It would seem that humanity is hungering for moral uprightness but cannot attain it because sin is a part of man's DNA.

The Era of Moral Law

There is an ancient Arabian proverb that says, "Sleep doesn't help if it's your soul that is tired." This would seem to be an accurate description of mankind throughout this time period of history. According to the Jewish calendar, civilization is now approximately 2500 years old and it has been an age of the survival of the fittest and the most cunning. There is something that reveals a unique trend that is happening throughout the earth during this time period. Moral law has begun to emerge amongst the nations as a way to stop the chaos and control the evil that was so prevalent in early civilization.

The Sumerian code of Ur-Nammu and Babylonian code of Hammurabi pre-date the Law of Moses, while Traditional Chinese law will follow in the decades after. It is as if the world was looking for some change to how humanity has lived. It was as though the earth was like a woman travailing in birth in the belief that a child would be born that would deliver the nations from the weight of its sin. Humanity was almost simultaneously preparing for a change and then it stopped. It makes one wonder if God Himself was setting the stage for the entire world and preparing it for the great revelation of His Son when the first covenant was offered. When thinking of mankind in this way, it is almost as though the 100-Monkey Principle that I wrote of earlier is having a similar intuitive effect throughout humanity. Change is coming to man, and mankind is almost subconsciously anticipating that a new era is in the making. Therefore, it finds itself moving towards this moral shift. Make no mistake about it, the world during this period is still violent and unforgiving with little regard for human life, but it does reflect a desire for change and a glimmer of hope for a new beginning, for a new era.

The Biblical View of the Three Ages of Mankind

Throughout this book, my goal is to show mankind in three ages. They are as follows; the world without covenant, the first covenant, better known as the Old Covenant and the age of the New Covenant in which we now live. So, a reasonable question to ask is, "Where in the scriptures is the basis to make this kind of assertion?" Let's read what Paul had to say on the subject when he compares the two covenants. He has begun the third chapter of Galatians by being shocked by the prospect that the Galatian church wants to return to the Law of Moses. He confronts their foolishness, and it is from that context that he explains the differences between the two covenants.

> Before this faith came, we were held in custody under the Law, locked up until faith should be revealed. So the Law became our guardian to lead us to Christ, that we might be justified by faith. Now that faith has come, we are no longer under a guardian. You are all sons of God through faith in Christ Jesus. For all of you who were baptized into Christ have clothed yourselves with Christ. There is neither Jew nor Greek, slave nor free, male nor female, for you are all one in Christ Jesus. And if you belong to Christ, then you are Abraham's seed and heirs according to the promise (Galatians 3:23-29)

What I am saying is that as long as the heir is a child, he is no different from a slave, although he is the owner of everything. He is subject to guardians and trustees until the date set by his father.

So also, when we were children, we were enslaved under the basic principles of the world. But when the time had fully come, God sent His Son, born of a woman, born under the Law, to redeem those under the Law, that we might receive our adoption as sons. And because you are sons, God sent the Spirit of His Son into our hearts, crying out, "Abba, Father!" So you are no longer a slave, but a son; and since you are a son, you are also an heir through God (Galatians 4:1-7).

Paul makes his point by using the description of a person who is an heir. There is a set date when the person would be of age and be able to access and enter into his or her full inheritance. Paul describes the period of not being able to access the inheritance as being enslaved by the base and immature cravings that drive the person. He then talks about this child coming to an age whereby he requires teachers and guardians who control access to the estate on behalf of the young person. These trustees will ensure that all of the instructions of the will are properly executed.

Are you seeing where Paul is going with this? The age without covenant is like a toddler during the period known to parents as the "terrible twos." The child's focus is on his or her own needs and can sometimes be out of control. The

131

child requires constant supervision by parents or as in Paul's analogy, tutors or guardians. That was the picture of early civilization; everyone was doing what they deemed was right in their own eyes. It seemed that little order was established except by violence at the hands of a harsh ruler or tyrant.

As that heir to the estate gets older and has gained some maturity, his teachers and guardians then groom the child for adulthood. The period of the emergence of moral law on the earth and God's covenant with the nation of Israel, mark for me a turning point in civilization. It was as though mankind is maturing and is readying itself for an era of adulthood. This is the picture that Paul the apostle is painting concerning the Old Covenant. It is in place, overseeing you until you reach the age of maturity as outlined in that will and testament.

The New Covenant is the age of maturity whereby you can enter all that God has made available to you through Christ. It is as though God was grooming mankind morally and socially so that all the peoples of the earth would be ready to hear the words of Jesus and receive Him. We tend to forget how extreme the message of love, mercy, and forgiveness must have seemed to the first-century world. Jesus was putting forth radical truths, which societies and peoples were now ready to hear. This is adulthood for humanity and the right of inheritance has come through our Lord Jesus in the New Covenant. According to the Jewish calendar, it has taken mankind almost four thousand years to reach the age of maturity whereby it was ready to enter the age of the New Covenant. Two thousand more years have taken place for this symbolic picture of mankind to grow in wisdom and maturity.

The chronological picture depicted through this allegory is to show us that until we receive the New Covenant reality, we can never enter into our inheritance. The only way to enter this covenant is by grace through faith in the finished work of redemption by Jesus Christ. Jesus is the rightful heir, and we come of age and become joint-heirs through Him. To live a form of Christianity that still holds out the doing of works for a standing of righteousness is to be fallen from grace. That is a road that leads you back to the Old Covenant and no longer of age to live in the inheritance appointed for you.

For if that first covenant had been without fault, no place would have been sought for a second. But when God found fault with the people, He said:

"Behold, the days are coming, says the Lord, when I will make a new covenant with the house of Israel and with the house of Judah.

It will not be like the covenant I made with their fathers when I took them by the hand to lead them out of the land of Egypt, because they did not abide by My covenant, and I disregarded them, says the Lord.

This is the covenant I will make with the house of Israel after those days, says the Lord.

I will put My laws in their minds, and inscribe them on their hearts.

And I will be their God, and they will be My people.

133

No longer will each one teach his neighbor or his brother, saying, 'Know the Lord,'

because they will all know Me, from the least of them to the greatest.

For I will forgive their iniquities and remember their sins no more."

In speaking of a new covenant, He has made the first one obsolete; and what is obsolete and aging will soon disappear (Hebrews 8:7-13).

This book began by addressing the subject of words. Each covenant is comprised of words that form the basis of an agreement. Once the agreement is ratified, it is then enacted into law. The knowledge of the rights that are contained within each treaty provides the heir with the authority to access those rights as outlined by the words of that covenant. Why is this important to the subject of spiritual warfare? If you do not understand the authority and executable rights of the covenant you are under, how then will you know what are those rights and provisions that are afforded you in the new treaty? Furthermore, you will also know what is not part of the treatise and any other restrictions or limitations that have been put in place. You are only empowered to enforce the words of the covenant that have been made with you through our Lord Jesus Christ.

You cannot live in both covenants, for it will always lead you to works and your subsequent judgment under the Law of Moses. Paul was a Pharisee from the strictest sect under Gamaliel; he understood this so completely that he warned the saints constantly against doing so in his letters. Grace through faith cannot be mixed with works for righteousness. It will always be as shifting sand under your feet and never provide the certainty of your standing in Christ, which is the difference between winning and losing in battle. We will cover these issues in greater detail in the later chapters.

Chapter 9

SUMMARY OF THE AGE OF THE FIRST COVENANT

The covenant between God and the children of Israel gave God the legal right to contend for mankind and to deliver them from their spiritual enslavement. When you think in terms of what that covenant could have been, that victory has a somewhat hollow ring to it. If Israel would have accepted the offer of a national priesthood, their service to man would have been the evangelizing of the world and making the Messiah known to all. Instead, they became a somewhat closed society wanting little to do with the Goyim; otherwise known as the Gentiles.

Demonic principalities and powers are largely unaffected by this first covenant as they work to keep Israel in a continual state of being in violation of the written code. That is their strategy of containment, to make the Law of Moses work against Israel and they are very successful in doing so. There was even an attempt by Satan to take the corpse of Moses and use it for some unrevealed purpose. However, Michael the archangel contended for the body of Moses and foiled that evil plan.

> *But even the archangel Michael, when he disputed with the devil over the body of Moses, did not presume to bring a slanderous judgment against him, but said, "The Lord rebuke you!"* (Jude verse 9).

You will notice again that there is no clash of swords, but rather, a clash of words. Within those words, each party would announce the right of authority. Moses belonged to God in life and in death. Michael breaks the legal stalemate by appealing to the highest authority and the decision brings the whole matter to a close.

In the book of Zechariah, we see a similar confrontation between the angel of the Lord and Satan. In this confrontation, Satan accuses Joshua the son of Jehozadak who was the high priest during the temple reconstruction period. Joshua stands before the angel of the Lord in filthy priesthood garments while Satan levels his charges against the man. Once again, we see no clash of swords, but rather, words of contention that lead to an ultimate rebuke from the Lord through the angel to Satan.

> *Then he showed me Joshua the high priest standing before the angel of the Lord, and Satan standing at his right side to accuse him. The Lord said to Satan, "The Lord rebuke you, Satan! The Lord, who has chosen*

Jerusalem, rebuke you! Is not this man a burning stick snatched from the fire?"

Now Joshua was dressed in filthy clothes as he stood before the angel. The angel said to those who were standing before him, "Take off his filthy clothes."

Then he said to Joshua, "See, I have taken away your sin, and I will put fine garments on you."

Then I said, "Put a clean turban on his head." So they put a clean turban on his head and clothed him, while the angel of the Lord stood by.

The angel of the Lord gave this charge to Joshua: "This is what the Lord Almighty says: 'If you will walk in obedience to me and keep my requirements, then you will govern my house and have charge of my courts, and I will give you a place among these standing here.

"'Listen, High Priest Joshua, you and your associates seated before you, who are men symbolic of things to come: I am going to bring my servant, the Branch. See, the stone I have set in front of Joshua! There are seven eyes on that one stone, and I will engrave an inscription on it,' says the Lord Almighty, 'and I will remove the sin of this land in a single day (Zechariah 3:1-8).

What is so absolutely striking about this passage is that the angel of the Lord (probably Michael the archangel) tells Joshua that his current life situation is also a spiritual picture of what is going to come. The priesthood of Israel stands before the Lord in filthy garments, which represent the righteousness of all mankind no matter what their position or status. The very name of the high priest is Joshua, which in Hebrew is *Yeshua* and is translated as Jesus into English. The angel tells Joshua son of Jehozadak that his life is a spiritual picture and reference is made to the "branch," which is the prophetic term used for describing the coming Messiah. This is the second time that we see this prophetic picture reveal itself in scripture. The name *Yeshua* (Joshua) translates to, "the Lord is salvation." Just as Joshua succeeded Moses, which represents the Old Covenant being succeeded by the New Covenant, the earthly priesthood represented by *Yeshua* son of Jehozadak will be replaced by the Messiah Yeshua who is the eternal High Priest for mankind.

This passage of scripture will continue to reveal that the earthly priesthood is to be cleansed and given new, clean garments, and sin is to be brought to an end in a day. That is what happened through Christ's redemptive victory. The shed blood of Jesus on the cross dealt with sin's damning testimony against man once and for all. Satan's legal right to accuse and bring man under judgment is brought to an end for all those who would receive His free gift of grace. The power of sin has been brought to an end and as believers, we should never give ear to Satan's accusations because he and his authority have been cast down; they no longer carry any legal weight or right. Only you can give him back that power, by heeding and believing his accusing lies.

That is what awaits mankind under the New Covenant, but under the Old Covenant little has been changed in the spiritual realm as Israel is the only open spiritual portal to the earth. During these first two ages, we have witnessed that the demonic ruling powers seem to have little restrictions placed upon them. Yet, they seem to have significant authority to hinder angelic activity on the earth. This is further exacerbated by the nation of Israel being led into sin depending upon which king is ruling at that time. We will read in the book of Daniel how the angel of the Lord is hindered from bringing Daniel's answered prayer. It is only after Michael the archangel, Israel's guardian breaks that delay on the 21st day that we can see how tenuous the spiritual realm was at that time.

> Then he continued, "Do not be afraid, Daniel. Since the first day that you set your mind to gain understanding and to humble yourself before your God, your words were heard, and I have come in response to them. But the prince of the Persian kingdom resisted me twenty-one days. Then Michael, one of the chief princes, came to help me, because I was detained there with the king of Persia. Now I have come to explain to you what will happen to your people in the future, for the vision concerns a time yet to come" (Daniel 10:12-14).

Aggression and war in the spiritual realm take the form of prevailing legal actions and rights as the context for a war of words. Every glimpse that we have seen from the scriptures alludes to a verbal confrontation, which ends in a prevailing word that brings about decisive actions. When these actions move into the natural realm on earth, their tendency is to move toward a physical response. What I find interesting from the last verse of Chapter 10 is a very gripping statement by the angel of the Lord to close out this prophetic passage.

> So he said, "Do you know why I have come to you? Soon I will return to fight against the prince of Persia, and when I go, the prince of Greece will come; but first I will tell you what is written in the Book of Truth. (No one supports me against them except Michael, your prince) (Daniel 10:20, 21).

This messenger angel is probably Gabriel as he has come to Daniel on a previous occasion to deliver to him a word from the Lord. He tells Daniel that he has no other support to enter the earth realm except through Michael the archangel who is called a ruling angel in this passage. There would only be one angel that would come to the angelic messenger's aid and free him from his detention. Why is that the case, could not God have sent a legion of angels to force their way through any blockade? As was stated in the previous chapter, Michael is the guardian cherub of Israel. He is the ruling spirit over the only people on earth who call Yahweh their God. They are an exiled people living in Babylon after being defeated by its armies subsequent to their breaking of their covenant with God. There is no longer an open heaven over the nation and this has severely limited the actions by God on behalf of His people. This is a rare view into the spiritual realm during the period of the Old Covenant, and it shows the kingdom of darkness in operation and seemingly as dominant as it was in the age before covenant.

This passage of scripture has given us a glimpse of the legal authority that is invoked in the spiritual realm. The prophetic decrees that God had given to King Nebuchadnezzar and also to Daniel in dreams and angelic visitations had become due. The time of their fulfillment was fast approaching, and they were about to reach their next level of fulfillment. These prophetic decrees revealed the change of empires as well as the completion of Jeremiah's prophecy of the 70 years of Israel's exile in Babylon. The warfare in the heavenly realm is to prevent God's decreed timetable from coming to pass as the ruling spiritual powers know the legal term of Israel's judgment is soon ending. The prince over Persia cannot withstand God's word from taking place and already, the prince over Greece is preparing to move in to exert its rule over Babylon. This brief passage reveals the interest by the principality that is over Greece in the affairs of Babylon even before the literal history of the earth has taken place. The armies of Alexander the Great will roll through the Middle East, defeat the Persians, and bring those prophecies to fruition some two hundred years later.

But wait, how can this be? Is not Satan the ruler of mankind and they do his bidding? How is it that mankind can also do God's bidding on the earth?

Conscience, Belief and the Will of Man

Even though man's conscience is seared and hardened through sin; it is still, nevertheless, a conscience. God will work past the walls that people have put up against Him and airdrop dreams into their souls. Those dreams are like parachutes containing His purposes and His will; they bypass the barriers of a hardened heart. It is from the book of Job we learn that God uses this vehicle to communicate with man through the realm of dreams. During this time of sleep, God speaks into the subconscious soul of a person and reveals His destiny and plans for his or her life.

> *A word was secretly brought to me, my ears caught a whisper of it.*
>
> *Amid disquieting dreams in the night, when deep sleep falls on people* (Job 4:12, 13).
>
> *For God does speak—now one way, now another — though no one perceives it. In a dream, in a vision of the night, when deep sleep falls on people as they slumber in their beds, he may speak in their ears*
>
> *and terrify them with warnings, to turn them from wrongdoing*
>
> *and keep them from pride, to preserve them from the pit, their lives from perishing by the sword"* (Job 33:14-18).

Man has a conscience and a will. He is still able to rise to any level of belief and change his own course or on an even greater scale, bring change to a nation. Throughout the scriptures, even as far back as with Abraham, we see God speaking into the lives of rulers and kings. He forewarns them of famines, wars, and sin that will bring their people into judgment. He gives them direction and even foretells the future to Pharaohs and kings who do not know Him. We read of God's interaction with rulers because of the impact their decisions have on a broad scale on the masses that make up their sphere of authority. We see this continually taking place in the scriptures, but on a lesser scale, be certain of the fact that God is certainly speaking and doing the same with the common person.

Why would the ruling principality over Greece accommodate the will of God and be a part of the downfall of the principality over Persia? As has been stated in the previous chapters, it is acted upon words and beliefs of a person that will bring them into engagement with the kingdom of God or the empire of death. So what has transpired that has moved Greece to do the will of God? We will have to look outside of the scriptures to read the writings of Josephus who was a Jewish historian for the Roman Empire.

From his writings on Jewish Antiquities, book 11.317-345 we read the following excerpts:

> So Alexander came into Syria, and took Damascus; and when he had obtained Sidon, he besieged Tyre, when he sent all epistle to the Jewish high priest, to send him some auxiliaries, and to supply his army with provisions; and that what presents he formerly sent to Darius, he would now send to him, and choose the friendship of the Macedonians, and that he should never repent of so doing. But the high priest answered the messengers, that he had given his oath to Darius not to bear arms against him; and he said that he would not transgress this while Darius was in the land of the living. Upon hearing this answer, Alexander

was very angry; and though he determined not to leave Tyre, which was just ready to be taken, yet as soon as he had taken it, he threatened that he would make an expedition against the Jewish high priest, and through him teach all men to whom they must keep their oaths. So when he had, with a good deal of pains during the siege, taken Tyre, and had settled its affairs, he came to the city of Gaza, and besieged both the city and him that was governor of the garrison, whose name was Babemeses.

Now Alexander, when he had taken Gaza, made haste to go up to Jerusalem; and Jaddua the high priest, when he heard that, was in an agony, and under terror, as not knowing how he should meet the Macedonians, since the king was displeased at his foregoing disobedience. He therefore ordained that the people should make supplications, and should join with him in offering sacrifice to God, whom he besought to protect that nation, and to deliver them from the perils that were coming upon them; whereupon God warned him in a dream, which came upon him after he had offered sacrifice, that he should take courage, and adorn the city, and open the gates; that the rest should appear in white garments, but that he and the priests should meet the king in the habits proper to their order, without the dread of any ill consequences, which the providence of God would prevent. Upon which, when he rose from his sleep, he greatly rejoiced, and declared to all the warning he had received from God. According to which dream he acted entirely, and so waited for the coming of the king.

5. And when he understood that he was not far from the city, he went out in procession, with the priests and the multitude of the citizens. The procession was venerable, and the manner of it different from that of other nations. It reached to a place called Sapha, which name, translated into Greek, signifies a prospect, for you have thence a prospect both of Jerusalem and of the temple. And when the Phoenicians and the Chaldeans that followed him thought they should have liberty to plunder the city, and torment the high priest to death, which the king's displeasure fairly promised them, the very reverse of it happened; for Alexander, when he saw the multitude at a distance, in white garments, while the priests stood clothed with fine linen, and the high priest in purple and scarlet clothing, with his mitre on his head, having the golden plate whereon the name of God was engraved, he approached by himself, and adored that name, and first saluted the high priest. The Jews also did all together, with one voice, salute Alexander, and encompass him about; whereupon the kings of Syria and the rest were surprised at what Alexander had done, and supposed him disordered in his mind. However, Parmenio alone went up to him, and asked him how it came to pass that, when all others adored him, he should adore the high priest of the Jews? To whom he replied, "I did not adore him, but that God who hath honored him with his high priesthood; for I saw this very person in a dream, in this very habit, when I was at Dios in Macedonia, who, when I was considering with myself how I might obtain the dominion of Asia, exhorted me to make no delay, but boldly to pass over the sea thither, for that he would conduct my army, and would give me the dominion over the Persians; whence it is that, having seen no other in that habit, and now seeing this person in it, and remembering that vision, and the exhortation which I had in my dream, I believe that I bring this army under the Divine conduct, and shall therewith conquer Darius, and destroy the power of the Persians, and that all things will succeed according to what is in my own mind." And when he had said this to Parmenio, and had given the high priest his right hand, the priests ran along by him, and he came into the city. And when he went up into the temple, he offered sacrifice to God, according to the high priest's direction, and magnificently treated both the high priest and the priests. And when the Book of Daniel was showed him wherein Daniel declared that one of the Greeks should destroy the empire of the Persians, he supposed that himself was the person intended. And as he was then glad, he dismissed the multitude for the present; but the next day he called them

to him, and bid them ask what favors they pleased of him; whereupon the high priest desired that they might enjoy the laws of their forefathers, and might pay no tribute on the seventh year. He granted all they desired. And when they entreared him that he would permit the Jews in Babylon and Media to enjoy their own laws also, he willingly promised to do hereafter what they desired. And when he said to the multitude, that if any of them would enlist themselves in his army, on this condition, that they should continue under the laws of their forefathers, and live according to them, he was willing to take them with him, many were ready to accompany him in his wars.
(-Josephus, Antiquities of the Jews, Book 11)

Alexander the Great had a dream from the God he did not know. He had seen what the representative priests had worn in his dream, and for the first time, he recognizes that it is the apparel of Israel's high priest. Yahweh was the God who revealed Alexander's destiny to him, and he bows to the ground to the representative of the God of Heaven. In the due course of time, Alexander will have fulfilled for God the prophecies over the nations through his conquest of the region. History records other such events, from dream encounters that would change the course of events in a person's life and even the world. Unfortunately, the vehicle of using dreams to shape one's destiny would also find its use by the enemy. But in the end, every dream must be believed and acted upon by that person to engage the destiny that is found in the dream.

The prophet Daniel had the distinct experience to serve under and bring counsel to two empires during his lifetime. He served Nebuchadnezzar and the Babylonian empire until its fall to the Medo-Persian Empire and served in the court of Darius I.

Daniel's prophetic book would have been in circulation for almost two hundred years before Alexander the Great would bring his armies against Darius III in 334 BC.

Israel did not suffer at the hands of Alexander's armies, and they continued to rebuild the nation just as it was promised. Malachi would be the last prophetic voice that would lead to a silent period lasting some 400 years. During this time, the empire of Greece would continue to be the occupying empire over Israel until its defeat by the Roman Empire. This will lead to another completed stage of Nebuchadnezzar's dream and Rome would be the occupying power at the time of Christ's birth. Things are about to change.

> In the time of those kings, the God of heaven will set up a kingdom that will never be destroyed, nor will it be left to another people. It will crush all those kingdoms and bring them to an end, but it will itself endure forever. This is the meaning of the vision of the rock cut out of a mountain, but not by human hands—a rock that broke the iron, the bronze, the clay, the silver and the gold to pieces.

> "The great God has shown the king what will take place in the future. The dream is true and its interpretation is trustworthy (Daniel 2:44, 45).

Daniel had interpreted Nebuchadnezzar's dream of four empires that will fall to a ruler who is a rock. This uncut stone, not made by human hands will strike the feet of this last empire (Rome), reduce it and all the other empires to dust and scatter that dust in the wind. This stone will grow into a mountain and fill the earth. This uncut stone is none other than Jesus Christ and of His kingdom there will be no end.

Chapter 10

JESUS THE SAVIOUR OF THE WORLD

For to us a child is born, to us a son is given, and the government will be on his shoulders. And he will be called Wonderful Counselor, Mighty God, Everlasting Father, Prince of Peace. Of the greatness of his government and peace there will be no end.

He will reign on David's throne and over his kingdom, establishing and upholding it

with justice and righteousness from that time on and forever. The zeal of the Lord Almighty will accomplish this (Isaiah 9:6, 7).

The First Shot across the Bow

The time has come; it is in the Lord's thirtieth year that the Father tells Jesus the moment has come to reveal Himself to Israel. Some fifteen hundred years before the Lord was born in Bethlehem, Moses had gone into the mountain wilderness of Sinai to fast 40 days and received the impartation of the details of the First Covenant. Jesus now goes into the wilderness and enters His 40-day fast. He receives all of the Father's heart and mind for the New Covenant. The perfect God/man Christ Jesus, will completely fulfill all of the Father's heart for the New Covenant while completely fulfilling the legal requirement of righteousness under the Old Covenant.

But before the Lord should begin His ministry Satan attempts to do to Jesus what he had succeeded in doing to Adam. He uses his tried and true tactics of temptation to try to thwart the purposes of God before Jesus goes on the offensive; the war is about to get underway.

> *Then Jesus was led by the Spirit into the wilderness to be tempted by the devil. After fasting forty days and forty nights, He was hungry.*
>
> *The tempter came to Him and said, "If You are the Son of God, tell these stones to become bread."*
>
> *But Jesus answered, "It is written: 'Man shall not live on bread alone,*
>
> *but on every word that comes from the mouth of God.'" Then the devil took Him to the holy city and set Him on the pinnacle of the temple. "If You are the Son of God," he said, "throw Yourself down. For it is written:*

154

*'He will command His angels concerning You,
and they will lift You up in their hands, so that
You will not strike Your foot against a stone.'"*

*Jesus replied, "It is also written: 'Do not put the
Lord your God to the test.'"*

*Again, the devil took Him to a very high
mountain and showed Him all the kingdoms of
the world and their glory. "All this I will give
You," he said, "if You will fall down and
worship me."*

*"Away from me, Satan!" Jesus declared. "For it
is written: 'Worship the Lord your God and
serve Him only.' Then the devil left Him, and
angels came and ministered to Him* (Matthew
4:1-11).

When Satan confronts Jesus on this occasion, he must have
felt quite assured in his position as the god of this world. This
is their first face-to-face confrontation that they would have
had in untold ages of time. Since Jesus' birth, Satan has
already made one recorded assassination attempt on Jesus'
life, which made the Lord and His family live as fugitives in
Egypt with a bounty on His head. The guardian of Israel,
Michael the Archangel has done his service to the Lord in
protecting Jesus through His childhood. Now, Jesus is ready
to begin His ministry. Up to this point, Satan has witnessed
Jesus grow into manhood without any recorded
confrontation with the Lord in scripture. I am sure that Satan
believed he had the situation under control and was now
poised to make his move.

The state of the world at large is right where he wants it to be and mankind is almost unrecognizable as God's creation because of sin. Much of the so-called civilized world of the 1st century is ruled by Rome, which is Satan's protégé whereby he can flex his muscles on the earth. The Israel of Jesus' day by the Lord's own admission, is a wicked and perverse generation. So, it is in that pompous state of arrogance and pride that the Devil feels strong enough in his rule, to confront Jesus.

The Devil will employ his four thousand-year-old strategy of using lust (the strong desire to have or want something) and the heady wine of pride. These two elements are found in the three temptations that Jesus will specifically face in the scriptural record. Jesus had just fasted forty days and was hungry. At that point, the enemy struck and sought to exploit any weakness in the Lord.

The enemy always seeks to exploit us when we are in weakened states physically or emotionally. That knowledge should be your spiritual cue to amp up the guarding of your heart and mind for battle.

The lust of the flesh does not have to be of a matter of engaging in some form of debauchery; it can be as simple as satisfying a basic human need by compromising from whom and how you meet that need. Jesus would rather hunger longer and be satisfied by God's hand than to take a shortcut away from God's purposes. Satan can quote the scriptures, but he cannot experience the sustenance that Jesus the Bread of Life provides. When Jesus told Satan that man shall live by every word that comes from God's mouth, He was making a statement. The first was that quoting scriptures does not make it the living word of God, for it must come from the living breathing mouth of God. Only the Holy Spirit can breathe the life of God into the written Word and Jesus was that voice of God on the earth. The second implied point of the Lord's response was, "I know the voice of God and yours isn't it." That was the first big shot to the gut of the god of this world and his rule.

The second temptation was to provoke any pride that might be found in Jesus to prove that He is, in fact, the Son of God. Satan wants the Lord to leap off the highest point of the temple and have the angels keep Him from falling. The Devil knows who Jesus is, but he is trying to get the Lord to justify Himself and provoke His ego to act. What the Devil is trying to produce is the very result that the scriptures teach, which is, "that pride goes before a fall." Satan is so full of himself to think the Lord could be so shallow and vain to fall for something such as the pride of life.

Lastly, the Devil tries to appeal to the lust of the eyes and the pride of life by showing Jesus all the nations of the world and offering them to Him. Satan thinks that he is one-upping God by offering all the nations in exchange for the Lord's worship. This reveals that Satan has no clue of the mystery of the gospel (as Paul called it) that Messiah would be the Redeemer for all people and all nations. The Devil has the same understanding that Israel had, which was that Messiah would be Israel's Redeemer and King. This shows us that Satan's acquired knowledge about God's purposes comes through what he can gather from man. There were no Gentiles in Israel's perception of Messiah's kingdom. So what was thought to be "the big offer" was, in fact, no offer at all. The only real temptation was that Jesus would have been tempted by was a pain-free alternative to possess the nations. If the Lord chose this option, it would have been at the expense of abandoning all hope for mankind. Jesus always leads from the front in battle and never takes the easy way out in the form of compromise. Every spiritual battle you will face in your life will always find its way back to a form of these temptations, so be watchful and alert.

Jesus has just modeled for us all of what spiritual warfare looks like. He would be tempted in every way as Adam was and never succumbed to sin.

"Jesus Leads from the front in every Battle"

This confrontation between Satan and Jesus reveals to us what we ought to be on the alert for when the enemy makes his move. The demonic realm comes at us with misapplied truths, questionings, and cunning to deceive us and bring us to a place of doubt. We overcome him by properly knowing the heart of God and staying in humility before God. In doing so, we use the scriptures as a sword to slay every falsehood and lie of the enemy. Sometimes, the obvious is hiding in plain sight and we can over complicate and over spiritualize what is at the root of the attack. It seems hard to believe that this would have been the enemy's best shot to exploit any weakness in the Lord. This should also reveal to us that Satan's arsenal is not loaded with super weapons; he can be easily countered if we choose to walk in the Spirit.

Combatants seek to always control the high ground to dominate the battlefield. For the believer that high ground is staying "in the day" with faith in God's goodness towards you and being armed with that knowledge through the Word of

God. The enemy's high ground is to create anxiety about tomorrow and fear about you and your family's wellbeing. He does this for the purpose of fostering unbelief and losing focus on today's battles.

> *So I say, walk by the Spirit, and you will not*
> *gratify the desires of the flesh* (Galatians 5:16).

At the end of the Lord's fast and His subsequent temptation, the scriptures record that angels came and ministered to Him. When Elijah was in the wilderness, the angel of the Lord came and brought him cool water and freshly baked bread before his forty-day journey. Would Jesus get any less treatment from the angels when they came and ministered to Him? Therefore, we also can be assured that the Lord will send His ministering angels to bring whatever provision we are in need of after we have withstood the enemy in battle.

It was now time for the Lord to go on the offensive.

Two Prophets, Two Proclamations — the Same but Different

Nothing will reveal the differences of the same truth of these two covenants more than the calling of Israel to repentance. John the Baptist is the last prophet of the Old Covenant; Jesus is the first prophet of the New Covenant. John is the forerunner and herald of the Messiah calling on the nation to turn from their sins and symbolically wash away those sins in the waters of baptism to make ready a people for their King. John's message flows out of the Law of Moses, and it reflects the harsh legal reality of a people under judgment because of failed works of righteousness.

He went into all the region around the Jordan, proclaiming a baptism of repentance for the forgiveness of sins, as it is written in the book of the words of Isaiah the prophet: "A voice of one calling in the wilderness, 'Prepare the way for the Lord;

make straight paths for Him.' Every valley shall be filled in,

and every mountain and hill made low. The crooked ways shall be made straight, and the rough ways smooth. And all mankind will see God's salvation."

Then John said to the crowds coming out to be baptized by him, "You brood of vipers, who warned you to flee from the coming wrath? Therefore produce fruit worthy of repentance. And do not begin to say to yourselves, 'We have Abraham as our father.' For I tell you that out of these stones God can raise up children for Abraham. The ax lies ready at the root of the trees, and every tree that does not produce good fruit will be cut down and thrown into the fire" (Luke 3:3-9).

The tone of the message has an all too familiar ring to it but there is hope because Messiah is soon to arrive. The traditional belief in Israel was that Messiah would free the nation from being crushed under the iron feet of Rome and usher in His kingdom. All evildoers within Israel will be dealt with severely and the nation will be cleansed of its filth. His rule will be a glorious age of peace and prosperity and every enemy that comes against Israel will be destroyed by Messiah's mighty power. There will be no other kingdom on the earth like it and it will surpass the glory that Israel enjoyed under David and Solomon. It will be in many ways a fearful display of the awesome might of God. It is for that reason the prophesied forerunner would come in the spirit of Elijah to prepare the people's hearts for His coming. The waters of baptism would be the symbolic action that hearts were being purified in anticipation of His coming.

John the Baptist preached this message with all of the urgency and severity, passionately imploring the people to repent and escape the judgment at Messiah's coming. After John was imprisoned, Jesus would continue to herald the same message and the baptizing through His disciples. However, the message carried a different tone.

> *After the arrest of John, Jesus went into Galilee and proclaimed the gospel of God. "The time is fulfilled," He said, "and the kingdom of God is near. Repent and believe in the gospel!"* (Mark 1:14, 15).

The Lord's words were not full of wrath, but rather, they were filled with hope. It wasn't condemning news; it was good news! His actions manifested the lovingkindness and tender mercies of a Heavenly Father to a people beaten down by their inability to satisfy the requirements of the law. The turning away from sin in the message from the Son of God carried with it no condemnation. The Greek word for repent, *metanoeó,* as translated from these two passages simply means for a person to change his/her mind.

Strong's Concordance

metanoeó: to change one's mind or purpose

Original Word: μετανοέω
Part of Speech: Verb
Transliteration: *metanoeó*
Phonetic Spelling: (met-an-o-eh'-o)
Short Definition: I repent, change my mind
Definition: I repent, change my mind, change the inner man (particularly with reference to acceptance of the will of God), repent.

Jesus was saying the same words as John but the tone of the message had a completely different ring to it. Who was right and who was wrong? Is there a right and wrong in either message? In fact, the truth is they both were right as each one was speaking from the paradigm of the covenant that they were living under. Jesus was fulfilling all the legal requirements of the Old Covenant while living in the New Covenant by faith. He was modeling it for all to see even though the New Covenant had not yet been ratified by His shed blood on the cross.

Though both were speaking the truth, which one do you think truly reflected the Father's heart? The answer to that comes from the context of where the quotation is taken from. What I find interesting are the two prophetic references about John the Baptist as the voice crying out in the wilderness. In Malachi's prophecy, the focus shifts to the sinfulness of man and his works, which carries within it John's voice to Israel from the Law of Moses.

The other passage concerning the ministry of John the Baptist comes from the book of Isaiah and is quoted directly in Luke's gospel. In this passage and throughout the entire 40th chapter, the emphasis is on the Messiah and the Father's heart for the children of Israel. Take notice of the context and heart of this prophecy, for this is the message of the New Covenant.

> *Comfort, comfort my people, says your God. Speak tenderly to Jerusalem, and proclaim to her that her hard service has been completed, that her sin has been paid for,*
>
> *that she has received from the Lord's hand double for all her sins.*
>
> *A voice of one calling: "In the wilderness prepare the way for the Lord;*
>
> *make straight in the desert a highway for our God. Every valley shall be raised up,*
>
> *every mountain and hill made low; the rough ground shall become level,*
>
> *the rugged places a plain. And the glory of the Lord will be revealed,*
>
> *and all people will see it together* (Isaiah 40:1-5).

Do you see it? Can you sense the Father's heart? Every time I read this passage, it almost always reduces me to tears. You see your Heavenly Father's heart of love for you as expressed in this most beautiful passage; it is the heart of the New

Covenant. We are so loved by God and how wonderful are the feet of those who bring this good news. The Old Covenant could not communicate the true heart of the Heavenly Father because you were always found being contrary to the Law, and therefore under judgment. Jesus is sharing the heart of the message of repentance from the context that the Father had always intended. It is a message of comfort, hope and an end of the hostility between God and man.

In the book of Hebrews, there is a Greek word that is only used once in the entire Bible, *hiketeria*, which is translated as "supplications or petitions."

> *During the days of Jesus' earthly life, He offered up prayers and **petitions** with loud cries and tears to the One who could save Him from death, and He was heard because of His reverence* (Hebrews 5:7).

The literal meaning of this word implies that an olive branch is held in the hand of the supplicant. In other words, Jesus Christ's life is the olive branch of peace that ended the hostility between God and man once and for all.

The most important understanding I can impart to you about spiritual warfare is found in the heart of this passage from Isaiah 40. All warfare serves one purpose and that purpose is the proclamation of the good news of Jesus, the Christ of God. Everything centers on Jesus and His free gift of salvation made available to all because of the immeasurable cost He paid on the cross. How can we set captives free if we still are trying to preach the Old Covenant message with a standard that is unattainable by mankind? Why would slaves accept a freedom of one type of bondage only to accept the bondage of another?

> *It is for freedom that Christ has set us free.*
> *Stand firm, then, and do not be encumbered*
> *once more by a yoke of slavery* (Galatians 5:1).

Do you understand that Paul the apostle made this statement to Christians who were considering a return to the Law of Moses? I think many Christians do not proclaim Jesus because they live under the condemnation and slavery of the Old Covenant. It has been the only message they have ever known and the impossible requirements of perfection that the Law of Moses demands has extracted any joy that they once had in Jesus. If the message of Jesus is not good news to us in this life, how then will it be translated from our lips to a lost and dying world?

Hear the forerunners' message in Isaiah Chapter 40, which reveals the Father's heart speaking tenderly to you with words of comfort, proclaiming to you that the debt of sin that you carry has been paid in full. Jesus is the greatest person anyone could ever hope to know, and His message is the greatest news anyone could ever hope to hear. His actions at Calvary put a dagger into the heart of the empire of death. Satan will do all that is within his power to silence that message by trying to keep Jesus from being known on the earth. Satan's greatest terror filled thought is that the church may one day wake up to the message of Jesus, which is the Good News. That truth is so dangerous to Satan's realm that it will be at the root of every attack against your life to keep you from knowing it and telling the world.

We find ourselves thinking that warfare is about our wellbeing, morality or some other noble cause, but if you think any of those things come before proclaiming Jesus, and His love for the lost, you have missed the mark. Faith works by love; if your intercession and prayer are not for the purpose of making Jesus known on the earth through the heart of the Father's love, it will be just one more prayer and one more meeting producing little to no fruit. This is the Great Commission and that is the calling of every believer to make His good news known. Ultimately, every spiritual battle will be fought over this issue for this is Spiritual Warfare 101.

The Isaiah 61 Mandate

The first message Jesus taught in the synagogue was what I call the Isaiah 61 mandate of the Messiah. As a young man growing up in his hometown, He would have often taken a turn in the reading of the scriptures at the synagogue. This time would be different because, after His 40 days in the wilderness, we are told that He returns in the power of the Spirit. It was now time to proclaim His message to Israel and it is our message to the world about the Son of God.

> *Jesus returned to Galilee in the power of the Spirit, and the news about Him spread throughout the surrounding region. He taught in their synagogues and was glorified by everyone. Then Jesus came to Nazareth, where He had been brought up. As was His custom, He entered the synagogue on the Sabbath. And when He stood up to read, the scroll of the prophet Isaiah was handed to Him. Unrolling it, He found the place where it was written:*

> *"The Spirit of the Lord is on Me, because He*

has anointed Me to preach good news to the poor.

He has sent Me to proclaim deliverance to the captives and recovery of sight to the blind, to release the oppressed, to proclaim the year of the Lord's favor."

Then He rolled up the scroll, returned it to the attendant, and sat down. The eyes of everyone in the synagogue were fixed on Him, and He began by saying, "Today this Scripture is fulfilled in your hearing" (Luke 4:14-20).

This is the "call to arms" of the kingdom of God; it is now time to undo all of the evil that the enemy has wrought on mankind. Jesus came to address this with good news to the poor that God is their provider, and His heart is for their wellbeing. He came to free every prisoner from whatever has held them in bondage. He came with healing for the blind spiritually and the blind physically. He came to set the oppressed free from every trouble and affliction. Those who are sick of heart, soul, and body will be made free through Him. And last but not least, He came to proclaim the year of His favor, which speaks of a complete era of His goodness; this symbolizes the age of grace, which is the New Covenant. This same mandate is the commission of every believer to proclaim our God in this way to the world. This is how we take the fight to the enemy.

When Jesus rose from the dead, He not only turned the world upside down but He forever changed the landscape of the spiritual realm. Everything that you learned about Satan's realm and his authority was crushed under the feet of Jesus our victor and mighty conqueror. In these remaining chapters, we will learn and understand that the status quo has changed, and we can now address the subject of spiritual warfare within the context of the New Covenant.

Under the Old Covenant, Satan the accuser ran rampant with his accusations to bring mankind under judgment. What was meant for man's safety was now being used against them because of sin. Jesus changed all that once and for all. Read this passage from John's gospel carefully and see how the tide has turned.

> But I tell you the truth, it is for your benefit that I am going away. Unless I go away, the Advocate will not come to you; but if I go, I will send Him to you. And when He comes, He will convict the world in regard to sin and righteousness, and judgment: in regard to sin, because they do not believe in Me; in regard to righteousness, because I am going to the Father and you will no longer see Me; and in regard to judgment, because the prince of this world already stands condemned (John 16:7-11).

Jesus has just told His disciples that three monumental changes will occur through His glorification that will affect mankind and the spiritual realm for all eternity. The Lord speaks of sin, righteousness, and judgment and so that there would be no misunderstanding, He explains what He meant by those three words. Jesus through the cross will deal with the issue of sin once and for all. The sins of all mankind were forever dealt with through the shed blood of Christ. Your sins, past, present, and future are covered and remitted by the blood of Jesus. Now the only sin that will keep you from being saved is to deny the Lord Jesus and thereby reject what He did for you on the cross.

His resurrection and the taking of His throne in heaven as the King of Righteousness ensure that you have been made righteous by His free gift of grace. By believing in His finished work of redemption on the cross, you have been made the righteousness of God in Christ. God sees you adorned in His robe of righteousness, given to you to wear with honor from the Lord Jesus. It is now by grace through faith that you are saved and no longer through fruitless works in an attempt to attain right standing with God. If the believer would truly embrace this truth, the accuser will be forever silenced in their lives and thereby nullify the source of Satan's authority and power. The grace of God is the sledgehammer to tear down every stronghold in your life. A stronghold is a belief that you negatively embrace about yourself, which has been fortified by the enemy's lies and your compliant actions. Even if as a Christian you are struggling with an area of sin in your life, do not own it. Renounce it at every turn even after sinning by repenting of that thought and action by declaring that you are the righteousness of God in Christ Jesus. Denounce it as evil and declare that sin as not being who you are and take back that ground in your life through Christ.

I remember hearing these words in my inner man once, "If a stronghold is in you, then you are in the stronghold." I immediately knew that it was through those things that I disparagingly believed about myself that in turn, those beliefs had imprisoned me. Wrong belief creates a cycle of defeat in the believer and places the focus of the issue of righteousness on your shoulders. Agree by faith in the finished work of His righteousness on the cross and His righteousness will shoulder and finish its work in you.

That is what Jesus did on the cross when He stripped Satan of his legal authority and the voice of accusation by casting him down from the heavenly places to the earth. Now, the accuser is the accused; he has been judged and the verdict has been reached. Satan is the one condemned for all eternity. Satan's right to throw accusation against us has been annulled; his voice as your prosecutor is over. His right to practice law has been revoked. He has been found guilty of perjury and malpractice and has been prosecuted. Your advocate is now the Lord Jesus and His blood is now the undeniable evidence that justice has been served for you and you are now pronounced, "Not Guilty!"

There is a legal term called "double Jeopardy," which prevents the courts from trying the same case twice based on the same facts that previously brought the results of a valid acquittal or conviction. For instance, in Canada and the United States this protection is a constitutional right and in most countries, the protection from this action is given by legal statute. If the world can't retry a case, how much more is this true for Christians who have the blood of Jesus protecting them from retrials by the accuser of the brethren? Stop listening to his condemning words and accept with joy that your name is written in the Lamb's Book of Life.

The enemy dreads the thought that you might be awakened with this truth and rise to battle as a victor in Christ and not a victim of Satan's lies. My prayer for us all is that we would be awakened with the light of His revelation with the same knowledge that Paul prayed for the church at Ephesus.

For this reason, ever since I heard about your faith in the Lord Jesus and your love for all the saints, I have not stopped giving thanks for you, remembering you in my prayers and asking that the God of our Lord Jesus Christ, the glorious Father, may give you a spirit of wisdom and revelation in your knowledge of Him.

I ask that the eyes of your heart may be enlightened, so that you may know the hope of His calling, the riches of His glorious inheritance in the saints, and the surpassing greatness of His power to us who believe. He displayed this power in the working of His mighty strength, which He exerted in Christ when He raised Him from the dead and seated Him at His right hand in the heavenly realms, far above all rule and authority, power and dominion, and every name that is named, not only in this age, but also in the one to come.

And God put everything under His feet and made Him head over everything for the church, which is His body, the fullness of Him who fills all in all (Ephesians. 1:15-23).

Chapter 11

THE ETERNAL AGE OF
THE NEW COVENANT

For you have not come to a mountain that can be touched and that is burning with fire; to darkness, gloom, and storm; to a trumpet blast or to a voice that made its hearers beg that no further word be spoken. For they could not bear what was commanded: "If even an animal touches the mountain, it must be stoned." The sight was so terrifying that even Moses said, "I am trembling with fear."

Instead, you have come to Mount Zion, to the city of the living God, the heavenly Jerusalem. You have come to myriads of angels in joyful assembly, to the congregation of the firstborn, enrolled in heaven. You have come to God the judge of all men, to the spirits of the righteous made perfect, to Jesus the mediator of a new covenant, and to the sprinkled blood that speaks a better word than the blood of Abel (Hebrews 12:18-24).

Few passages in scripture show us the contrast of covenants as this passage from the book of Hebrews. The images are stark with the Old Covenant being pictured with trembling and fear for those who live under it and the New Covenant represented as a festive and joyful assembly. This passage of scripture is also the identifiable trait that marks the Christians and reveals the covenant that they are mostly influenced by. Under the Old Covenant and the era before its implementation, mankind lived under the accusing finger of Satan. Your sins were his expert witnesses that brought testimonies against you and brought the enforcement of the laws that governed you. Jesus perfectly fulfilled all of those laws and abolished them through His death on the cross. For all who would believe in Him, it is as though they also died in Him and when He rose from the dead you rose with Him in newness of life. Jesus has brought all who would believe in Him into a resurrected life as a new creation; the laws of God are now written on your heart. This is the gospel of grace; this is the New Covenant and that is why it is a celebration of the greatest news mankind could ever hear.

You have been made the righteousness of God through Christ. It is not about your works of righteousness; it is solely about His righteousness. Never stray in your thoughts from this truth; abide in Him and joyfully receive this good news. If you sin, renounce the folly; run quickly to the Father without delay, and place yourself under this truth. Do not run away from Him in shame and hide in the shadows. This is how Satan lurks as a predator, seeking out those who get separated from the herd, he then plans his attack. Remain in Christ, arm yourself with this knowledge, and the enemy will gain no power over your life. If you think that I am belaboring the point, you're right — for I am doing it with purpose. The critical moment in all of the battles you will fight in your life will be decided by what you believe about yourself. If you stumble and fall into some state of believed unworthiness, you will not stand firm in the day of evil. But, if your trust is always in His righteousness that is bestowed upon you as a gift and not of merit, you will still be standing at the end of that day.

What is Covenant?

The oldest legal agreement between two parties is the given oath or words of promise. In the ancient world, a formal ritual of that oath would make those words sacred to both parties and those who would witness it.

A covenant is the most ancient authoritative legal agreement between two parties known to man. I do not find it a coincidence that in the region known as the Fertile Crescent, we find blood covenants used by all peoples and nations. These are the lands of the Bible, known as the cradle of civilization. Every tribe and kingdom practiced and finalized pacts and agreements in a blood oath by animal sacrifice. In the book of Genesis, we see this practice being conducted and initiated by God with Noah and Abraham, and it is inferred in animal clothing provided by God in the aftermath of Adam's fall. It was to be an irrevocable pact between two parties and to break a covenant led to the violent severing of all ties between the two parties. Depending on the severity of the offense, it could also lead to the death of the covenant breaker.

There are several recorded covenants that were made between God and man promising blessings, protection, and every other type of provision. Every covenant in the ancient world was ratified by blood. An animal would be divided and each party would walk through its blood citing their part of the agreement. The animal would then be offered by fire unto God or the gods that the parties worshipped. Even today, we still use the ancient vernacular when describing an agreement, when we say, "Let's cut a deal." Before I understood the origin of that phrase it made me wonder why you wanted to sever something as opposed to joining something in making a deal?

God has made several recorded covenants with individuals in the Bible, but a covenant with a nation began with Israel. The book of Hebrews describes the covenant between God and the nation of Israel as the First Covenant, which Christians essentially understand to be the writings of the Old Testament. As stated many times before, Jesus fulfilled all requirements of the Old Covenant in order to perfectly ratify the New Covenant. His shed blood would end the need for sacrifice because in offering Himself, He ended the old and ushered in the new. His blood would stand for all eternity, once and for all, and end any further requirement of sacrifice.

Furthermore, it is impossible to have two covenants active on the same issue for mankind. One must end before the other can be enacted. When Jesus said, "It is finished" on the cross, the Old Covenant came to an end and within three days, the New Covenant was enacted. In the ancient world, a covenant could never be amended with additions and or subtractions as we see taking place in our day. It stood in place until one of the parties died or its complete fulfillment had been achieved. Jesus fulfilled all of the requirements of the first covenant and perfectly completed the holy treaty through His death.

> *Brothers, let me put this in human terms. Even a human covenant, once it is ratified, cannot be canceled or amended. The promises were spoken to Abraham and to his seed. The Scripture does not say, "and to seeds," meaning many, but "and to your seed," meaning One, who is Christ. What I mean is this: The Law that came four hundred thirty years later does not revoke the covenant previously established by God, so as to cancel the promise. For if the inheritance depends on the Law, then it no longer depends on a promise; but God freely granted it to Abraham through a promise.*

> *Why then was the Law given? It was added because of transgressions, until the arrival of the seed to whom the promise referred. It was administered through angels by a mediator. A mediator is unnecessary, however, if there is only one party; but God is one* (Galatians 3:15-20).

God replaced the first covenant, which was temporal, with

an entirely new agreement that is eternal, thus ending the Old Covenant. The covenant that He made with Abraham was now fulfilled in and through Christ.

> Now if the ministry of death, which was engraved in letters on stone, came with such glory that the Israelites could not gaze at the face of Moses because of its fleeting glory, will not the ministry of the Spirit be even more glorious? For if the ministry of condemnation was glorious, how much more glorious is the ministry of righteousness! Indeed, what was once glorious has no glory now in comparison to the glory that surpasses it. For if what was fading away came with glory, how much greater is the glory of that which endures!

> Therefore, since we have such a hope, we are very bold. We are not like Moses, who would put a veil over his face to keep the Israelites from gazing at the end of what was fading away.

> But their minds were closed. For to this day the same veil remains at the reading of the old covenant. It has not been lifted, because only in Christ can it be removed. And even to this day when Moses is read, a veil covers their hearts. But whenever anyone turns to the Lord, the veil is taken away.

> Now the Lord is the Spirit, and where the Spirit of the Lord is, there is freedom. And we, who with unveiled faces all reflect the glory of

> *the Lord, are being transformed into His image with intensifying glory, which comes from the Lord, who is the Spirit* (2 Corinthians 3:7-19).

To further clarify the point, the word translated as "fading away" is from the Greek word *katargeó*, which is interpreted as follows:

Strong's Concordance

katargeó: to render inoperative, abolish

Original Word: καταργέω
Part of Speech: Verb
Transliteration: *katargeó*
Phonetic Spelling: (kat-arg-eh'-o)
Short Definition: I bring to naught, sever, abolish
Definition: (a) I make idle (inactive), make of no effect, annul, abolish, bring to naught, (b) I discharge, sever, separate from.

One covenant is brought to an end and a new covenant is enacted.

The Covenant 2.0

If the Old Covenant was a software program that was flawed, the manufacturer could provide upgrades with patches and fixes to remedy the operating problems. But what do you do when it is not the software that was flawed; rather, it is the users who are contaminated with viruses, trojans, backdoors, and malware? How do you replace the user and what fixes can you provide them?

This was precisely the problem of the Old Covenant. The Law was perfect but unfortunately, man was not; therefore, he was incompatible with the terms of the holy treaty. The Adam of the garden of Eden could have successfully operated the software before the fall, but now, mankind has no ability to execute the programmer's manual or even grasp the understanding or intent of its developer.

Israel had experienced nearly 1500 years of futility trying to obey the Law of Moses. In trying to do so, they created a vast interpretation of the Law in the form of the Oral law (Mishnah) and the written interpretation of the law called the Talmud. The five books of Moses were added with these interpretive traditions, which created a library of rules and regulations resembling something like your grandparent's set of encyclopedias. Jesus called these additions, "the traditions of men," and He found Himself continually at odds with these religious edicts. Yet, for all of this religious zeal and effort, it only led its leaders and people to become hardened in their hearts towards God through their failure to attain righteousness.

In the book of Romans, Paul uses the example of the death of a spouse in a marriage as the freedom to move on into a new marriage covenant.

> *Do you not know, brothers (for I am speaking to those who know the law), that the law has authority over a man only as long as he lives? For instance, a married woman is bound by law to her husband as long as he lives. But if her husband dies, she is released from the law*

of marriage. So then, if she is joined to another man while her husband is still alive, she is called an adulteress; but if her husband dies, she is free from that law and is not an adulteress, even if she marries another man.

Therefore, my brothers, you also died to the Law through the body of Christ, that you might belong to another, to Him who was raised from the dead, in order that we might bear fruit to God. For when we lived according to the flesh, the sinful passions aroused by the Law were at work in our bodies, bearing fruit for death. **But now, having died to what bound us, we have been released from the Law, so that we serve in the new way of the Spirit, and not in the old way of the written code** (Romans 7:1-6).

The death of the Old Covenant made it possible for you to join yourself in marriage to another. Jesus stands as the groom awaiting anyone who would accept His proposal of marriage in the New Covenant.

Jesus the Perfect User for a Perfect Written Code

No human being on the face of this earth has ever been able to perfectly execute[i] the requirements of the written code, which was the Law of Moses. Jesus, being fully God and fully man, would take on the task to fulfill the Law of Moses and then terminate it in His body on the cross. In using Paul's analogy, all mankind became widowers as the marriage to the Law of Moses was brought to death in the body of Jesus on the cross. Then, all mankind became free to be joined into a new marriage covenant to the risen Jesus, with His hand of marriage being extended to all who would receive His invitation.

So, to flip back to computer analogy, Jesus now dwells in us, and we become new users in Him. We no longer have to try to use a manual that is impossible to operate; instead, the user manual is an extension of the Lord Himself in the form of the new birth and the code is now written on our hearts.

> For you have been born again, not of perishable seed, but of imperishable, through the living and enduring word of God (1 Peter 1:23).

What Effect Did the Cross Have on the Spiritual Realm?

I can think of no better spiritual picture to explain what happened on the cross and the overall activity of what would follow in the New Covenant, than what is portrayed in Revelation 12. The entire chapter is a synopsis of the spiritual realm and the warfare that the church is now engaged in and will be in until the Lord returns. Those who have struggled to interpret this chapter have done so because they do not follow it chronologically and thereby jump out of its clear message in trying to make their eschatology fit. This has led to considerable confusion as to what was truly accomplished on the cross. These doctrines place events to a future time, instead of what was immediately won for us on the cross by Jesus. Let's examine and review in brief this chapter in its entirety and in its stated chronology.

> *And a great sign appeared in heaven: a woman clothed in the sun, with the moon under her feet and a crown of twelve stars on her head. She was pregnant and crying out in the pain and agony of giving birth.*
>
> *Then another sign appeared in heaven: a huge red dragon with seven heads, ten horns, and seven royal crowns on his heads. His tail swept a third of the stars from the sky, tossing them to the earth. And the dragon stood before the woman as she was about to give birth, ready to devour her child as soon as He was born.*
>
> *And she gave birth to a son, a male child, who will rule all the nations with an iron scepter; and her child was caught up to God and to His throne. The woman fled into the wilderness, where God had prepared a place for her to be nourished for one thousand two hundred sixty days* (Revelation 12:1-6).

The key to interpreting spiritual symbolism is found in the scriptures; the beautiful thing about this chapter is that most of the imagery has been used elsewhere in the Bible. It has not only been used elsewhere, but we have been given through those scriptures, the interpretation of the symbols used.

The scene opens with a woman who is clothed with the sun, the moon under her feet, and a crown of twelve stars. In

Genesis, we read of Joseph's dream where the sun, moon, and eleven stars bow to him. The dream's interpretation was obvious to everyone in his family. Joseph's parents and brothers would bow to him one day and it pleased no one in the family including Israel, his father. God used the stars to describe to Abraham how large and without number his offspring would be on the earth. From this symbolic interpretation, we know this woman is Israel, and she is about to give birth.

The red dragon with seven heads is represented as Satan and the heads, crowns, and horns represent authority, nations, and power. The dragon is red, which is the color of war to depict that Satan is at war against Israel. If I were to use history as a guide, I would tell you that it just so happens that seven empires had vexed Israel as a nation up to the day that Jesus made His entrance onto the scene of humanity. The seven dragon heads/empires would be as follows: Egypt, the Amorites that comprised the nation states of the land of Canaan, the Assyrians, the Babylonians, the Medes-Persians, followed by Greece, which then brings us to the Roman Empire. While the history matches the symbolism, that is not the interpretation of this passage, although we will end up with the same result.

The angel of the Lord in Revelation 17 tells John plainly the interpretation of the symbolism used in this passage. He describes that the seven heads represent seven hills or mountains and says that these are also seven rulers, which are to be understood as part of its dual meaning. The Greek word *oros* is used here and is translated into English as a mountain or hill. For those of you who have been to Israel, you will probably recall from your tourist literature that the three-hill ridge to the east of Jerusalem is called the Mount of Olives. It is this same Greek word that is translated as "mount" in every scriptural reference. If you type into your favorite search engine the phrase "city of seven hills," you will be brought to numerous tourist pages for the city of Rome; for that is the historic name for which it is known. In Chapter 17, the angel describes a prostitute who is sitting on the beast. She is the city-state of Rome and the beast is the military power of the Roman Empire.

In the story of Romulus and Remus whom folklore suggests were the abandoned baby twins that would later found the city of Rome. It was said that a wolf nursed the boys until the day they were found by a shepherd who would raise them as his own sons. The Latin word for a female wolf is *Lupa,* which is also a Latin slang term referring to a prostitute. The Romans prided themselves on the notion that a fierce predator sustained its founders. I can't help but think that God is insulting their heritage by using the other use of the word and calls Rome a whore in depicting the nature of that ancient city-state.

The great whore is called "Babylon" in Revelation 17, which was the code word used by the early Christian church in Rome. In the first century, if you were caught with any literature that painted Rome in a negative light, that parchment could be deemed as seditious and cost you your life. In scripture, we see Peter passing on greetings from the church at Babylon in his writing. It is a known fact that in 148 BC, Babylon ceased to exist and the city was completely depopulated. There would be no misunderstanding to Peter's readers when he wrote his letter some two hundred years later as to whom he was referring.

A third of Israel's population has suffered over time at the hands of Satan's oppressors and the dragon is now poised to destroy the child that is about to be born.

That child is the Lord Jesus, and He will be taken up to heaven to take His place on the throne. The 3½-year (1260 days) period, symbolizes the earthly ministry of Jesus who has completed His mission on the earth. He takes His throne in heaven and enters His reign as King of kings and Lord of lords. The spiritual victory has been completed. The continuation of His victory in the natural realm is ongoing and being conducted by His church. Lastly, the prophecy declares that Israel as a people will be preserved in the wilderness. The symbolism of the wilderness should not be lost on anyone as it speaks of the forty-year journey to its Promised Land. Jesus is the end of the wilderness wandering for every Jew when He is received as their Messiah. It is not the end for this historic people, as they will be brought to a place where they will have their hope set before them, once again.

> Then a war broke out in heaven: Michael and his angels fought against the dragon, and the dragon and his angels fought back. But the dragon was not strong enough, and no longer was any place found in heaven for him and his angels. And the great dragon was hurled down—the ancient serpent called the devil and Satan, the deceiver of the whole world. He was hurled to the earth, and his angels with him (Revelation 12:7-9).

Take special notice of who is now on the offensive; it is the

186

kingdom of God. Jesus brought about the invasion of the earth through His ministry and it remains ongoing through His saints. Satan tries to fight back but he and his angels are overwhelmed. How is he overwhelmed? Jesus declared His message and through His sinless life, His words, and His manifest authority and power, the kingdom of darkness was crushed in battle. No longer would Satan control the heavenly places over mankind and no longer is he the voice of accusation to incite judgment against mankind as heard at heaven's gates. Satan's accusations against mankind no longer carry any legal authority because of what Jesus accomplished on the cross in taking on Himself the sins of the world. How freeing this would be to an enslaved world that lives under the weight of their sins. O, if they would only hear the true message of His grace; it is, for this reason, we are called to tell the world the truth of what Jesus has done for them. Jesus has defeated and disarmed His enemies and that victory is shown forth in the lives of all believers who manifest this truth to the world.

So, are angels and demons in a clash of swords or a clash of authority over words? In the spiritual realm, swords are words backed by authority. At the cross, Jesus stripped every demon and Satan himself of the authority that they once had over mankind and the domain wherewith they ruled.

> *When you were dead in your trespasses and in the uncircumcision of your sinful nature, God made you alive with Christ. He forgave us all our trespasses, having canceled the debt ascribed to us in the decrees that stood against us. He took it away, nailing it to the*

cross! And having disarmed the rulers and authorities, He made a public spectacle of them, triumphing over them by the cross (Colossians 2:13-15).

Paul described to the Colossian church exactly what John had seen in his revelation. The war in the heavenly places took place during the time of Jesus' ministry and that is what is depicted here. This is Satan's kingdom at its zenith, and Jesus through the cross is dealing it its fatal blow. Do you remember in scripture when Jesus had sent out seventy-two of His followers to minister throughout Israel and they returned with awesome testimonies of the power of God? What did Jesus say?

The seventy-two returned with joy and said, "Lord, even the demons submit to us in Your name."

*So He said to them, "**I saw Satan fall like lightning from heaven.** See, I have given you authority to tread on snakes and scorpions, and over all the power of the enemy. Nothing will harm you. Nevertheless, do not rejoice that the spirits submit to you, but rejoice that your names are written in heaven"* (Luke 10:17-20).

Jesus had just released the kingdom of God in a sample version through His disciples and the results sent Satan crashing to the earth. Picture in your mind for a moment these seventy-two individuals. They had become followers of Jesus and stayed connected to His ministry. The Lord's death on the cross had not yet happened; therefore, Jesus was not yet in His glorification and so these people were not born again or filled with the Holy Spirit. These unnamed individuals carefully followed the instructions of Jesus and saw the manifestation of the kingdom of God. They preached His message and witnessed healings taking place through their prayers. The disciples marvelled at the sight of devils being cast out by the authority in their words. These followers have just been told by Jesus after their joyfully successful mission that the Lord had given them authority over all the power of the enemy. If, by carefully adhering to the Lord's instructions meant the release of God's power for followers of Jesus who were not yet born again, how much more is it true for a born again believer who is indwelt with the Holy Spirit? This was a prophetic picture of the church in operation, and we read that it brought the Lord great joy.

> At that time, Jesus rejoiced in the Holy Spirit and declared, "I praise You, Father, Lord of heaven and earth, because You have hidden these things from the wise and learned, and revealed them to little children. Yes, Father, for this was well-pleasing in Your sight.
>
> All things have been entrusted to Me by My Father. No one knows who the Son is except the Father, and no one knows who the Father is except the Son, and those to whom the Son chooses to reveal Him."
>
> Then Jesus turned to the disciples and said privately, "Blessed are the eyes that see what you see. For I tell you that many prophets and kings desired to see what you see but did not

see it, and to hear what you hear but did not hear it" (Luke 10:21-24).

In His prayer to the Father, Jesus calls these warriors who have trodden upon devils, "little children." Little children in knowledge, understanding, and faith have just knocked Satan out of the sky and sent him crashing to the earth like a fighter jet being taken down by a shoulder-fired missile from a foot soldier. They were given authority by Christ, which endued them with overwhelming power that hurled Satan down to the ground. The prophetic word given to Adam about a coming Redeemer who would crush the head of the serpent, has now been witnessed by the Father's future children. This happened as they simply did what Jesus told them to do. We should never minimize "the little" that God gives us because it is far greater than you can possibly imagine. The powers of darkness tremble at the thought that one day, you too might come to believe that this is true for you. They dread the thought that you may push through the clutter of doctrines and teachings that make you believe that this is not your reality. For on the day that you believe this as truth for your life, you too will live out the imagery of seeing Satan and his minions crashing to the earth.

Jesus was seeing the fullness of His day when He defeats the empire of evil. That day is the prophetic day of His cross and His resurrection marking the start of the New Covenant. The passage from Luke went on to describe how the testimonies from the disciples brought joy to Jesus when He heard it. We know from the book of Hebrews that faith pleases God. Now, by using your faith to proclaim Jesus and manifest His works to a suffering world, you can know that you have brought the Lord pleasure and joy. How awesome is that? By manifesting His love to the world, we have the privilege of bringing joy to our Lord's heart. His victory at Calvary ended the legal right of Satan's rule over man and has forever changed the course of human history. The kingdom of darkness will now operate as a rogue empire on the earth, operating wherever man still yields to it in servitude. He will hold the title as "god of this world" but that world is only as far as his influence will reach.

In another passage from John's gospel, we read of what appears to be a timing trigger point for Jesus when the Greeks sought to meet with Him. The Gentile world wants to meet with Jesus but the Lord must first complete His mission to the Jewish race and fulfill all that was written of Him in the Law and the prophets and in the psalms.

> *Now there were some Greeks among those who went up to worship at the feast. They came to Philip, who was from Bethsaida in Galilee, and requested of him, "Sir, we want to see Jesus." Philip relayed this appeal to Andrew, and both of them went and told Jesus.*
>
> *But Jesus replied, "The hour has come for the Son of Man to be glorified* (John 12:20-23).
>
> *Now My soul is troubled, and what shall I say? 'Father, save Me from this hour'? No, it is for this purpose that I have come to this hour. Father, glorify Your name!"*
>
> *Then a voice came from heaven: "I have glorified it, and I will glorify it again."*

The crowd standing there heard it and said it had thundered. Others said that an angel had spoken to Him.

*In response, Jesus said, "This voice was not for My benefit, but yours. Now judgment is upon this world; **now the prince of this world will be cast out.** And I, when I am lifted up from the earth, will draw all men to Myself." He said this to signify the kind of death He was going to die* (John 12:27-33).

Again, Jesus sees the defeat of Satan through His cross with the result being the harvest of souls from the earth. The work of the cross has successfully driven out the authority, which was behind Satan's rule. The phrase that is translated as "will be cast" is from the Greek word *ekballo*, which implies the thought of banishment. Now the passage in Revelation 12 shows that heaven resounds in a proclamation of praise and worship. It is then revealed to us how we continue in that victory and defeat the enemy on a daily basis.

And I heard a loud voice in heaven, saying:

"Now have come the salvation and the power and the kingdom of our God, and the authority of His Christ.

For the accuser of our brothers has been thrown down, he who accuses them day and night before our God.

They have conquered him by the blood of

the Lamb and by the word of their testimony;

and they did not love their lives so as to shy away from death.

Therefore rejoice, O heavens, and you who dwell in them! (Revelation 12:10-12a).

This passage now gives every believer the unfailing strategy that keeps Satan under your heel as the defeated foe Jesus so gloriously triumphed over. Once again, you will see that it is not a clash of swords but it is most certainly a clash of words. Live this truth, and you will always display the conquest and victory of Jesus Christ the Righteous.

This is what the cross of our Lord has purchased for us; Jesus has ushered in His kingdom on the earth and has cast down Satan, the accuser of the brethren. The Devil's accusations no longer have any legal authority against us and the followers of Jesus are now empowered to triumph over the Devil. This will always be the case when we believe God's words of truth over the Devil's lies. The beauty of this passage lays out how this victory takes place. The blood of Jesus ratified the New Covenant and purchased our redemption for us. We, who have believed in Jesus and have accepted His free gift of salvation, are now citizens of the kingdom of heaven. We are no longer slaves, prisoners, or a population of serfs owing any allegiance to the kingdom of darkness because our redemption was paid in full by the shed blood of Jesus. We proclaim these words of His warfare as our testimony to the truth and uphold it with our very lives, no matter the cost. We do this for the purpose of making known this victory to every man, woman, and child.

Paul said it like this:

> *Being strengthened with all power according to His glorious might so that you may have full endurance and patience, and joyfully giving thanks to the Father, who has qualified you to share in the inheritance of the saints in the light. He has rescued us from the dominion of darkness and brought us into the kingdom of His beloved Son, in whom we have redemption, the forgiveness of sins* (Colossians 1:11-14).

Satan no longer has any legal claim against you. As an ambassador for Christ, you have diplomatic immunity on this earth and the Devil no longer has any right to go through your baggage.

Therefore we are ambassadors for Christ, as though God were making His appeal through us. We implore you on behalf of Christ: Be reconciled to God. God made Him who knew no sin to be sin on our behalf, so that in Him we might become the righteousness of God (2 Corinthians 5:20, 21).

We now have a testimony that says, "*I have been crucified with Christ, and I no longer live, but Christ lives in me. The life I live in the body, I live by faith in the Son of God, who loved me and gave Himself up for me*" (Galatians 2:20).

We who have entered into this covenant are now righteous in Christ and our lives are abandoned to the purposes of God. Now, we must continue the struggle to free other prisoners, who are the victims and casualties of this war by proclaiming Jesus to those who have not yet truly heard the good news.

Satan no longer has any legal claim against you. As an ambassador for Christ, you have diplomatic immunity on this earth and the Devil no longer has any right to go through your baggage.

> But woe to the earth and the sea; with great fury the devil has come down to you, knowing he has only a short time."
>
> And when the dragon saw that he had been thrown to the earth, he pursued the woman who had given birth to the male child. But the woman was given two wings of a great eagle to fly from the presence of the serpent to her place in the wilderness, where she was nourished for a time, and times, and half a time.
>
> Then from the mouth of the serpent spewed water like a river to overtake the woman and sweep her away in the torrent. But the earth helped the woman and opened its mouth to swallow up the river that had poured from the dragon's mouth. And the dragon was enraged at the woman, and went to make war with the rest of her children, who keep the

commandments of God and hold to the
testimony of Jesus (Revelation 12:12b-17).

Pride goes before a fall and so, once again, Satan assumes his usual position. There is no time in the dimension of the spiritual realm; time is restricted to the earth. Satan had authority on the earth and in the spiritual realm through the fall of man but now he is on the clock, having been cast down to the earth. It could be said that the realm of darkness had gained ascendancy as far as the gates of the kingdom of heaven and it was from outside those walls and gates that the accuser railed against God and man. God could have easily ended the noise from the outside of those walls, but it would have been at the cost of mankind. Now, Satan has been cast down to earth after suffering his eternal defeat at the hands of Jesus and what is left of his domain is now clear. His dominion in the heavenly places is over and his realm of operation is reduced to being over the earth. The Devil knows the earth clock is ticking and his time is short.

There is one reason and one reason only that the Jewish people have been the subject of so much hatred and violence. That reason is that they were the people who had the promise that the Messiah would come through them and they brought forth the Savior of the world. Satan will never stop pursuing them in his fury and hatred because of that glorious privilege given to them by God. It is for this reason that God will never forget them, no matter how hardened to Jesus they may seem, God will always have a remnant from that nation on the earth. Evil men will create new reasons to justify their hatred of the Jewish race but the DNA of all that hatred is because Satan seeks revenge against this people who were the portal to bring Jesus into the world.

You will notice that a description of eagle's wings is used to portray how God would place those wings upon the nation and take them into the wilderness. Those eagles' wings were also used to describe how God delivered Israel from the Egyptians and brought them to Sinai.

> *Then Moses went up to God, and the Lord called to him from the mountain and said, "This is what you are to say to the descendants of Jacob and what you are to tell the people of Israel: 'You yourselves have seen what I did to Egypt, and how **I carried you on eagles' wings and brought you to myself**** (Exodus 19:3, 4).

The nation of Israel is protected from every evil flood of destruction and is carried by God to a wilderness location. He has brought them back to the place where He first invited them to become a kingdom of priests and a holy nation. This is not a coincidence. Israel as a people has been preserved and they are brought back to the place of God's original intention for this great people. Now they must be re-grafted into the olive tree as part of the spiritual Israel of God through Jesus the Messiah into the New Covenant.

The enemy in his fury will now vent his rage against those who have accepted the offer to become a kingdom of priests and a holy nation. And so, the battle continues on to this day but you have the supreme advantage. This passage of scripture has shown you how you win every battle in the war that has already been won.

When I think of these things, it reminds me of what the allies knew in late 1944. They knew that Nazi Germany was defeated and after the Battle of the Bulge, Hitler did as well. With the Third Reich in ruins, Hitler wanted to see the annihilation of Germany as a nation; he wanted it to perish with him. In like manner, Satan fights for little else than to destroy everything that God loves and causes as much ruin as he can before his days are ended. That is why we persevere and fight on with purpose to see Jesus receive His full inheritance from the earth and labor in the harvest fields with swords in hand.

Chapter 12

THE CHURCH AT WAR

Christians, whether they are aware of it or not are in the midst of a genocidal war. As we have read in the previous chapter Satan is raging, and he seeks to destroy physical Israel and the body of Christ also known as spiritual Israel. As a Christian, you are either in the fight or you are a potential victim of the collateral damage of war. There is no neutral country to flee to and no escape from this war. God has laid out the blueprint of a victorious battle plan, which always leads us to our place in Him. It is from that vantage point of being seated with Him in heavenly places that we can see beyond our troubled circumstances. These challenges in our lives can be like the fog of war, which are the uncertainties that cloud our perspectives. When we calm our hearts through prayer and elevate to be with the Lord by taking our seats in heavenly places, we can then see with a birds-eye view what is shaping up and taking place in and around our lives. Good reconnaissance always leads to an advantage in warfare.

"And God raised us up with Christ and seated us with Him in the heavenly realms in Christ Jesus" (Ephesians 2:6).

From this spiritual vantage point, we can now wage a good warfare and position ourselves under the leadership of the Holy Spirit to take the fight to the enemy. So then, what exactly does that mean in spiritual terms?

Evangelism, Evangelism, Evangelism

Consider for a moment what this world would be like if every believer engaged in battle as a good soldier of Christ Jesus. That person's life would be one that is not entangled with the world and maintains a readiness for the fight. The answer to the question, "What exactly is the fight?" is quite simply: the proclamation of the gospel. All warfare of the kingdom of God finds its marching orders from the one commission of the Lord Jesus and that is,

> Then Jesus came to them and said, "All authority in heaven and on earth has been given to Me. Therefore go and make disciples of all nations, baptizing them in the name of the Father, and of the Son, and of the Holy Spirit, and teaching them to obey all that I have commanded you. And surely I am with you always, to the very end of the age" (Matthew 28:18-20).

The primary focus of all spiritual warfare is not about taking up causes related to Jesus; it is about telling one and all about the good news of Jesus. In so many ways Christendom is confused about how it conducts itself because it is confused about what covenant it lives under. In the Old Covenant, you had to get your life right before you came to God. In the New Covenant, you come to Jesus just as you are and He makes you right before God. When we are confused about this basic truth, it often leads to believers trying to fix the world's ills first; in the belief that only then will God's favor and blessings be released. That kind of thinking is the essence of the Law of Moses and the reason why the proclamation of the gospel is way down the list of the social agenda and identity of many local churches. Jesus in a person's life changes their culture and brings transformation; it grows out of that initial seed, which is Christ in us. Jesus is faithful to produce the plant that has in it His DNA within that seed. Our commission is to sow that seed and see it through to harvest; that is our primary purpose.

In World War 2, the United States military fielded a force of over 6 million persons. Of that number, only about 36% were men in combat. The remaining 64% of those forces were logistical support and supply, officers, and administration. All in all, the number was slightly more than two million men in harm's way. If the body of Christ in every city and town had 3 or 4 out of every 10 believers passionate about bringing the kingdom of God to their communities, what do you think the outcome would be?

Our intercessors are crying out for revival on a scale that would be like a wave sweeping up the lost in its wake. But what if as the people of God we would simply walk in our commission leading one person to the Lord at a time. That new believer then impacts his family and friends and in a short period of time, the results will compound; you will then reach critical mass.

O God, raise up the dread warriors that carry the fire of the Isaiah 61 mandate to this world –in Jesus' name!

Fighting on Several Fronts, Depletes the Enemy's Resources

The Devil is not all-knowing or all-powerful and he is limited to being in one place at any given time. He does not have a limitless resource of demons at his disposal and as the earth's population grows and the kingdom of God expands; his numbers remain static. God can create more angels to service the growing population of His kingdom and so expansion and growth are not an issue at all to Him. What if the numbers of Christians already outnumber the demonic forces? That would mean the enemy cannot deploy a familiar spirit to shadow every single person; therefore, he would have to use one spirit to cover a family or a group. This would severely hinder his ability to gather information. For Christians not to be active proclaimers of the Lord Jesus, they are inadvertently helping the Devil manage his resources judiciously. He can divert his forces to those giving him the most trouble and later take out the non-combatants.

Can you picture the mayhem in the realm of darkness if the body of Christ would awaken to their calling and mandate? Jesus would be everywhere through His church in power pulling down strongholds by rescuing the lost, one person at a time.

The Kingdom of God and the Anti-kingdom

In my first book, I shared an experience that I had in the Lord concerning the kingdom of God in a given city and its evil counterpart.

In those early morning hours, I saw a building that was square in its foundation being erected vertically from its base. As the vision zoomed in for a more detailed inspection, I could see that the stones of the building were like a crystal with living faces within these blocks. It reminded me of those decorative glass blocks that are used in home construction. I recognized some of the faces that made up these living stones. It was obvious to me then, that what I was seeing was a picture of the body of Christ in the city I was living in. In Peter's epistle, he writes of this symbolic picture:

> *As you come to Him, the living stone, rejected by men, but chosen and precious in God's sight, you also, like living stones, are being built into a spiritual house to be a holy priesthood, offering spiritual sacrifices acceptable to God through Jesus Christ* (1 Peter 2:4, 5).

Paul wrote,

> *Therefore you are no longer strangers and foreigners, but fellow citizens of the saints and members of God's household, built on the foundation of the apostles and prophets, with Christ Jesus Himself as the cornerstone. In Him the whole building is fitted together and grows into a holy temple in the Lord. And in Him you*

> *too are being built together into a dwelling place for God in His Spirit* (Ephesians 2:19-22).

The structure was not flashy by any means and its solid austerity resembled almost something of a fortress-like structure. As I was viewing this scene before me, the vision then panned across the landscape to another fortress or castle-like structure that had in its appearance something that was comprised of dark black glass. As the scene zoomed in for closer inspection, I could see its black stones were of a similar glass block design that I described earlier. Just as the first structure, it too had within it, living faces, some of whom I also recognized. I knew I was looking at a spiritual principality ruling within my home city. I had never thought or considered that the enemy's stronghold could carry in its imagery, something similar to the picture of the church of God. But behind the walls of those living stones, sat a power ruling in relative safety, shielded from the arrows of intercession that were being volleyed against it. I knew that in order to dethrone that ruler, we would have to breach the walls.

As the good news of Jesus was being proclaimed to those people who made up the stones of the black wall, I watched as a stone moved out from its structure, was transformed into a clear glass block and then transferred into the crystal wall of the kingdom of God. With every stone and group of stones that were removed from the wall of the enemy, his fortress was weakened. With every stone removed from the enemy's wall, the kingdom of God's structure continued to grow vertically. I also realized that any outpouring of the Spirit within the city could create a significant breach in the wall and transfer those stones out of the darkness into the structure of light.

I came to the realization that the protection a principality, power or ruling spirit maintains over a specific locale is, in fact, a human shield. Those held captive or those who choose to be under the power and influence of the realm of darkness become the source of protection for the demonic realm.

These forces were defeated at the glorious victory of the Lord Jesus on the cross. He restored all that the Father had gifted to man and placed the choice of rule back into the hands of mankind. If they choose the darkness over the light, they do so because they still have yet to hear the Good News or they have used their freedom of choice to continue to reject the One who gave His life for them. Either way, if a person remains in darkness, this is the only way Satan can cling to any power in a city or region. He operates his rogue state within the boundary of the earth, which is now, once again, the legal domain of the kingdom of God.

We live in a day that has just witnessed what a rogue empire looks like while operating in nations that are recognized as sovereign countries. During the writing of this book, our world has witnessed ISIS, which came into power and claimed territory within Iraq and Syria and operated as its own nation within those sovereign boundaries.

The picture of the two competing kingdoms within a region changed my perspective of how spiritual warfare is to be conducted in the New Covenant. If the spiritual leadership within our cities would focus its attention on intercession and evangelism, we will see a change in our communities. We need intercession that binds the enemy's ability to blind the eyes, plug the ears, and block the understanding of the gospel from penetrating people's hearts. We need to stop attacking the people in our prayers, but rather cry out for mercy. We need to proclaim the Good News in all of its forms of evangelism and bring that invitation to those communities in word and deed; we will then be able to breach the spiritual walls that hold those citizens captive.

We need to move from a fixed model of warfare like that of the Great War, where each side is entrenched and separated by a "no man's land" and move to a new perspective of that of a mobile strategy, engaging the lost with the manifest love of God in word, power, and deed. We need to crossover and bring the kingdom of God to those who are held captive and set them free in Jesus' name!

Further to these impressions and thoughts, I would like to share something that the late John Paul Jackson said he received from the Lord by a revelatory dream. When he first shared this, I must tell you that I emphatically disagreed with him. I argued that Satan is crushed under the feet of our Lord Jesus; therefore, the Devil no longer had any legal right and thus, no authority in the spiritual realm to maintain rule. This, of course, was before I had any understanding of how man still cedes the authority of rule over to Satan. With permission from great folks at Streams Ministries, here is what John Paul Jackson shared from a dream he received from the Lord:

Throwing Hatchets at the Moon

It was night; the sky was blue-black except for
a huge luminous moon that filled the horizon.

In the remote blackness, several figures were silhouetted against the moon. Each figure stood on a circular platform and preached to a small group of people. With great emotion, these leaders pointed and shouted at the moon, urging others to follow them. Gradually, each leader's platform rose higher as the crowds grew larger. Some platforms rose above the crowds to precarious heights. Others lifted only slightly off the ground. Resembling gunslingers, the leaders stood on the platforms with holsters strapped to their hips. But instead of guns in the holsters, there were hatchets tucked inside. As the leaders began to preach, crowds of people gathered around them. Then, each leader grabbed a hatchet, waved it around, and hurled it at the moon. But the hatchet never hit the moon; it simply fell into the darkness that lay beyond. After some time, the leaders grew weary. Eventually, each lay down on his or her platform and fell asleep. Then with undetected stealth, several dark figures dropped off the moon's surface. They crawled up poles which held up the platforms, sneaked over, and began to attack the leaders with extreme viciousness. Since the platforms were large and lofty, no one had been alerted to the coming devastation. Soon, blood-curdling cries came forth from the leaders—cries for their families, their children, their churches, and their ministries. (Page 16)

"Somebody help me, I'm dying," someone pleaded. It was a terrifying sight and sound. Then, the dream faded to black. In the stillness that followed, God spoke to me:

To attack principalities and powers over a geographic area can be as useless as throwing hatchets at the moon. And it can leave you open to unforeseen and unperceived attacks.

God's words echoed in my mind. These leaders did not foresee principalities counterattacking them. They believed they were doing something great for God. They failed to comprehend the nature of the enemy's authority to retaliate with fierceness (Page 17, from John Paul Jackson's book *The Needless Casualties of War*)

John Paul described that shortly after receiving that dream, he received calls from pastors from all over the nation with distressing tales of how the enemy was attacking their families and ministries. In each case, the churches were found to be attacking demonic, spiritual authority without authorization from the Lord. We must remember the words of Paul when he spoke of how people who choose the darkness of sin over coming into the light of the glorious gospel would see the eventual withdrawal of the Spirit of God from their lives. Three times in Romans Chapter 1 in verses 24 through 26, we see the phrase, *"God gave them over."* There is a point where God will withdraw from a person's life and allow him or her to fully experience life under Satan as god. When man cedes legal right over to the realm of darkness and should those spirits of wickedness convert a great segment of the population over a locale, he then gains legal right over that town, city, state or even that nation. Satan can exercise no control or rule on the earth except for what he can re-acquire through man.

When we attack spiritual powers in this kind of warfare engagement, we are merely throwing hatchets at the moon and falling far short of the target. What we are more likely to hit are the human shields that provide the enemy's authority and protection. The direction of our intercession is to cry out for mercy on behalf of the lost and ask that their hearts would be open to the message of Jesus. We bind spiritual forces that are trying to suppress that proclamation and keep the message from being heard. We also need to proceed with caution as to how we seek to bring our values through political means to a world that is hostile to God and alienated from His ways. The world only perceives this as an attack on their freedom and right of choice. They aggressively respond by resisting the morality of a God they do not recognize. These also turn and accuse the church of bigotry because they see that the church is trying to use secular laws to enforce their religious beliefs. The church, in nations where it once held prominence, has now been trying to change people from the outside-in to preserve the values it once knew. This is not how Jesus modeled warfare for us. By proclaiming the Good News and manifesting the Isaiah 61 mandate of His ministry, He will change hearts from the inside-out.

The Strongman's House and Goods

> *Knowing their thoughts, Jesus said to them, "Every kingdom divided against itself will be laid waste, and every city or household divided against itself will not stand. If Satan drives out Satan, he is divided against himself. How then can his kingdom stand?*
>
> *And if I drive out demons by Beelzebul, by whom do your sons drive them out? So then, they will be your judges. But if I drive out demons by the Spirit of God, then the kingdom of God has come upon you.*
>
> *How can anyone enter a strong man's house and steal his possessions, unless he first ties up the strong man? Then he can plunder his house* (Matthew 12:25-29).

The Lord had miraculously healed a man who was blind and mute but the religious leaders claimed it was a work of the Devil. This was the backdrop of this key revelation from Jesus as to how to overpower a spiritual enemy within his fortification. What did this man's healing have anything to with binding a strongman and plundering his goods?

The weapons that the enemy uses on humanity are those things that seek to rob, kill, and destroy. In the case of the blind and mute man, it was his physical disability. Every time the power of God comes in the form of healing and deliverance, it literally disarms the enemy of a weapon he relies on to hold a person in bondage. When the Isaiah 61 mandate of Jesus is manifested in a person's life, it disarms the Devil. The kingdom of God coming in word and power neutralizes the enemy's weapons and clears the way to bind that evil spirit and take him prisoner. That is how Jesus acted against a stronghold of the enemy that was holding a person's life captive through his infirmity.

Jesus had revealed the strategy that was to be used to take a strong man's house. Now, let's take the view from the paradigm of a person living behind the walls that he or she erects in his or her life. We can also use this to describe a group of people as a walled town or a city, like that of that earlier description of the fortress or castle. In the context of the passage that Jesus spoke of overpowering and taking the strongman's assets, He had just been accused of deriving His source of power from the Devil. In refuting their evil claims, the Lord reveals two strategic keys about warfare with the Devil. First, if his ranks are divided, their position of strength will fail. Second, if you bind the strongest opponent, you can then strip him of his wealth.

So, if we want to apply this in practical terms, how do we divide the enemy's defenses and bind the strongest foes? We also need to ask, what are those possessions that he trusts in?

Let's use the same analogies in our answers as those given from The Lord's words on the subject from a personal perspective. The walls people put up in their lives are based on their beliefs and their life experiences. A person then uses those very things as building blocks to be insulated and protected from potential vulnerability or further hurt. It is through those believed thoughts, words, and experiences that the castle walls are erected; that person resides behind them and is enslaved to the strong man who rules his or her thought life. Satan uses fear, mistrust, deception, and lies as the essential building materials for the structure with an almost certain high degree of thoughts that cast doubt against God. Lies are sown in the form of thoughts, such as, *if God is truly real, why then has all of this befallen them*? Another common claim is that God did not love the person enough to save them from trouble. The usual lie that Christians are told is that they were under judgment by God and that is the reason for His apparent absence.

On a corporate level such as a community, city or even a state, province or nation it is the collective beliefs and acceptance of the things of good or evil that will define the given region. The people themselves make up the very walls of that structure where the strongman resides. Whatever the people are known to love or that they give themselves to becomes the known collective trait of that locale.

How then do we divide the enemy's house, breaching the structure and facilitating its downfall? The following two passages of scripture show us how we accomplish this task on a personal and corporate level.

> *For the word of God is living and active. Sharper than any double-edged sword, it pierces even to dividing soul and spirit, joints and marrow. It is able to judge the thoughts and intentions of the heart* (Hebrews 4:12).

> *For though we live in the flesh, we do not wage war according to the flesh. The weapons of our warfare are not the weapons of the world.*

Instead, they have divine power to demolish strongholds. We tear down arguments, and every presumption set up against the knowledge of God; and we take captive every thought to make it obedient to Christ (2 Corinthians 10:3-5).

It is the truth that sets the captive free and that truth is the Word of God. As we have addressed in previous chapters, it is words that are believed that will divide truth from lies or expose lies against the truth. The proclamation of the good news about Jesus and His manifest power disarm a person's hostile thoughts about God. From personal walls to national walls, it will be the truth about Jesus in love that will breach any barrier, divide their houses and bring down that principality or ruler over a given region. It will be the proclamation of His message and His mandate that will accomplish this from those who have received His commission with hearts overflowing with love and mercy to a people expecting to only hear wrath, judgment, and hatred. If ever a term such as "lethal smart bomb" exists, there is no defense that the enemy can match against the passionate love of Jesus for the lost. When we bring the true knowledge of God that is found in the New Covenant, it will destroy the walls, which are their arguments against following Jesus.

Do you want to bring down a demonic stronghold or kingdom? Divide his house with truth; for unity is the strength of all spiritual strongholds. When unsaved people begin to question their lifestyles, morals, and the reality of Jesus, this positive uncertainty is the beginning of dividing that house. This is the time we can plunder the enemy's works in their lives and unite them to Jesus.

After evangelism has breached the walls, we can focus our attention on the strongman. If he were a man in battle, the easiest way to deal with him would be to slay him. The strongman is a spirit and is eternal; therefore, he cannot be slain, so he must be bound or restrained from carrying on his rule. So then, how does one bind a spirit that cannot be held by any natural means?

There are three main passages from the New Testament that are used as the basis for the spiritual warfare teaching on "Binding and Loosing." We have already read the passage from Matthew 12 on binding the strongman, so here are the two other scripture passages that are used.

> *Truly I tell you, whatever you bind on earth will be bound in heaven, and whatever you loose on earth will be loosed in heaven.*
>
> *Again, I tell you truly that if two of you on the earth agree about anything you ask for, it will be done for you by My Father in heaven. For where two or three gather together in My name, there am I with them"* (Matthew 18:18-20).
>
> *Simon Peter answered, "You are the Christ, the Son of the living God."*
>
> *Jesus replied, "Blessed are you, Simon son of Jonah! For this was not revealed to you by flesh and blood, but by My Father in heaven. And I tell you that you are Peter, and on this rock I will build My church, and the gates of Hades will not prevail against it. I will give you the*

keys of the kingdom of heaven. Whatever you bind on earth will be bound in heaven, and whatever you loose on earth will be loosed in heaven" (Matthew 16:16-20).

The word "bind" is used 43 times in scripture and is translated below into English.

Strong's Concordance

deó: to tie, bind

Original Word: δέω
Part of Speech: Verb
Transliteration: *deó*
Phonetic Spelling: (deh'-o)
Short Definition: I bind
Definition: I bind, tie, fasten; I impel, compel; I declare to be prohibited and unlawful.

What I found interesting is that whenever the text was placed in a natural context, the implication of fastening or tying was obvious. But when the context moved into a spiritual context, the implication always seemed to be a legal declaration and action. Binding, is a rabbinical idiom in the Aramaic language that uses that term to forbid, prohibit or declare something as illicit. All three passages used seemed to carry that implication as well. These passages indicate a legal authority to enforce the edicts of the will of God by the believer into the natural realm.

Just as the angel of the Lord under the Old Covenant enforced the will of the Lord by saying the "the Lord rebukes you" and thereby ceasing the intended action of Satan, believers use the authority that is given to them in the name of Jesus. To the enemy, that spoken authority is as though the Lord is saying it to them directly. The demons know this and tremble at the very thought that one day, we may believe this to be true as well. This is the New Covenant reality of legal enforcement in the realm of the spirit through prayer and intercession. Jesus told the disciples that one day, they will preside in judgment in the land. We are, even now, a spiritual nation of kings and priests unto our God. This authority is not to lash out and abuse the body of Christ or the lost. This authority is to restrict the demonic realm's activity from lashing out and abusing people whether they are saved or lost. To truly stand in the gap for people in intercession is to express to the Father the true heart of Jesus on behalf of the people. If your theology still holds the paradigm of the Old Covenant, you will find yourself contrary to the very heart of Jesus who you are trying to honor in your service to Him.

Our human tendency is to lash out at our opponents for the things that are taking place against us or the things that are taking place in the world. But how did Jesus model intercession and warfare for us? For after all, everything that the enemy has plotted to do against God and His creation found its target on the Lord Jesus. Everything that the church faces in warfare is because the enemy and the world hated Jesus first. The Lord warned us not to be surprised when this happens; for this is all part of the battle.

The Lord's teaching on binding the strongman gives us a picture of warfare in both realms. The vertical warfare takes place in the spiritual realm through prayer and intercession. The horizontal warfare is the proclamation of Jesus to the world in the natural realm. We engage principalities and powers through intercession, binding them with the legal authority that is ours in Christ. We then divide the enemy's stronghold with the truth about Jesus bringing down the lies that fortified the stronghold. By binding the demonic influence over a person or a populace, we then can move in with the gospel to take the spoils, which are those lives that are now made free by the love of God.

Chapter 13

THE HEART OF THE WARRIOR

Therefore, since we are surrounded by such a great cloud of witnesses, let us throw off every encumbrance and the sin that so easily entangles, and let us run with endurance the race set out for us. Let us fix our eyes on Jesus, the pioneer and perfecter of our faith, who for the joy set before Him endured the cross, scorning its shame, and sat down at the right hand of the throne of God. **Consider Him who endured such hostility from sinners, so that you will not grow weary and lose heart.**

In your struggle against sin, you have not yet resisted to the point of shedding your blood. And you have forgotten the exhortation that addresses you as sons:

"My son, do not make light of the Lord's discipline, or lose heart when He rebukes you.

For the Lord disciplines the one He loves, and He chastises everyone He receives as a son." **Endure suffering as discipline;** *God is treating you as sons. For what son is not disciplined by his father? If you do not experience discipline like everyone else, then you are illegitimate children and not true sons. Furthermore, we have all had earthly fathers who disciplined us, and we respected them. Should we not much more submit to the Father of our spirits and live?*

Our fathers disciplined us for a short time as they thought best, but God disciplines us for our good, so that we may share in His holiness. No discipline seems enjoyable at the time, but painful. Later on, however, it yields a peaceful harvest of righteousness to those who have been trained by it.

Therefore strengthen your limp hands and weak knees. Make straight paths for your feet, so that the lame will not be debilitated, but rather healed (Hebrews 12:1-13).

I find the 12th chapter of Hebrews a remarkable passage of scripture. The chapter is often taught from the perspective of a father disciplining his children when they get out of line, for God loves us too much to let us go astray. I see no problem with that, but consider for a moment some key points to the context of this exhortation. The writer of Hebrews is first addressing us to shed our lives of the distractions of this world. Then he talks of Jesus enduring great hostility from sinners; yet, He stayed the course of His mission, which was the cross. It is from the example of Jesus that we are then exhorted to accept the discipline of the Lord and endure the hardships of the discipline. Are you getting the picture? I think if you have served in the military at some point in time, you just got it.

When a new recruit enters military service, he goes directly into basic training. The difficult regimen of life as a soldier now begins with strict military discipline. The training he or she receives and the repetitive knowledge that is being ingrained into them is for the purpose that once he or she enters battle, the embedded disciplines will take over and produce the reactions that may well save the soldier's life and those in combat with his or her unit. I am sure we could not count how often a struggling private in battle has the words from his NCO, "remember your training."

In like manner, the Father is telling us, His children, to follow the example of Jesus in His conduct in the midst of a hostile world. We are exhorted to maintain that example of discipline in our lives when we face the challenges that will surely come our way. The chastising circumstances are not candy-coated by the Lord; they are unpleasant to be sure. But, like basic training, you will be made strong through the experience and will produce the end results we are seeking Him for.

Now look at Paul's words to Timothy, and you see a similar context to his exhortation to this young leader.

> *You therefore, my child, be strong in the grace*
> *that is in Christ Jesus. And the things that you*
> *have heard me say among many witnesses,*

> *entrust these to faithful men who will be qualified to teach others as well.*
>
> *Join me in suffering, like a good soldier of Christ Jesus. A soldier refrains from entangling himself in civilian affairs, in order to please the one who enlisted him* (2 Timothy 2:1-4).

Paul was telling Timothy that this world with all of its distractions leads to a life of entanglement. That Greek word *emplekó* creates the picture of being woven into something, like that of being intertwined with the world. Oftentimes, as we try to be so culturally relevant, the distinction of who we are gets lost in the translation. We need to put Jesus front and center in our motives with the desire to be a living book that reads His life in us in every chapter. For a soldier, keeping your mind in the fight is often the difference between winning and losing. For us, keeping our minds centered in Christ is to be kept by Him.

How did Jesus react and respond to a world that was so hostile to Him? His response will be our key to follow after as we seek to break down the enemy's defenses in our lives and in the world.

The Mantle of the Warring Intercessor

> *During the days of Jesus' earthly life, He offered up prayers and **petitions** with loud cries and tears to the One who could save Him from death, and He was heard because of His reverence* (Hebrews 5:7).

222

I quoted this verse in an earlier chapter, but now it bears repeating as it relates to our hearts in prayer. What is so powerful about this verse was how Jesus prayed for His enemies and a world that was mostly indifferent or fervently hostile towards Him. The word that is only used once in the entire Bible and therefore is solely His signatory mark is the Greek word, *hiketéria*. As seen from the *Strong's Concordance* description: The intercession of Jesus was as an offering of the olive branch of peace to the Father. Should not our intercession as His body on the earth be the same?

Strong's Concordance

hiketéria: **supplication**

Original Word: κετηρία, ας,
Part of Speech: Noun, Feminine
Transliteration: *hiketéria*
Phonetic Spelling: (hik-et-ay-ree'-ah)
Short Definition: supplication, entreaty
Definition: (originally: the olive branch held in the hand of the suppliant), supplication, entreaty.

The meaning of the word "sin" in its most literal translation from the Greek is, "to miss the mark." The Greek word *entugchanó* translated as "interceding" literally means "hitting the mark" as referenced by Paul in the verse below. He uses this word to describe Jesus in His intercession for us.

> *He who did not spare his own Son, but gave him up for us all—how will he not also, along with him, graciously give us all things? Who will bring any charge against those whom God has chosen? It is God who justifies. Who then is*

the one who condemns? No one. **Christ Jesus who died—more than that, who was raised to life—is at the right hand of God and is also interceding for us** (Romans 8:32-34).

Sin is representative as the arrow of mankind missing the target of righteousness. The prayer of Jesus for mankind was that the world would find that target of righteousness through Him. His prayer was not offered up in judgment as that verse indicates; rather, His intercession is for mercy. If we seek to see our intercession hit the mark as an arrow striking the intended target, we must be of the same heart and mind that was in the Lord. His heart was one that continually petitioned the Father with the image of the extended olive branch. It was a cry for mercy, not judgment. It was a cry for forgiveness, not vengeance and it was a cry for restoration, not destruction. That is what the Lord modeled through His life and His words.

> *You have heard that it was said, 'Love your neighbor and hate your enemy.' But I tell you, love your enemies and pray for those who persecute you, that you may be sons of your Father in heaven. He causes His sun to rise on the evil and the good, and sends rain on the righteous and the unrighteous. If you love those who love you, what reward will you get? Do not even tax collectors do the same? And if you greet only your brothers, what are you doing more than others? Do not even Gentiles do the same? Be perfect, therefore, as your Heavenly Father is perfect* (Matthew 5:43-45).

The actions Jesus modeled for us go against every natural human reaction to the offenses that occurred against Him. In fact, we would completely consider it acceptable and within our rights to demand and seek vengeance on our enemies.

Jesus would have been well within His right as under the Law of Moses to demand the retribution rights granted under "the eye for an eye, bruise for bruise and wound for wound" principle as stated in the book of Exodus. He would have in no way violated the law He was to fulfill. He would have been just using one of its provisions given to offended parties. Instead, He lets us look into the New Covenant and shows mercy to those who hate Him and He offers forgiveness to every offender.

When we take up the mantle of warfare in prayer and intercession, which covenant does it resemble and does it follow the Lord's example? If the intercession of your prayer group does not have the olive branch of peace being offered to the Lord on behalf of your enemies and the world that opposes you, you may need to search your heart. A judge's gavel in hand with demand for vengeance and justice places you within the wrong covenant.

In the last hours that Jesus spent with His disciples, He gives us some of the most powerful truths about the Father, Himself, and the Holy Spirit. He also reveals what the disciples' lives will be like in Him after He is raised from the dead. In John's gospel, Chapters 13-17 reveal the final hours before His crucifixion, and Jesus will speak of the most important things that He wants His disciples to remember.

If you had mere hours to live and you called your family together, you would want to relay to your loved ones the most important things that they can hold on to and remember. It would take the writing of another book to do justice to those thoughts that the Lord was saying, but I will merely highlight the keys given by Jesus for intercession and prayer.

Love is the Key of Release in Prayer

I would ask you before we go further in this teaching that you put this book down and go and read the Gospel of John, Chapters 13-17. It is important that you grasp the context and heart of Jesus before we come back and focus on these verses listed below.

> *Truly, truly, I tell you, whoever believes in Me will also do the works that I am doing. He will do even greater things than these, because I am going to the Father.* ***And I will do whatever you ask in My name, so that the Father may be glorified in the Son. If you ask Me anything in My name, I will do*** *it* (John 14: 12-14).*

> *As the Father has loved Me, so have I loved you. Remain in My love. If you keep My commandments, you will remain in My love, just as I have kept My Father's commandments and remain in His love. I have told you these things so that My joy may be in you and your joy may be complete.*

> *This is My commandment, that you love one another as I loved you. Greater love has no one*

226

than this, that he lay down his life for his friends.

*You are My friends if you do what I command you. No longer do I call you servants, for a servant does not understand what his master is doing. But I have called you friends, because everything I have learned from My Father I have made known to you. You did not choose Me, but I chose you. And I appointed you to go and bear fruit—fruit that will remain—**so that whatever you ask the Father in My name, He will give you. This is My command to you: Love one another*** (John 15:9-17).

*In that day you will no longer ask Me anything. Truly, truly, I tell you, whatever you ask the Father in My name, He will give you. **Until now you have not asked for anything in My name. Ask and you will receive, so that your joy may be complete*** (John 16: 23, 24).

I trust that in reading those chapters, you can sense the passion and emotion coming from the Lord Jesus on that fateful night. As much as He felt love for any disciple that night, He feels that same way towards you. You too were in His heart on that night of nights. There were no trivial or idle words from the Lord; there never were, but one can only imagine the intensity in His eyes and the emphasis in the words that He spoke. So often in the past, the disciples just wouldn't get it, and the teaching moment would pass only to be brought up again at a later date. Not so for this night, they had to get it and get it right then and there.

I have highlighted from these three verses what I want to focus on, which is the asking in prayer and the unquestioned receiving of that prayer, as answered. Now I want to ask you some questions:

1. Are there any preconditions to the answering of these prayers?

2. Are our prayers in the intercession ministry answered and our joy complete?

3. Are all your personal prayers, answered and your joy complete?

If, on questions 2 and 3, you responded with, "Not yet, but I believe that they are in the process of being answered" that would be a commendable and proper response to your faith. But, if there were times when prayer went unanswered, how do we reconcile these verses.

Over the three years Jesus spent with His disciples, He pounded away at the subject of belief and unbelief. Therefore, I am assuming that it was embedded in their understanding of how the kingdom of God functions and operates. As it relates to the rest of us, I am sure that we all share that general understanding of belief and unbelief as well. So the point can be made that though it was unstated as a precondition, you have to believe the words that Jesus said in order to see the manifestation of His words.

But that is not what I would like to point out to you. The whole context of these chapters is that they are drenched with His love for His disciples and His desire for our joy to be fulfilled. Jesus then gives to them His commandment to love as He loved. It should be noted that the Lord has only two newly stated commandments as given in the New Testament.

Beloved, if our hearts do not condemn us, we have confidence before God, and we will receive from Him whatever we ask, because we keep His commandments and do what is pleasing in His sight. **And this is His commandment: that we should believe in the name of His Son, Jesus Christ, and we should love one another just as He commanded us.** *Whoever keeps His commandments remains in God, and God in him. And by this we know that He remains in us: by the Spirit He has given us.* (1 John 3:21-24)

One could rightly imply that the great commission is a commandment, but the Greek words used do not place it in the same authoritative context like that of the Ten Commandments. Jesus did however place new illumination on how a person operating through love, would not be able break a commandment.

One of them, an expert in the law, tested Him with a question: "Teacher, which commandment is the greatest in the Law?" Jesus declared, "'Love the Lord your God with all your heart and with all your soul and with all your mind.' This is the first and greatest commandment. And the second is like it: 'Love your neighbor as yourself.' All the Law and the Prophets depend on these two commandments." (Matthew 22:35-40)

The fact of the matter is this: if you obey His commandment to love as He loved, you can't break any of the other commandments of the Law of Moses. It is when we move in God's love for others that we will mirror the same fruit from our prayers that Jesus had when He walked upon the earth. God is love and everything He does proceeds from His great love. Paul wrote in Galatians *"faith works by love,"* and it is for that reason everything Jesus spoke came to pass. My point to all this is if we tangibly manifest the heart of Jesus through our intercession, we will see every prayer also come to pass if it was prayed through His heart of love.

Unfortunately, so much of corporate intercession often resembles a complaint against humanity session. With a fervent spirit, individuals call out for judgment to be meted out on the listed sins and offenses by governments, institutions, groups, and individuals. Is that kind of activity following the example of our Lord?

Near the end of the Lord's ministry, Jerusalem became a dangerous place for Jesus and His disciples. The disciples no longer wanted to go there and endure death threats, potential stoning, and the continual attacks that came from the religious establishment against the Lord.

Jesus knew that no prophet had been killed outside of Jerusalem and it would be in that great city that He would fulfill His destiny. As He came to Jerusalem for one of the last times, He wept intensely over the city. Was it for the stones, bricks, and mortar that He was so troubled? Of course not, it was for the people who were most indifferent towards Him and others who were incited with hostility towards Him from their religious leaders. Every tear shed was a cry from His heart that wanted to show mercy and not judgment. He cried that their ears would be open to hear, their eyes being opened to see and their minds being opened to understand. That is the heart of love from our Mighty Warrior; that is how He intercedes for us all.

When I was a young man, my prayers were from a heart that

was willing to cast the first stone. When I preached, I thought I had orated a great sermon if I made you feel what I thought was conviction and see many of the congregation being laden with shame. I was zealous for God like a Saul but was in desperate need of a transformation to become like a Paul.

In my mid-twenties, I had an experience whether half awake or half asleep; it was so long ago, I am unsure. I saw in my mind's eye a picture of the Lord standing at my four-tier filing cabinet, which contained my teachings and sermons. As the Lord reviewed each file, He would not return them to the cabinet but dropped them on the floor. One file after another, they found their way to the floor, except one file and a page or two from another. I stood there stunned not understanding what I was seeing because I believed that I was a stickler for the Word and those teachings were filled with scriptures. Finally, I piped up and said, "But Lord, that is your scripture on the floor," and He responded and said, "It may be the scriptures, but it is not my heart being expressed through those scriptures." That was it, the scene was gone, and I was left stunned to ponder what it all meant.

In the years that followed and especially within the past ten years, the Holy Spirit has been ever so gracious to help me understand how to express the Lord's heart. To give you an example of what I am trying to say, I will use the healing of the woman on the Sabbath from Luke's gospel.

> *One Sabbath Jesus was teaching in one of the synagogues, and a woman there had been disabled by a spirit for eighteen years. She was hunched over and could not stand up straight. When Jesus saw her, He called her over and*

said, "Woman, you are set free from your infirmity." Then He laid His hands on her, and immediately she straightened up and began to glorify God.

But the synagogue leader was indignant that Jesus had healed on the Sabbath. "There are six days for work," he told the crowd. "So come and be healed on those days and not on the Sabbath."

"You hypocrites!" the Lord replied, "Does not each of you on the Sabbath untie his ox or donkey from the stall and lead it to water? Then should not this daughter of Abraham, whom Satan has bound for eighteen long years, be released from her bondage on the Sabbath day?"

When Jesus said this, all His adversaries were humiliated. And the whole crowd rejoiced at all the glorious things He was doing (Luke 13:10-15).

I am embarrassed to say that in the past, my entire focus of this passage was about Jesus confronting the establishment. I would have celebrated that Jesus had just shamed the religious leaders by healing on the Sabbath. "Stick it to the man Jesus; let them know who is boss!" God had just flexed His muscles and there's more where that came from, so watch out! But was that the motivating factor for Jesus to release that miracle into that woman's life? Was it just to humiliate the religious leaders? Jesus performed many miracles on the Sabbath because that was the day when people would come together at the synagogue. The Lord wasn't focused on the religious leaders; He was focused on the afflicted woman. His heart was moved with compassion after seeing this dear woman who had not known a Sabbath rest in over eighteen years while suffering from her condition. Jesus, out of His loving kindness and tender mercies gave this woman what everybody else had on the Sabbath; He gave her rest by healing her affliction. My emphasis in the past was placed on things that were not what the Lord was emphasizing; He was moving in compassion but my mind was on judgment.

We need to change the way we think about God and understand what His heart is towards His people and the lost. The intercession of Jesus holds within His hand the olive branch of peace as He stands in the gap for humanity. We need to go and do likewise. In so doing, we will carry His warrior heart into battle and win the day.

The Warfare of the Kingdom is a War Waged out of Love

Never at any time when I felt that I should write this book on spiritual warfare did the subject of love cross my mind. And yet, when stepping back and looking at it with perspective it makes total sense. The kingdom of darkness has no sustainable defense, no cover, and no weapon that can counter the love of God. Over time, it will erode every defense that is exposed to it and it will absorb every attack of the enemy. The manifest love of God only gets stronger until it eventually consumes all the nations of the earth for the purpose of making Jesus known as King of kings and Lord of lords.

Just as Satan has no equal to combat the love of God, he also has no weapon to counter mercy. The book of James declares that mercy triumphs over judgment. The accuser loves judgment; it advances his kingdom steadily but mercy will defeat him every time. In spiritual war, mercy achieves the triumph in battle and brings honor, praise, and glory to our King. Oh, that we would unleash these terror weapons on the enemy every day of our lives.

The Reality of the Two Worlds in Which We Dwell

In light of these things and the reality of the fallen world we live in, I have pondered if a devout Christian should ever take the seat as an earthly king. Jesus said *"My kingdom is not of this world"* and the decisions that kings make during war in the earthly realm cannot easily be tempered with love. The ideals of a civilized worldview do not translate well into the language of war if the other combatant does not espouse those same ideals. For instance, in World War 2, the U.S Air Force opted for a strategy of the daytime bombing of military targets only, when they first entered the war. The thought of attacking civilian targets was unthinkable to Bomber Command in those early days of the air war. The cost of bombing during the daytime to avoid civilian casualties took a terrific toll on US Airmen and the losses climbed at an alarming rate of men and machines. The ferocity of a merciless war would eventually see the change of strategy that led to cities being bombed and eventually the atomic bomb being dropped on Japan. What began as a civilized approach to war rooted in Christian values and ethics soon gave way to matching the ferocity of unrelenting viciousness and the determination that was being meted out by the enemy.

In the annals of the worst despots of human history, Joseph Stalin will certainly find himself on its top ten list. 43 million of his own citizens would die under his regime. It is estimated that he purposely starved over nine million Ukrainian peasant farmers to confiscate their land for his plan to mechanize agriculture. Stalin's response to those statistics was to say, "The death of one man is tragedy, the death of a million is a statistic." Life held no value to him; he had no moral compass. He made the comment regarding the ruthless acts he performed by saying, "My hand does not quiver." To have Mao Zedong rising to power along with Hitler and Stalin already in power all at the same time is an unimaginable horror, but that was the reality of World War 2.

We live in a day where Christian morality and ethics are challenged and rejected by secular humanism, other nations, and other religions. These are not the days of the "so-called" Christian kings of Europe engaging in the "so-called" civilized wars and warfare, which was pure myth anyways, and laden with atrocities. So, even if a nation holds the moral high ground such as the United States had when war was declared upon them in WW2, they were soon left with no choice but to match and exceed the ferocity of their enemies. That is why I have considered that God purposely places those in leadership over nations that may not wholly espouse His ways in times of war. To me, Winston Churchill is a perfect example of one who was a political pariah in times of peace; yet, was one of the greatest leaders in history in a time of war. In 1945, less than two months after Nazi Germany surrendered, Churchill was voted out of power. His life was a preparation for war, which he fulfilled as a man of destiny. History has marked him as one of the greatest leaders in the modern era, and I believe God had raised him up as the right leader for that perilous time. God places men in the seats of power and sometimes it makes no sense in the present until future events begin to unfold. So in light of this, we ought not to be so quick to judge things before time weighs in with its opinion.

In Council to the King

In scripture, what seems to hold water for me, is how God placed His councilors in key positions within the ruling government and close to its leader. Those kings, by our standards of today, would be considered ruthless dictators. Yet, God strategically placed His people in positions of influence with them. Furthermore, God would directly get involved with those rulers by dreams and supernatural encounters to speak to them and direct His plans through them. We see this with Pharaoh and Joseph, Nebuchadnezzar and Daniel, Darius and Daniel, Nehemiah and Artaxerxes, and Cyrus and Ezra to name a few. In Israel, whether the king was listed as doing evil in the sight of the Lord or one who did right in the eyes of the Lord, there was always a prophet of national influence speaking into his rule.

Even history recorded outside of the Bible reveals these encounters as still taking place, even to our current day. I realize this kind of thinking goes against the current thought of evangelical Christendom, but I see this as the biblical pattern with a purpose. In the natural realm when God is engaged in battle, He takes responsibility for the battle and the war. The children of Israel witnessed this first hand in their deliverance from the Egyptians in the days of Moses, Gideon against the Amorites and Hezekiah against Sennacherib and the Assyrians. The Lord fought those battles for Israel when the nation was too weak naturally (militarily) to defend itself or engage in war.

In terms of covenant, the weaker party has the assured right of protection from the avowed stronger party. The weakness of the lesser is made complete or perfect by the strong and is the very essence of covenant. When Paul wrote about his thorn in his flesh, he recorded these words that the Lord said to him:

> But He said to me, "My grace is sufficient for you, for My power is perfected in weakness." Therefore I will boast all the more gladly in my weaknesses, so that the power of Christ may rest on me. That is why, for the sake of Christ, I delight in weaknesses, in insults, in hardships, in persecutions, in difficulties. For when I am weak, then I am strong (2 Corinthians 12:9, 10).

God was answering Paul in covenant language that the ancient world understood completely. Today, its meaning is all but lost to us, but it was not misunderstood in their day. In terms of covenant, God had avowed to Paul the same rights of petition that the ancient world had in their covenants.

That is how the weaker is made strong; it is because of the binding oath between the two parties. Through Jesus, we are in an irrevocable eternal covenant with the God of all creation. He has bound Himself to His oath to be our rock of defense.

Israel's Earthly History and Spiritual Allegory

There are essentially only two periods of war that Israel's army actually engaged in battle in partnership with God. Those wars were led initially by Moses and then carried on by Joshua and the other was under Saul who gave way to David. These two transfers of power speak spiritually and prophetically of the Old Covenant and the New Covenant. The children of Israel in the Sinai wilderness wanted a compromise to the covenant offered by God, which became the Law of Moses. The New Covenant through Jesus would restore God's original offer of covenant to Israel and to all nations of the earth to create a priesthood nation.

In the era of the Judges in Israel, the nation of Israel wanted a king to preside over them to be like all of the other nations. God, who was their King, gave Israel what they wanted and Saul was named king. Saul's failing rule would give place to David who was the prophetic picture of God choosing His king over the nation. Jesus is called the Son of David in recognition of His prophetic calling as the Messiah King. The wars that were fought by Joshua were to take back the Land of Promise that was vowed to Abraham. For David, it was to break the oppression of the surrounding nations and restore freedom and independence to Israel. These two symbolic pictures reveal to us the picture of Jesus leading His people in war to take back that which was promised by God and to break off the yoke of bondage from the rulers who enslaved them.

As a final footnote to tie these thoughts together, the rest of Israel's history of wars were fought from a national perspective that had its heritage rooted in God. That would give way to the influence of the surrounding nations with their culture and their gods. This to me is a picture of what the western world is like today. The politics, the cultural dilution of Christian influence and morality are not those of what can be called a Christian nation. Furthermore, even the wars that they engage in, citing the interests of national security, cannot be likened to the rule or extension of the kingdom of God in any way. The nations of this world are set to an earthly agenda; the agenda of the kingdom of God is to proclaim Jesus to that world and rescue the hearers that respond to His message. The Messiah came to Israel and the nation did not see it because they looked for an earthly kingdom. Western Christianity has followed Israel's path in looking for their nations to be an earthly manifestation of the kingdom of God. We should remind ourselves that Jesus said that His kingdom is not of this world.

Let us all seek to bring God's kingdom to whatever country we were born in; for all the nations of the world are His inheritance. Let us all become one of those dread champions that make up the army of God who are of the same heart and mind as the Lord. And let us seek to be trained in the tactics and weapons of the kingdom of God to adeptly engage in spiritual battle.

Chapter 14

LEADERSHIP AND COMMAND

You may be reading this book because you are looking to be more engaged in the purposes of God and recognize that spiritual warfare is an unavoidable component of your service. Another may be a seasoned veteran of war in the spirit who is looking to further equip his or her knowledge and understanding on this subject. To both, I have tried to give a biblical and historical backdrop of the spiritual realm that traverses the three ages as described in scripture and to show the differences in the spiritual realm during those eras. We have then been presented with our glorious King's victory and have learned of His heart as we have explored what this means for us as those who live in the New Covenant. So now, it is time to personalize this, get familiar with the command structure, distribute the weapons and military kit or gear, and help you recognize the company you have been assigned to serve in.

The Commander-in-Chief

In the army of God, all officers follow the Lord's example and lead from the front in battle. Jesus never asks anyone to do something that He hasn't done or would not do Himself. His will is conducted on the earth just as it is in heaven; the rules do not change because the environment is different, which is why we can always trust His leadership. We have not entered this war having to be concerned whether victory is in doubt; that outcome was decided over two thousand years ago. Jesus is the victor and the key contest has been decided decisively. The army of God is now in battle cleaning out the last resistance and occupying the recaptured land until He returns.

There was a monumental change in the spirit realm that took place at the glorious victory by our mighty King Jesus. The Old Covenant was a temporary covenant, The New Covenant and all that Jesus wrought for us through it, is eternal. The body of Christ whether individually or corporately wherever they are in the world can now live under an open heaven. No longer are the lines of communication and shipping lanes, supply lines, and roads only opened and available for mankind when Israel as a nation is walking uprightly. Now, all access points for supplies and communication are spiritually open wherever two or more are gathered in His name in agreement. In reality, that agreement number can be as small as you being in agreement with God and His Word. How's that for having a prayer partner? Jesus our intercessor and you in agreement with His will being done on earth as it is in heaven.

In Matthew 28, Jesus gave us the Great Commission; He said that *"all authority in heaven and earth"* had been given unto Him. Now for a math question: if you possess all of something, such as 10 marbles out of a total of ten marbles, how many marbles does the other party have? Do you get the picture? Satan was stripped of all of the authority that man ceded to him at Eden. Jesus took it all back and returned it to mankind through His body, the church. The victory on the cross was not a battle won with mixed results; it was a crushing defeat by overwhelming force by Jesus our conquering hero. He stands over Satan having crushed his head under the power of His heel, once and for all.

To the Victor Goes the Spoil

> But *thanks be to God, who always parades us triumphantly in Christ and through us spreads everywhere the fragrance of the knowledge of Him. For we are to God the sweet aroma of Christ among those who are being saved and those who are perishing. To the one, we are an odor of death and demise; to the other, a fragrance that brings life. And who is qualified for such a task?* (2 Corinthians 2:14-16).

I love Paul's references to Jesus as our mighty conqueror. He uses the analogy of what a Roman Triumph was — an all-day victory parade through the streets of Rome. Throughout the long history of the Roman Empire, the "Triumph" as it was known, was the epitome of honor and acclaim for a Praetor, a commander of the army or Caesar. To qualify to be given a Triumph by the Senate of Rome, the victory had to be decisive and glorious with proven heroism along with the spoils of war being brought back to Rome. This wealth was comprised of the national treasures of their enemies along with their territories and lands. Furthermore, the defeated nations were then brought under Roman rule and an untold host of slaves would be taken to serve the victorious people.

The victory parade would be led by a marching band of trumpeters with the senators of Rome filing past the celebrating crowds. The vanquished humiliated army of prisoners would follow along with the spoils of war that were showcased before the people. Smaller gifts would be distributed to the crowds as the procession passed by. Then the victor would come next on a spectacular chariot drawn by four horses, followed by his family and his officers, all to the praise of the adoring crowds. The entire army would follow, marching unarmed to the thunderous cheers from the citizens of Rome. Flower petals would be laid before the feet of the victorious conqueror and his soldiers. The combination of the scent of the flowers and the burning of incense gave off a pleasing fragrance to the victors.

To the citizens of Rome, that fragrance would have represented the sweet smell of success. For the defeated prisoners marching through those same streets, it would be the smell of defeat and their soon demise. The symbolic picture reveals that our testimony of our Lord's victory is like the spreading out of the fragrant petals, which is the beautiful scent of His life. But to the realm of darkness and those that are perishing, it is the odor of death.

> *When you were dead in your trespasses and in*
> *the uncircumcision of your sinful nature, God*

> *made you alive with Christ. He forgave us all our trespasses, having canceled the debt ascribed to us in the decrees that stood against us. He took it away, nailing it to the cross! And having disarmed the rulers and authorities, He made a public spectacle of them, triumphing over them by the cross* (Colossians 2:13-15).

How did Jesus strip away all authority and power from Satan? He did this by removing the debt of charges against us, nailing it to the cross, and thereby erasing the debt. So, the Devil is described here as a cruel lender who has thrown you into a debtors prison leaving you languishing there with no hope or ability to pay the debt in and of yourself. But here comes Jesus who is known as the kinsmen redeemer and takes complete and total responsibility for the offense and the debt. Satan has no case against you; justice has been served through the cross of Christ. No case means no accusation and no accusation means, no power.

The defeated king and his armies would be marched through the streets of Rome as a public humiliation with the citizenry hurling insults and debris at them. In the imagery of that victory parade Paul is describing, Satan is made the public spectacle before all the ages as he is revealed in the shame of his crushing defeat.

We need to understand that the power of the enemy was eternally shattered in the realm of the spirit. Satan has been cast down to the earth, and it is on this little blue planet amidst this vast universe that he is desperately trying to cling to any form of power. He can only access power through that which he can reacquire from man. His propaganda campaign is in full force declaring himself mighty and increasing in power and strength, but it is all just "fake news" to coin the pop culture phrase that is used today. I cannot emphasize this enough: as far as the realms of darkness are concerned, it is not what is true that matters; it is entirely about what they can get you to believe. The risen Jesus is our conquering Lord and King and to this day, He is setting in order his leadership to manifest the kingdom of God on earth.

The Officers Corps

Every believer from the most senior and respected leader in the body of Christ down to the newly born again believer all have the same commission. The proclamation that Jesus is the Christ of God and what the Good News means for every person are your direct marching orders given to you by the Lord. That is how you take the fight to the enemy in this war and no matter what office you serve or ministry you feel called to, that commission is the same for all.

> Now to each one of us grace has been given according to the measure of the gift of Christ. This is why it says:
>
> "When He ascended on high, He led captives away, and gave gifts to men."
>
> What does "He ascended" mean, except that He also descended to the lower parts of the earth? He who descended is the very one who ascended above all the heavens, in order to fill all things.

And it was He who gave some to be apostles, some to be prophets, some to be evangelists, and some to be pastors and teachers, to equip the saints for works of ministry, to build up the body of Christ, until we all reach unity in the faith and in the knowledge of the Son of God, as we mature to the full measure of the stature of Christ.

Then we will no longer be infants, tossed about by the waves and carried around by every wind of teaching and by the clever cunning of men in their deceitful scheming.

Instead, speaking the truth in love, we will in all things grow up into Christ Himself, who is the head. From Him the whole body is fitted and held together by every supporting ligament. And as each individual part does its work, the body grows and builds itself up in love (Ephesians 4:7-16).

Once again, Paul uses the picture of the ancient victory parade to cement the understanding in our minds. Just as the commander of the armies or Caesar would parade through the streets of Rome displaying the spoils of war and small gifts would be distributed to the crowds that lined the streets, in like manner, the imagery is that of all humanity held captive is now God's spoil of the war, and it is the Lord who is distributing His gifts of conquest, to His people. The victory is that the way to the Father has once again been opened. The free gift of salvation has made way for the restoration of man's authority on the earth. The Lord also gave gifts of His appointed individuals that will make known to the church what He has accomplished, equipping them, that they, in turn, will make it known to all the world. The Lord's ministry gifts will reveal His heart and mind and help to ensure that the soldier of the Lord is fully equipped, fully trained and brought to his or her full maturity in the army of God. The subject of the five-fold ministry cannot be fully addressed here, but in using the context of this writing, we will touch on some key relevant points.

In keeping with the military theme, I would liken the apostolic ministry to the field command of Military Headquarters. It is from there that strategic operations are coordinated and battle plans are assessed. Those plans are then formulated and are logistically calculated with orders released to prosecute the war. The Greek word for apostle is the word *apostolos*, which literally means, to be "commissioned" or to be "sent out." Paul called himself a wise master builder and through the scriptures, we see that the commission can vary depending on what the person is sent by the Lord to do. The sphere of your authority could be worldwide or it could be solely to a given locale. Paul called himself the apostle to the Gentile world while Peter felt called as an apostle to the circumcision, which is in reference to the Jews. To one, their commission may be to restore a truth and return it to the forefront of their generation. To another, it may be to found a work or ministry with its scope of operation determined by the Lord. In the simplest of terms, it is a mantle to execute with authority, the Lord's command on the earth.

In the structure of the kingdom of God, the Father appointed Jesus as the first apostle who is the head of His body, the

248

church.

> *Therefore, holy brothers, who share in the heavenly calling, **set your minds on Jesus, the apostle and high priest whom we confess.** 2He was faithful to the One who appointed Him, just as Moses was faithful in all God's house* (Hebrews 3:1, 2).

Jesus then appointed his 12 apostles from among His followers and they became the foundation stones on which the whole building of living stones (the church) would be built.

> *Therefore you are no longer strangers and foreigners, but fellow citizens of the saints and members of God's household, built on the foundation of the apostles and prophets, with Christ Jesus Himself as the cornerstone. In Him the whole building is fitted together and grows into a holy temple in the Lord. And in Him you too are being built together into a dwelling place for God in His Spirit* (Ephesians 2:19-22).

The Holy Spirit, throughout the ages and to this very day is appointing and setting in place apostles and the ministry gifts to affect His work in every generation.

> *In the church at Antioch there were prophets and teachers: Barnabas, Simeon called Niger, Lucius of Cyrene, Manaen (a childhood companion of Herod the tetrarch), and Saul. While they were worshiping the Lord and*

> *fasting,* **the Holy Spirit said, "Set apart for Me Barnabas and Saul for the work to which I have called them."** *So after they had fasted and prayed, they laid their hands on them and sent them off.* (Acts 13:1-3).

In continuing the military analogy, the prophetic ministry is like Recon, Military Intelligence and Communications. The prophetic office differs from the prophetic gift that can be used by all for the edification of the church. The office of the prophet in proper function would in many ways mirror that of military intelligence in the field. They stay connected to HQ receiving information and orders and in turn provide valuable reconnaissance as to the movement of the enemy. They, like in ancient in times, serve as watchmen on the walls, keeping a discerning eye to any silhouettes on the horizon.

The office of the evangelist is that of a field commander taking the fight to the enemy. Just as the evangelist herald's the truth of the good news about Jesus, the enemy fires back with words of falsehoods against the knowledge of God. This warfare is a battle of words and each soldier enters into the conflict contending for the truth.

The office of a teacher would be likened to the officers who serve the same function to teach and instruct in the ways of war. Whether it is weapons training, field tactics or situational instruction, their role is to fulfill the mission and help keep you alive in the fight. In the US Marine Corps, the non-commissioned officers (NCO's) are considered the backbone of the Corps and are the vital link between the commander and his officers and the enlisted marine. In the unofficial NCO creed in an excerpt from Warrior Culture of the U.S. Marines, copyright 2001 Marion F. Sturkey, it reads:

> I am an NCO dedicated to training new Marines and influencing the old. I am forever conscious of each Marine under my charge, and by example will inspire them to the highest standards possible. I will strive to be patient, understanding, just, and firm. I will commend the deserving and encourage the wayward. I will never forget that I am responsible to my Commanding Officer for the morale, discipline, and efficiency of my Men. Their performance will reflect an image of me.

Few words would need to be changed to make this a good creed for use by any leader. Paul encouraged the churches that he founded to follow him as he follows Christ and those that have been tried in battle have the same confidence to ask those whom they lead to do the same.

I think in these military analogies the office of the pastor is going to be quite obvious to all. If the office of the teacher serves to train the soldier to help him or her stay alive, the office of the pastor is to care for the wellbeing of that soldier. The Army Medical Corps serves to provide both the emotional and physical care of the soldier. From medics in the field, MASH units in combat areas on through to military hospitals; preserving the life of the soldier is their primary objective. Pastoral ministry not only attends to the needs of the wounded but it also equips the saints to operate out of that same heart of love. For it is out of God's love that all faith and ministry proceeds in fruitfulness and power. The example of love that the pastoral ministry models to the church is the core message in manifesting the life of Christ. Without this, we have no message; we are just the unpleasant sound of clanging brass to those around us.

Identifying Leadership

There are those who have felt called to military service and have enrolled in military academies with the intent of making it their career. Upon their graduation, they receive their commission as officers; in the US, it is usually the rank of second lieutenant. Enlisted persons earn their promotions and authority by rising through enlisted ranks. They begin as privates and through merit and conduct, work their way up those ranks in peacetime and war. It can be a long process to move from the status of NCO to that of a commissioned officer.

As it relates to the church, rising through the ranks of the local church through one's service seems to be the common model. While it is good to build relationships with believers and raise those from your own ministry, we need to also recognize those whom the Lord has prepared. They are like those who are trained in His academy of the wilderness and need acceptance and integration with the local church. Good leaders are those who have hearts to develop and release other leaders. They are not threatened by another's gift, calling or maturity in the things of God. They are keenly aware that there are never enough laborers for the harvest field, which all the more provokes them to equip as many saints as possible.

Conversely, any leadership that exercises authority from insecurity or fear is not the example of leadership that Jesus modeled. People who operate that way tend to maintain their leadership through a spirit of control that leads to micromanaging at every level. This kind of leadership only frustrates the saints and inhibits the growth and life of the church.

There is an emerging leadership that serves with the goals that are presented from this passage from Ephesians. They are endeavoring to release fully mature believers who are grounded in the knowledge of Christ in both Word and Spirit. The fruit of which releases an army of the Lord, which to Satan looks like Jesus on the earth. When you do this, the new crop of leaders that your ministry has yielded will be the endorsing letter and seal to your ministry.

Chapter 15

THE EQUIPPED WARRIOR

The Lord saw it, and it displeased him that there was no justice. 16 He saw that there was no man, and wondered that there was no one to intercede; then his own arm brought him salvation, and his righteousness upheld him. 17 He put on righteousness as a breastplate, and a helmet of salvation on his head; he put on garments of vengeance for clothing, and wrapped himself in zeal as a cloak (Isaiah 59:15b-17).

In this prophetic passage, Isaiah wrote about the Messiah, and we read that there was no one who could stand in the gap to bring forth His justice on the earth so he decided to do it Himself. In His righteousness and salvation, He armed Himself with fiery zeal to take up the fight and take out His vengeance on the enemy. Jesus did precisely what this passage spoke of and unleashed His vengeance upon the kingdom of darkness. Now, being armed with His zeal and passion, we likewise carry His heart and message to the lost and plunder the enemy's goods. I wonder if this passage was on Paul's mind when he instructed us to put on the full armor of God.

> *Finally, be strong in the Lord and in His mighty power. Put on the full armor of God, so that you can make your stand against the devil's schemes. For our struggle is not against flesh and blood, but against the rulers, against the authorities, against the powers of this world's darkness, and against the spiritual forces of evil in the heavenly realms.*

> *Therefore take up the full armor of God, so that when the day of evil comes, you will be able to stand your ground, and having done everything, to stand. Stand firm then, with the belt of truth fastened around your waist, with the breastplate of righteousness arrayed, and with your feet fitted with the readiness of the gospel of peace. In addition to all this, take up the shield of faith, with which you can extinguish all the flaming arrows of the evil one. And take the helmet of salvation and the sword of the Spirit, which is the word of God* (Ephesian 6:10-17).

> *But since we belong to the day, let us be sober, putting on the breastplate of faith and love, and the helmet of our hope of salvation* (1 Thessalonians 5:8).

As Paul closes his letter to the Ephesians, he tells them to be strong and uses three different Greek words that all indicate power. If we took the emphasis of each word in its use, we could read it in this way, "Finally, be empowered in the Lord and in the supremacy of His might." If as His church, we would keep our minds stayed on His mandate, His message and His works, we would know the spiritual reality of the supremacy of His might. But what is all too often the case is that we find ourselves being drawn into battles on the enemy's turf and into an ambush on battlefields that we were never to be on in the first place. You may have the most powerful weapons in the arsenal of human history but if you are drawn into a battle where you cannot deploy them, your strength is neutralized. These are known as killing zones and the situation only worsens when you have to fight in unfamiliar territory at the place of the enemy's choosing. During the Vietnam War, the United States learned that although they had the most powerful military in the world, they could not use it to their advantage in a guerrilla war. We should no longer play into the enemy's strength; rather, be strong in the Lord and make the enemy fight on the ground of our choosing. That place will always be the solid ground of God's righteousness.

In Christ We Stand

First and foremost we must be in Christ, living our lives centered on Him and if necessary shed ourselves from the trappings of this world. We then need to focus our attention on His commission, which is the proclamation of gospel with the power of God in manifestation. Our warfare is not in the realm of this world, which Paul categorizes as flesh and blood; for our enemies are not people. Whether they are haters of our Lord Jesus, political opponents, evildoers or anyone who opposes our values, they are loved by Lord and sought out for, by Him. The Lord has appointed you with His physician's heart to reach out to them with the cure that will make them alive in Christ.

Paul refocuses the church at Ephesus to realize that their enemies are the spiritual entities and powers that bring their influence and actions to bear upon the society. These forces of evil are at work and are always anti-Christ in their propaganda and rule. They set their sights on taking down Christians before they awaken to the call to arms, and then, in turn, take them down.

After telling us to be in Christ and engage the rightful use of His power, Paul now tells us to put on armor. Not just any kind of armor, but armor that in his description, revolves around beliefs and believed words. This is not a war fought in the manner that earthly wars are fought; these are confrontations of beliefs against our faith by spiritual powers that inflect their rule over an area. They do this through the hearts and minds of the people caught in their web of deceit. The actions of the people will be the result of what they have come to accept, believe, and embrace as truth for their lives. It will lead them to act upon that belief and the depth of those actions will be to the degree they have given themselves over to it.

We live in a day where it seems that it takes very little to move from a disagreement into a violent confrontation. The reality is that wherever there is an erosion of Christian ethics and morality or where the gospel has not yet been received, it reflects a contention of that ground in the realm of the spirit. Whenever there is an advance by the kingdom of God, these principalities and powers will deploy an anti-Christ strategy from the moment that Jesus is embraced by a person, family or group. It is for that reason that Paul admonishes the church to take on the armor of God and be ready for battle on that evil day.

The Armor of God

> The night is nearly over; the day has drawn near. So let us lay aside the deeds of darkness and put on the armor of light. Let us behave decently, as in the daytime, not in carousing and drunkenness, not in sexual immorality and debauchery, not in dissension and jealousy. Instead, clothe yourselves with the Lord Jesus Christ, and make no provision for the desires of the flesh (Romans 13:12-14).

Paul tells us that the armor of God is the armor of light, which radiates the glory of the One who is the Light of the World. He then also exhorts us to be clothed in the Lord Jesus in the gleaming, brilliant white robes of His righteousness. This is not exactly the picture of a camouflage kit that will enable you to blend in with the terrain and operate in the shadows. But maybe, in a spiritual sense, it is precisely a type of camo gear.

If you wore your night vision goggles in a darkened house and someone turned on the lights, the effect would be an indistinguishable wash of light. So let's carry the analogy further. To the realm of darkness when you live your life in Christ and rely solely on His righteousness, you radiate an indistinguishable light of His glory. The enemy is uncertain if Christ is present and certainly wants no trouble with Him.

Now, consider what the opposite might be in the light of this analogy. When we entertain sin in our lives, it marks us with darkness, which obscures the light of God's glory. Through the lens of the enemy's surveillance, we send out a distinguishable image that clearly marks our weaknesses. There is no spot on the Lord, no shadow of darkness, so it is not Him, and the sniper then loads his round and takes aim for the shot. Paul uses the word provision to describe the giving of yourself to a sin. When you were born again, you were freed from the enslavement of sin. You have the authority and power in Jesus name to resist sin; for its appetite is met only if you feed it. That is not who you are, you are the righteousness of God in Christ. So do not allow your mind to roam in the shadows of darkness where you can be made a clear target of the enemy.

The armor of God has been described as light and in the passages that we will now read from, we will see that its description can vary. They differ because all of its depictions lead you to one clear point of understanding that Christ is your armor, so be in Christ. Each of the described imagery will lead you to an attribute of the Lord that can only be received by believing in all that He has done for us. Throughout this book, the definition of what spiritual war is always finds its root in believed words that are generated into actions. If the warfare is about believed words then the weapons and armor will also reflect that reality and that is precisely the case.

Loins Girded with Truth

Since the Roman army was the occupying force of much of the first-century world and therefore, the most identifiable, I will assume that Paul uses their armor for the exampled imagery. The first item of a Roman's soldier's kit was his undergarment called a subligaculum. To try to describe this, it would be like wrapping a towel around your waste after coming out of the shower and then folding it up between your legs and over your waist like tying a tie or an ascot. This was wrapped securely and became a protection of sorts for the soldier's waist and the lower loin area.

In spiritual terms, Paul refers to this protection and the securing of the lower internal digestive organs and reproductive organs in "truth." Some translations use the word "belt" in their descriptions, which is quite weak in portraying what Paul was describing from a first-century perspective. How interesting, that the protection of the organs that are vital for our body's development and for expelling the unwanted remains, also serves a role of guarding the ability to process food. Jesus is the Bread of Life and His words are the spiritual food that sustains us. Also protected are the reproductive organs, which in spiritual terms is the ability to spiritually procreate. The proclamation of the good news of Jesus is that fertile spiritual seed.

> *Righteousness will be his belt and faithfulness*
> *the sash around his waist* (Isaiah 11:5).

This verse from Isaiah is a part of a prophetic passage about Jesus the Messiah. He girds Himself in His own righteousness and faithfulness. Because of His grace and through faith in His righteousness, we are made righteous in Him. We must never be deceived into returning to a form of Christianity that resembles the Old Covenant in works and practice. The joy of the good news of Jesus Christ is sucked out of us like that of the air being drawn out by a vacuum sealer when we lose sight of the true gospel. Living under the accuser of the brethren's condemnation for our every shortfall is a sure way to spiritual impotence. Do not allow yourself to be neutered from the joy of telling others about Jesus. A glad heart comes from the knowledge, when you truly know it is all about what the Lord has done.

> For the law was given through Moses; grace and truth came through Jesus Christ (John 1:17).

We need to understand which covenant we have been born into and uphold the gospel of grace and truth. The very fact that Paul even mentions truth as a part of the soldier's kit is to warn us that Satan will seek to attack and quiet the message of the gospel in our lives. If he can accomplish this, he can make our lives spiritually impotent and, therefore, pose no reproductive threat to him.

Breastplate of Righteousness

The issue of righteousness takes on an even more formidable picture, as it is now the armor of our torso. Our hearts and other vital organs are covered with protection from weapons that could potentially evade our shields. The breastplate of Christ's righteousness is an armor that the enemy cannot penetrate. It is for that reason the enemy seeks to have you take up the shield of your own righteousness, which to the powers of darkness is like you putting on costume armor. Satan loves to draw people back into a lifestyle belief of the Law of Moses. Look what he was able to do to Israel by continually bringing them under judgment of the law. Jesus fulfilled the law and its requirements perfectly. The Law of

Moses expired on the day that Jesus uttered, *"It is finished"* and then died. The Lord rose from the dead ushering in a New Covenant that makes every person who believes in Him righteous in Christ. It is not about your best days or your worst days because His truth is unchanging. That knowledge is what destroys the work of the Devil in a believer's life because his weapon of accusation has been disarmed. If we believe the truth that we have been made the righteousness of God in Christ Jesus, then even in failure, we can quickly run to the throne of grace and get all the help we need from the Father to immediately get back on track. The attack is swiftly absorbed and the bruise heals quickly. There is no lingering threat of infection and you are quickly returned to your station to stand your ground.

This is not the case for those who try to stand in the battle in their own righteousness. When their papier-mâché breastplate fails them and they sin, they are fallen on the battlefield and writhe in the poison of condemnation. Over time, and after numerous repetitions of this scenario, they scarcely have any desire to get back into the fight. Cynicism is the scar that hardens the heart and the joy to proclaim the good news is in doubt because the Christian life seems too difficult to live out with joy. This is the cycle and pain of an unwitting victim who has lived under the heavy yoke of a gospel (so-called) of works of righteousness. Changing what you believe and by simply receiving the truth about His righteousness will adorn you with God's armor so that you can go out in confidence, knowing that you are well protected. Paul also describes this breastplate as faith and love, which speaks of what you believe and how you wear it. To walk in love is to walk free of the sinful life. That love will constrain you from violating another, and it always keeps your faith locked, loaded, and ready to be used; for faith works by love. Never take off this breastplate armor of His righteousness.

Feet Shod in Readiness

The Roman Caligae was a cross between a sandal and a boot. It had very thick soles that had iron hobnails hammered into the bottom of the sole for extra traction and reinforcement. Those hobnails would also prove to be very effective weapons against a fallen enemy. The leather strapping on the boot was designed for good airflow and to minimalize blistering making it suitable for long marches. The spiritual subject matter of the shoe is for war, but the result of its use, brings peace. The foot soldier will march into battle, take his place in formation and stand his ground awaiting further orders.

Paul is encouraging the believers to lace up their boots and stand ready for battle against spiritual powers. Those hobnails will come into use for placing your spiritual enemy underfoot while you proclaim the good news. Setting captives free and leading them to a true peace that is only found in Christ are your marching orders for battle. In doing so, you have plundered the enemy's goods; for his spoils are the lives that the forces of evil have enslaved.

The Shield of Faith

There were different types of shields used by the Roman army, but the most notable shields were those used by Legionaries. They were the large rectangular shields that provided full body protection and reinforced with metal to stop those fiery projectiles. They also had metal domes at the center, which was also used as a thrusting ram in close combat. I would think that this is the kind of a considerable shield of protection that Paul was picturing when he wrote this letter.

> *In truthful speech and in the power of God;*
> *with the weapons of righteousness in the right*
> *hand and in the left* (2 Corinthians 6:7).

I would have thought that the subject of faith might be more suited as an overt offensive weapon such as a sword, a pilum, javelin or spear. But here in Paul's symbolism, it is about what we hold on to in order to protect ourselves from the enemy's weapons. Like all our military kit, we are once again brought to matters of belief and whose words we believe. The fiery missiles of doubt, unbelief, vice, and fears are meant to move you from your position of standing in Christ. Numerous times in scripture God has described Himself as a shield for His people,

> *Every word of God is flawless; he is a shield to*
> *those who take refuge in him* (Proverbs 30:5).

David wrote these two passages about the Lord,

> *The Lord is my rock, my fortress and my*
> *deliverer; my God is my rock, in whom I take*
> *refuge, my shield and the horn of my salvation.*

> *He is my stronghold, my refuge and my*
> *savior—from violent people you save me* (2
> Samuel 22:2, 3).

> *Praise be to the Lord my Rock, who trains my*

hands for war, my fingers for battle. He is my loving God and my fortress, my stronghold and my deliverer, my shield, in whom I take refuge, who subdues peoples under me (Psalm 144:1, 2).

Our shield of faith is a person — Jesus. When we position our hearts and minds in Him, He stands in front of us, absorbs, and quenches the fiery darts of the enemy. We can place our trust in Him for our safety and wellbeing. It is a trust that the goodness of God far outweighs and is so much greater than the evil that the enemy has conspired against us.

The Helmet of Salvation

There is a continuity of thought as every part of armor and weapons provides an almost seamless pattern of defense. The helmet protects the head from where every action of defense or offense receives its instruction. Your sensory organs send the acquired information to the mind for processing and assessment, which in turn, sends out the necessary response. Any injury to the head can severely disrupt this vital link to the body's defenses and almost ensures certain death.

In light of that reality, the metal that comprises the helmet of the spiritual warrior is made of salvation. The Greek word used here for salvation is the word, *sótérios,* which implies that something is being saved or that salvation is being brought to it. This fits the descriptive role of the helmet, but what does salvation mean? The Greek word used to describe the noun salvation is the word, *sótéria.* The word contains multiple meanings: welfare, prosperity, deliverance, preservation, salvation, and safety. This helmet of salvation that God has provided for you is made from a metal that comprises all of those elements that make up this high-grade alloy for your protection. The enemy would like to inflict a blow to your head creating a fear that contradicts the alloyed composition of your helmet of salvation. Instead, focus your trust in the God who has provided you with the necessary protection for whatever need you may be facing in your life. Whether the attack is against your emotional or physical health, finances, or your all-around wellbeing, this helmet is designed to guard God's truth of His favor on your life. From that living hope, you can go into battle and appropriate whatever you need in this life by faith to overcome the attack of the enemy.

The Sword of the Spirit

The Romans used a shorter sword than most of their opponents in battle. This two-edged sword was designed for close quarters combat. A soldier would lead with his shield and then thrust with his sword. You are so close that you can look into the eyes of your enemy and see his every emotion. In like manner, the Word of God is like this two-edged sword. To spiritual forces, it is the unleashing of violence on one side of its blade; yet, on its other side, to the person hearing that same word, it is a message of grace and truth being wielded in love.

The scriptures are the words of God for the ages. The gifts of the Spirit in operation are the words of God for the moment. When both are working together, they become a powerful weapon to set the captives free because they reveal to a person the one true God and that He personally knows and cares about that individual's needs. When words of knowledge, words of wisdom, discerning of spirits, and the prophetic gifts are in operation, they speak directly into the here and now. They open up the hearers to believe and change their minds about God. When the power gifts are in operation they show that these words are not just more words in a world filled with words and opinions, but that they are, in fact, God's words. The operation of the power gifts of faith, healing, and miracles brings the Lordship of Jesus into that person's present moment, revealing the Lord to them. Now Jesus is no longer just a person of antiquity; He is the manifest, living God of the here and now.

> Brothers who are beloved by God, we know that He has chosen you, because our gospel came to you not only in word, but also in power, in the Holy Spirit, and with great conviction—just as you know we lived among you for your sake (1 Thessalonians 1:4, 5).

> For the kingdom of God is not a matter of talk but of power (1 Corinthians 4:20).

I feel I am not doing any justice to so many of these important subjects with these brief descriptions. The Gifts of the Spirit is one of those topics and there is much to write, but I am acutely aware that this book is not meant to be an encyclopedia.

It is from this foundation of His truth that we hold in our hearts, that we are given a weapon that offers both offensive and defensive capabilities. Furthermore, we can be assured of one thing: the sword is a weapon of war and in like manner, the Word of God is also a weapon of war.

Whoever acknowledges me before others, I will also acknowledge before my Father in heaven. But whoever disowns me before others, I will disown before my Father in heaven. "Do not suppose that I have come to bring peace to the earth. I did not come to bring peace, but a sword. For I have come to turn 'a man against his father, a daughter against her mother, a daughter-in-law against her mother-in-law—a man's enemies will be the members of his own household (Matthew 10:32-36).

The proclamation of the gospel of Jesus Christ is the weapon with which we engage and contend with spiritual forces. For every time a person receives Jesus and believes in Him, principalities are weakened, powers are diminished and ruling spirits have suffered the loss of one of their subjects. Their retaliation will be swift and often, the resistance will come from that person's family. Their attempts to reconvert them often lead to broken relationships within the family. Through this passage, Jesus is clearly pointing out that this is spiritual war. In other cultures and religions, a conversion to Christ can be a death sentence with the consent of that person's family. Wielding the sword is the preaching of the gospel in love and power.

My last thoughts on this subject are for those who deliver the Word in public ministry. As one that has through the decades sat and listened to hundreds, if not thousands of messages and teachings, I would offer this advice — It is apparent that a definite refinement has taken place in the area of public speaking, which has come with each new crop of leaders.

While this is helpful to the hearers, I would rather listen with attentive ears to those whose words carry the weight of having been with Jesus. Paul was a good speaker but when he arrived in Greece, he found himself judged as being a poor speaker because that culture made public speaking an art form. It was not the delivery of the words that broke through the nation; it was words laden with the power of God. I am reminded of the religious council's words after they had arrested Peter and John and put them before a hearing. They knew that they were unlearned fishermen, but they also knew and recognized that these men had been with Jesus. Let the true mark of your ministry be that people know you as one who has been with Jesus.

When they saw the boldness of Peter and John and realized that they were unschooled, ordinary men, they were astonished and recognized that they had been with Jesus (Acts 4:13).

Prayer and Intercession – Long Range Projectiles

A Roman soldier would also carry long-range weapons such as pilums, javelins, and spears. Where he was positioned on the line determined what additional weapons he would be required to carry. A soldier at the front of the formation would often carry two spears. The first one for hurling at the enemy and the other as a thrusting weapon as the armies engage each other. Paul's admonishment to the Ephesians to pray and intercede evokes in me the image of those long-range weapons.

Praying in the Spirit with All Kinds of Prayer

> *Pray in the Spirit at all times, with every kind of prayer and petition. To this end, stay alert with all perseverance in your prayers for all the saints. Pray also for me, that whenever I open my mouth, divine utterance may be given me, so that I will boldly make known the mystery of the gospel, for which I am an ambassador in chains. Pray that I may proclaim it fearlessly, as I should* (Ephesians 6:18-20).

Paul continues by urging the church to pray in the Spirit at all times. He uses different words to describe different types of prayer, which, unfortunately, are all just translated as "pray or prayer" in many versions of the Bible. Paul is asking the Ephesians to break out the arsenal of heavy weapons to repel the attacks of the enemy so the gospel can be preached without opposition. He then asks the church to pray that he would have divinely inspired words to proclaim the gospel fearlessly and with great boldness. It is interesting to me that as I read scriptures such as the fourth chapter of the book of Acts or early Christian writings on prayer, they were offered along these lines of Paul's request to the Ephesians. Boldness to proclaim the gospel far outweighed the prayers for personal safety even in the midst of intense persecution. Jesus had told the disciples that they would receive persecution on account of Him so, in their minds, it was a settled issue.

Praying in Tongues

It was Paul who made the claim that he used the gift of speaking in tongues more than anyone else in the Corinthian church. He did so because he understood its immense value in prayer and the recharging or edification of his own spirit. Your spirit is more in tune with the Holy Spirit than your understanding is in a given situation. So as your spirit is praying, it is accurately speaking with God about that situation. When we pray from our own understanding, we often add our emotions, opinions, and judgments that can frequently muddy the lines of communication. When your spirit is praying, your mind is disengaged from the exercise, and it keeps the intent clear of your own perceptions.

Praying in the Spirit is like deploying a precision-guided missile instead of using a conventional munition. Both are lethal, but tongues will accurately find its mark every time. Another important benefit of the gift of tongues is that it is like sending out your communication in an encrypted code, indiscernible to the enemy. The gift of tongues can be in earthly languages, which can benefit the hearers as we can read in Acts Chapter 2 or it can be in a heavenly language as in the instances that I am referring to. We should all challenge Paul's claim as to who prays in tongues more; if we did, the impact on the enemy's works would be devastating and immediate.

Petitions, Prayers and Intercessions and Thanksgivings

> *First of all, then, I urge that petitions, prayers, intercessions, and thanksgiving be offered on behalf of all men for kings and all those in authority, so that we may lead tranquil and quiet lives in all godliness and dignity. This is good and pleasing in the sight of God our Savior, who desires all men to be saved and to come to the knowledge of the truth.*
>
> *For there is one God and one mediator between God and men, the man Christ Jesus, who gave Himself as a ransom for all—the testimony that was given at just the right time* (1 Timothy 2:1-6).

I must confess that there was a time in my life that my prayer for the world and those in government was more of an indictment and call for judgment; it had very little resemblance to Paul's instruction about prayer. I had completely missed the Lord's heart and purpose that He modeled for us as our intercessor.

Today, unfortunately, many prayer meetings would be unrecognizable to Jesus or Paul as being a place where prayer is being offered. You might be reasoning in your mind by saying, "But Paul, you have no idea how wicked the sins of the people are or how evil and corrupt our government is." You may or may not be surprised to know that when Paul wrote this letter to Timothy, he was in Rome and Nero was the Emperor. Under Nero's rule, the church suffered greatly in persecution and pagan Rome was probably near its zenith for its debauchery. It is from that place of difficulty that Paul gives this instruction to his young disciple. He teaches this for the purpose of seeing that an environment of favor, peace, and safety would be brought upon the Christian community. The gospel could then go forth without opposition from the people or the authorities.

Paul continues by saying that to offer prayer in this manner pleases God and is endorsed by Him as being proper and good. He ends his instruction by telling Timothy to offer up prayers without dispute or anger.

Sadly, I must say that Paul's lessons about how we should pray are unheeded in many places and churches. Spewing hatred against political leaders and on those who do not yet know the grace of our Lord Jesus gives off a foul-smelling incense before the Lord. This is not the model of our Lord's intercession that we discussed in an earlier chapter and is not pleasing to Him. Calls for judgment align us with the accuser, and it places you within the context of the Old Covenant. Make no mistake; to judge will bring judgment upon you. Instead, cry out for mercy and mercy will always find you. If this mind would be in you and your ministry, I can assure you from the scriptures that your prayers, supplications, entreaties, petitions, and thanksgivings will be fragrant and pleasing offerings unto the Lord, and they will be heard.

The Prayer of Faith

When our hearts are aligned with the Lord's heart as it relates to people and not issues, we are now in a position to pray with maximum effect. It is then that we can focus on the Lord to be directed to what to pray for and how to pray for a situation. Intercession that embraces His heart and is spoken in faith will release His will on earth as it is in heaven. Those prayer laden words carry authority and manifest in power. When they are believed and acted upon, they release the creative power of God to be brought to pass into the natural realm.

> Have faith in God," Jesus said to them. "Truly I tell you that if anyone says to this mountain, 'Be lifted up and thrown into the sea,' and has no doubt in his heart but believes that it will happen, it will be done for him. Therefore I tell you, whatever you ask in prayer, believe that you have received it, and it will be yours (Mark 11:22- 24).

Words that are believed, spoken out, and acted upon make up our understanding of what faith is. Hearing it, believing it and living it, completes our portion of the cycle of faith. It becomes like a seed that is planted and then breaks through the soil, growing to its full maturity. The fruit that leads to harvest is the result of that process and it is the Lord who will complete the cycle.

> The prayer of a righteous man has great power to prevail. Elijah was a man just like us. He prayed earnestly that it would not rain, and it did not rain on the land for three and a half years. Again he prayed, and the heavens gave rain, and the earth yielded its crops (James 5:16b-18)

Elijah was a great prophet of the Old Testament; yet, the Bible records his victories and struggles as a man of faith. James says you're no different in your walk with God; for He shut the heavens from yielding rain in response to Elijah's word. James is basically saying if He did it for him, He'll do it for you. Do you remember what Jesus said of John the Baptist?

> *I tell you, among those born of women there is*
> *no one greater than John, yet even the least in*
> *the kingdom of God is greater than he* (Luke
> 7:28).

John was the last and greatest prophet of the Old Covenant. Jesus is saying that anyone, no matter how seemingly insignificant you may see yourself, you are greater than John because you live in the New Covenant. So be bold; believe for great things for it is the Father's good pleasure to give you the kingdom.

Standing in Readiness or an Army of Navel Gazers?

Paul began his teaching on the armor of God with a call to stand ready for battle. He was teaching those new believers about spiritual warfare with the intent of raising them up as warriors in the kingdom of God. I can't help but think back to another army that it was prophesied was to be raised up.

If we think back to Ezekiel's vision of the valley of dry bones, it is the rebirth of a mighty army of the Lord. As those bones came together and received sinew and flesh, they were then filled with the breath of God. Can you imagine that after all that had taken place to revive a might army to the point where they now stand in battle array, that they would stop, lift up their armor and begin to gaze at their navels? An army raised from the dead is not an army that is trying to reconcile its past. Instead it moves forward in newness of life. Unfortunately, this is a picture that is repeated often in the body of Christ. The enemy in all its rage stands before the army of God and while this is occurring, believers are trying to bring resolution to their past. How can an army that was once dead and is now alive, even consider such a thing?

> *I have been crucified with Christ, and I no*
> *longer live, but Christ lives in me. The life I live*
> *in the body, I live by faith in the Son of God,*
> *who loved me and gave Himself up for me. I do*
> *not set aside the grace of God. For if*
> *righteousness comes through the Law, Christ*
> *died for nothing* (Galatians 2:20, 21)

If you have ever had a conversation with a dead man (I am being facetious), I am sure his past would be silent except for what is found in the annals of his personal history. You are a new creation in Christ, your past died with Christ when you believed in Him. Together, you live a brand new life in Him and through Him. To dig up the past in a morbid belief that somehow you can make it better and deal with issues that Christ fully dealt with on the cross, is to miss the mark. The modern church needs to be renewed in the revelation of what happened on the cross. The past is not just the past, for you in Christ; the past is dead.

Paul the apostle held firmly to this belief as he set his eyes on Christ and the future that was found in Him.

> *Not that I have already obtained all this, or*

have already been perfected, but I press on to take hold of that for which Christ Jesus took hold of me. Brothers, I do not consider myself yet to have laid hold of it. But one thing I do: Forgetting what is behind and straining toward what is ahead, I press on toward the goal to win the prize of God's heavenly calling in Christ Jesus (Philippians 3:12-14).

We should follow Paul's example and keep our eyes focused on the challenges that are ahead. Stand in the readiness of Christ, and you will never be caught off guard.

Chapter 16

ENGAGED IN BATTLE

Timothy, my child, I entrust you with this command in keeping with the previous prophecies about you, so that by them you may fight the good fight, holding on to faith and a good conscience (1 Timothy 1:18, 19a).

In Paul's first letter to the Corinthians, we learned that all of the weapons that we are equipped with are infused and anointed with divine power. In their proper use, they will pull down demonic fortresses and change population centers. When that takes place, we call it revival, but it is in fact, the kingdom of God advancing no matter what the size or scale. Those fortresses that are being brought down are the lies and arguments that resist and war against the knowledge of Jesus Christ as Savior and Lord. The root cause for all spiritual warfare centers on this sole issue, and it will continue until every word and belief is taken captive and brought under God's rule.

> *For though we live in the flesh, we do not wage war according to the flesh. The weapons of our warfare are not the weapons of the world. Instead, they have divine power to demolish strongholds. We tear down arguments, and every presumption set up against the knowledge of God; and we take captive every thought to make it obedient to Christ (2 Corinthians 10:3-5).*
>
> *See to it that no one takes you captive through philosophy and empty deception, which are based on human tradition and the spiritual forces of the world rather than on Christ* (Colossians 2:8).

In light of these verses, Paul wants the church to recognize that the enemy's arsenal is also made up of words with a different purpose. Those words are to foster unbelief and doubt that leads to fear and every form of vice. We demolish those arguments with the manifest love of God in truth. We need leadership that will not confuse the order of the battle; we need to focus our warfare on proclaiming Jesus, which is in harmony with Paul's instruction. In our day, many churches have little focus on evangelism and place a high emphasis on social and moral issues. As noble as these causes are, the world sees this as an imposition of our morality on them, which results in a vigorous pushback. We need to introduce people to the Lord Jesus and let the Holy Spirit do the work of transforming a believer into the image of Christ.

If you carefully examine the ministry of Jesus, you will see that this is the example He sets through His words and ministry. The only people He continually found Himself in contention with were the self-righteous, religious of His day. He drew attention to their sins and that of the religious establishment because they thought they were righteous before God and held all others in contempt.

Think about that for a moment, Jesus could have gone through the crowds naming the sins of everyone and justifiably rebuke them all and call them to repent. Instead, He spoke about love, hope, and true faith and manifested it to all through His works. In John's gospel, we read of the Lord's encounter with the Samaritan woman at the well. He knew everything about her; yet, instead of condemning the woman, He commended her for speaking the truth in response to His question. When He told her all about her marital history, it was not in a judging spirit that would have driven the woman away; in fact, the opposite happened. He related the facts in such a way that she felt no scorn of judgment, and it led to a religious discussion about the Messiah. It is then that Jesus clearly states to her that He is the Messiah, which He rarely ever revealed directly to anyone. His handling of that situation caused an adulterous woman to turn to Him as Messiah and that very day, she became an evangelist to her hometown. A move of God took place in that town and it all began over a cup of water.

The Winning Strategy

This is why the Son of God was revealed, to

destroy the works of the devil (1 John 3:8b).

You yourselves know what has happened throughout Judea, beginning in Galilee with the baptism that John proclaimed: how God anointed Jesus of Nazareth with the Holy Spirit and with power, and how Jesus went around doing good and healing all who were oppressed by the devil, because God was with Him (Acts 10:37, 38).

If you feel that I have continually drawn your attention to the fact that the focus of all spiritual warfare is the proclamation that Jesus Christ is Lord and Savior of the world then I feel that this book has been a success. We are crying out to Heaven for revival in our lands; yet, our primary purpose takes a continual backseat to other things. Every changed life influences others with the result being that demonic strongholds will begin to weaken and become unstable. At the point when critical mass is achieved through lives that are changed, those structures will fall to earth. Then, after the hearts of people are changed, the Holy Spirit will begin the work in their lives from the inside out.

The kingdom of God cannot be imposed or forced upon a person as is the case in other religions. Only through the personal encounter of receiving Jesus as Lord and being born again does a person gain entry into the kingdom. We know this; yet, we try to legislate our morality to the world. As honorable as those causes are, from the perspective of the New Covenant, it is putting the cart before the horse.

Your Great Commission is to preach the good news, heal the sick, cast out demons and proclaim that the time of God's favor has come to them through Jesus Christ.

The Traditions of Men

In many ways, as leaders, we have embraced Christian philosophies that cause believers to move to the sidelines instead of joining in the ministry of the kingdom. We tell the church, "Well brother, there is a high cost for the anointing." There is — and Jesus paid that high cost. From the day you received Jesus, you were sent out with His commission to go into all the world without preconditions. People who are newly born again lead more people to Christ in those first few months than older Christians because their hearts are filled with praise and thanksgiving and they want to let everyone know it. They move in the anointing and God is with them with signs following because they have not yet been taught otherwise. When they are told that they haven't paid the cost as yet, and they look introspectively at their lives, they then disqualify themselves. Subsequently, another voice for Jesus goes quiet and heads to the sidelines. The unperceived subtlety of that message is that achieved piety brings the favor of God. In doing so, you have returned to works of righteousness to earn merit before God. To believe that is to depart from the gospel and the knowledge that it is entirely by grace through faith and not of works of righteousness.

The delivered Gadarene demoniac is an extreme example of a person being sent out by Jesus to go to his hometown and testify of the mercy and goodness of God. That man wanted to stay with Jesus and become a disciple but Jesus sends him out to evangelize his family and friends. He left with little more than the knowledge that Jesus was his deliverer and his personal testimony of God's goodness. The Samaritan woman at the well that we read of earlier is another example of someone going out armed with nothing more than a belief in Jesus and a testimony of His impact on their life. Jesus told the disciples when He sent them out in pairs that it would be the Holy Spirit who would do the work; they just had to obey the Lord in going out. That is simple faith in action but we in leadership want to complicate things with works of piety and recognizable spiritual fruit as the qualification for ministry.

> But because of His great love for us, God, who is rich in mercy, made us alive with Christ, even when we were dead in our trespasses. It is by grace you have been saved! And God raised us up with Christ and seated us with Him in the heavenly realms in Christ Jesus, in order that in the coming ages He might display the surpassing riches of His grace, demonstrated by His kindness to us in Christ Jesus. For it is by grace you have been saved through faith, and this not from yourselves; it is the gift of God, not by works, so that no one can boast. For we are God's workmanship, created in Christ Jesus to do good works, which God prepared in advance as our way of life. Ephesians 2:4-10

When you were born again, you took a place in the spirit of being seated with Christ. There was no earned requirement for that honored place in Christ to display His grace to you. You immediately became His handiwork and it is He, by His Holy Spirit who performs those good works through you.

Another philosophy that makes Christians feel they are ill-equipped and unprepared to go out and evangelize is that they feel that they do not have enough prayer covering. Therefore, they will be vulnerable to retaliation from the enemy. While there is some truth in these words, they are usually laced with testimonies of fear, which cause potential warriors for Christ to draw back, lay down their boldness and become apprehensive. Let's be clear about one thing, if people hated Jesus, some will surely hate you. The Lord has already told you of this in advance. Satan will try to stop the proclamation of Jesus and thus, attempt to quiet your voice in order to stop you from tearing down his works. That is why you have the spiritual armor of the truth of God. Put it on and keep it on! You will absorb and defeat every attack of the enemy. When Satan attempts to retaliate against you it is because he is more afraid of the powerful "Christ in you" and does so in the hope that you won't realize the dreaded champion that you are in Christ. Your prayer of faith is enough to bind any host of darkness arrayed against you and send them fleeing at the name of Jesus. The key is to be watchful in prayer without fear. As you do that, you will not be caught off guard or unprepared for any of plot of the Evil One.

My mind is drawn to the apostle Paul and all of the people who sailed with him and were shipwrecked off the island of Malta. Everything that Paul had forewarned concerning the voyage had come to pass and everyone knew it. Now, Paul is giving them the word of the Lord, affirming that all lives would be saved even though the ship would be lost. They all took courage, ate, and got ready for what would happen next. All were saved, and you can well imagine how positively all those people who went through that ordeal with him perceived Paul and his God. I am sure a great many gave their hearts to Jesus, which caused Satan to set his sights on retaliation. The people of Malta made a great bonfire for those 276 survivors and treated them all favorably. As Paul was gathering more sticks for the fire, a viper fastened its fangs on the hand of Paul. The people then concluded that Paul must have been an evil criminal because justice had finally found him. Paul merely shook it into the fire knowing he would not die from the venom of this poisonous snake. How was he so certain? The Lord had told him that he would stand before Caesar; therefore, he did not fear. He most assuredly would have prayed and then carried on with stoking the fire.

The people who were watching the unfolding drama, no longer considered him a criminal, but they were convinced that Paul was a god. This opened the door for Paul to proclaim Jesus to inhabitants of the island with signs and wonders following. This move of God happened as a result of the enemy's retaliation. Do not give place to fear concerning the enemy's backlash against you. Stay vigilant but be assured of this; the Lord will enable you to thoroughly punish the realm of darkness as a result of any attack.

I love corporate prayer and would never want to say anything to diminish it, but we have made a philosophy of strength in numbers that is contrary to the teaching that we see about the kingdom of God. I would rather be joined with one or two faith-filled prayer partners in full agreement in Jesus' name, than a mixed multitude of opinions, beliefs, and fears. Social Media posts are a great example of this when people put out prayer chains and requests during a personal crisis. Reading some of the posts of those who respond with fear-filled responses or critical judgments is hardly the atmosphere of the prayer of agreement.

We quote, "One shall send a thousand to flight and two, ten thousand" implying that strength grows exponentially as more join in the fight. The context of that passage from Deuteronomy 32, actually speaks of what would happen to Israel if the nation falls into idolatry; it will be the enemy's few who scatter Israel's strength. In Leviticus 26, we read that if Israel would faithfully keep the commandments of God; He then, would bless the nation and preserve it. No matter how small their numbers would be, they would still send their enemies to flight in battle. That was part of the blessing as found in those first thirteen verses. But, if they disobeyed the covenant and broke God's laws and decrees, her enemies would rout Israel in battle and flee even when no one is chasing them. The lesson to be extracted from this Old Covenant shadow is that we who are in Christ, no matter how small in number we may be can send to flight the armies of darkness.

God does not espouse the philosophy of strength in numbers; but rather, will choose subtraction if necessary to find true agreement in order to release His power.

God reduced the army of Gideon from 30,000 men to 300 warriors of like heart and mind and then proceeded to rout the enemy with them. Fear is poison in battle; it paralyzes clear thought and decisive action. It is also contagious, affecting the rest of those who are joined with you. Have you noticed that when Jesus was ministering He did not ask for everyone to join with Him in prayer? In fact, He did the opposite. He had an entourage of followers who went with

Him wherever He went and, of course, He had His twelve disciples with Him. But you will notice that in certain situations, He would only take Peter, James, and John with Him and would remove everyone else from the room or situation. The exception to this would be the situation with the parents of a child who was in need of healing or a miracle; they were invited to join Him.

> When Jesus had again crossed by boat to the other side, a large crowd gathered around Him beside the sea. A synagogue leader named Jairus arrived, and seeing Jesus, he fell at His feet and pleaded with Him urgently, "My little daughter is near death. Please come and place Your hands on her, so that she will be healed and live."

> So Jesus went with him, and a large crowd followed and pressed around Him (Mark 5:21-24).

> While He was still speaking, messengers from the house of Jairus arrived and said, "Your daughter is dead; why bother the Teacher anymore?"

> But Jesus overheard their conversation and said to Jairus, "Do not be afraid; just believe." **And He did not allow anyone to accompany Him except Peter, James, and John the brother of James.**

> When they arrived at the house of Jairus, Jesus saw the commotion and the people weeping

and wailing loudly. He went inside and asked, "Why all this commotion and weeping? The child is not dead, but asleep." And they laughed at Him.

After He had sent them all out, He took the child's father and mother and His own companions, and went in to see the child. *Taking her by the hand, Jesus said, "Talitha koum!" which means, "Little girl, I say to you, get up!" Immediately the girl got up and*

began to walk around. She was twelve years old, and at once they were overcome with astonishment. Then Jesus gave strict orders that no one should know about this, and He told them to give her something to eat (Mark 5:35-43).

You will notice that Jesus does not even allow His full team into that critical moment in prayer and certainly removed those who scoffed at His words. The Lord could have called maybe several dozen people at that time to join with Him in prayer. Instead, He made sure that those who joined with Him were of the same heart and mind on the issue. The demonic interference of unbelief will work to inhibit the prayer of faith. Even Jesus experienced the effects of this negative force while He was ministering.

Then Jesus told them, "A prophet is without honor only in his hometown, among his relatives, and in his own household." So He could not perform any miracles there, except to lay His hands on a few of the sick and heal them. And amazed at their unbelief, He went around teaching from village to village (Mark 6:4-6).

Well, you may say that Jesus did not require prayer assistance because, after all, it was Jesus doing the ministry. Let's read and see if the disciples followed the Lord's example?

In Joppa there was a disciple named Tabitha (which is translated as Dorcas), who was always occupied with works of kindness and charity. At that time, however, she became sick and died, and her body was washed and placed in an upper room. Since Lydda was near Joppa, the disciples heard that Peter was there and sent two men to urge him, "Come to us without delay."

So Peter got up and went with them. On his arrival, they took him to the upper room. All the widows stood around him, weeping and showing him the tunics and other clothing that Dorcas had made while she was still with them.

Then Peter sent them all out of the room. He knelt down and prayed, and turning toward her body, he said, "Tabitha, get up!" She opened her eyes, and seeing Peter, she sat up. Peter took her by the hand and helped her up. Then he called the saints and widows and presented her to them alive (Acts 9:36-41).

These dear believers who loved their friend Dorcas had enough hope and faith to call out to Peter for help. When Peter arrives, the scene is charged emotionally with sorrow and loss at the passing of this dear saint. So how did Peter respond to the situation? Did he have them all lay their hands on her or all join hands in prayer together with him? No, he saw that they were all too affected emotionally with grief and sent them all out of the room. Peter was alone when he prayed the prayer of faith in that room and saw the woman raised from the dead. An atmosphere of faith in prayer is critical to the release of the miraculous.

As you can see by these scripture passages, you are in no way inhibited by a lack of numbers in prayer support or covering from doing the works of God. Only, be sure that the one who is agreeing with you, shares that same belief in prayer. If there is no one else, you have "The Intercessor" our Lord Jesus agreeing and delighting to respond to your prayer of faith. I say all this with the full knowledge that there are few things I treasure more than those who faithfully pray and cover my ministry; I receive it and consider it a high honor. But be assured of this, even if you feel that you are all alone, you are never alone in God; for He is with you to will and to do His good pleasure.

Guard your heart and mind against every well-meaning Christian tradition that does not solidly offer the sure foundation of the Word of God. For it is the half-truths or our biased add-ons to the Word of God that make us vulnerable to attack. These things are the exposed chinks in our armor that Satan seeks to exploit in us, just as he did with Eve in the garden when she added words to the commandment of God.

The Battle Within

> *Beloved, I urge you as foreigners and exiles, to abstain from the desires of the flesh, which war against your soul. Conduct yourselves with such honor among the Gentiles that, though they slander you as evildoers, they may see your good deeds and glorify God on the day He visits us* (1 Peter 2:11, 12).

> *What causes conflicts and quarrels among you? Don't they come from the passions at war within you? You crave what you do not have. You kill and covet, but are unable to obtain it. You quarrel and fight. You do not have, because you do not ask. And when you do ask, you do not receive, because you ask with wrong motives, that you may squander it on your pleasures* (James 4:1-3).

Desire is always lurking at the door, but you are empowered to always prevail should you choose to do so. As we read in Ephesians, the armor of God addresses all of the vulnerabilities of our humanity in a fallen world. The difference between success and failure is in the wearing of the armor and being in the posture of battle readiness. That means keeping your mind on the Lord and then, He will keep you in His perfect peace because there is no peace when our minds stray from Him.

Peter and James tell us that the "passions of the flesh war against the soul." The lust of the flesh and God's love for the person in question are completely incompatible; one will displace the other. If your passions are for the things, which the world loves, it will be at the expense of your wellbeing in God. Staying with the war analogy: when we give place to sin, the enemy of lust rushes through that breach in our defenses and goes on a mission to disrupt lines of communication; it attempts to sabotage our supply lines in its earliest stages of the battle. Therefore, quickly close that breach by repentance and take down the enemy within your lines.

We have discussed throughout this book the tactics the enemy uses against the saints to bring about a fall. This knowledge is of little value if a person does not apply it to his or her life. There is an old saying, "To be forewarned is to be forearmed"; therefore, ready yourself to stand in the evil day so that you will never be taken by surprise. I think it should be of no shock to anyone that David, Israel's great warrior king, had his worst moments of moral failure when he was away from the battlefront. There were too many distractions and pleasures vying for his attention in the city, and it was then that he let his guard down. Passions are called passions for a reason, and they can become inflamed at a moment's notice. Be wise and know that it is presumption and folly to think that you can dance with your eyes closed at the edge of a slippery slope.

> *Therefore do not let sin control your mortal body so that you obey its desires. Do not present the parts of your body to sin as instruments of wickedness, but present yourselves to God as those who have been brought from death to life; and present the parts of your body to Him as instruments of righteousness. For sin shall not be your master,*

> *because you are not under law, but under grace* (Romans 6:12-14).

I want to draw your attention to the word "instruments" that is used twice in this passage. The Greek word is *hoplon*, which literally translates as a tool or weapon of war. In this sixth chapter of Romans, which is where this passage comes from, Paul is speaking about what the spiritual reality is for those who have died with Christ are now born again. For us to go back and entertain the things we are already dead to, is like changing sides in the midst of battle. To any believer that is an unthinkable scenario. In the light of that thought, let us guard ourselves in mind and deed, to only be used as weapons of righteousness.

If you do fall, repent quickly and be renewed again in your mind concerning to whom you belong and quickly get back in line with those you serve with. When you hear veterans speak of what it was like for them in battle, they strongly affirm one thing. They may have been terrified in battle, but they just could not bear the thought of letting their buddies down. During those harrowing firefights, they were not fighting for flag, country or even their own personal safety; they were fighting for their friends. Let us be of that same mind and remember that we have family and friends who are depending on us. Not only that, but we contend for those people who need to be rescued from the bondage of Satan's evil regime. Most importantly, we carry on the struggle of the freedom cry of our Lord Jesus who moved each one of us out of harm's way and took that bullet for us.

I would add here a word concerning those who are wounded warriors. It is time to rise up, be healed, and take your place in your calling that was given to you by God without repentance. There is an unimaginable grace that has been prepared for you, which the religious mind cannot comprehend; this grace carries within it everything you need to be healed and restored. You were a target of the enemy because of the threat you posed to him and you are far too valuable to remain sidelined and cast down. The Father gives no orders to shoot His wounded; this is a regrettable tragedy committed by those who think they are being of service to God. Worldly nations place medals on their wounded even if it happened because of a lack of good judgment on the part of the soldier. Unfortunately, the church has a record of placing a badge of shame on its soldiers but this too is coming to an end. The body of Christ is awakening to the realities of spiritual war and is showing signs of providing the greatest medical care through Christ the Healer. No longer are these wounded warriors discarded, but now, they are being loved back to health and restored to their destinies.

Shame is not found in the medical kit of the kingdom of God and so likewise, it should not be found in yours.

The Battle Without

I became a servant of this gospel by the gift of God's grace, given me through the working of His power. Though I am less than the least of all the saints, this grace was given me: to preach to the Gentiles the unsearchable riches of Christ, and to illuminate for everyone the stewardship of this mystery, which for ages past was hidden in God, who created all things.

> *His purpose was that now, through the*
> *church, the manifold wisdom of God should*
> *be made known to the rulers and*
> *authorities in the heavenly realms,*
> *according to the eternal purpose that He*
> *accomplished in Christ Jesus our Lord*
> (Ephesians 3:7-11).

This passage could well be the best picture of what is happening in the natural and spiritual realm as it relates to our warfare. As has been expressed throughout this book, evangelism in proclaiming Jesus to the world is the reason we fight. But you will notice that there is clear instruction on how to deal with spiritual principalities and powers. Paul writes that we are commissioned by the Lord to make known the mystery of the gospel to those ruling spirits. Why would He be telling us, the church, to do that to demonic powers?

The mystery of the gospel is to make it known to all the peoples of the earth that they too have been purchased by Jesus' redemptive blood. Satan and his kingdom only understood what Israel understood concerning the Messiah. They thought that Jesus was only the Messiah of the Jews, and they were quite prepared through their defeat to accept and concede to that reality. That is why we enforce to those rulers the unveiled mystery that Christ died for all and take the gospel to the nations to give Jesus His full inheritance.

Legion, Leviathan, and Jezebel

In many circles of Christendom, much attention seems to be given to demonic spirits, their work of spreading havoc in the world and their attacks against the body of Christ. These fallen spirits almost have a twisted renown among some Christians as if they are something to be feared. If Satan is cast down then how much more so are they? These demons have been cast out of Heaven, stripped of their heavenly identities and now are known only by an identifying trait of the evil service they offer Satan. In the scriptures, fallen spirits are identified as "spirit of infirmity," "deaf and dumb spirit," or "tormenting spirit" to name a few. Satan was Lucifer, a bearer of light and now he is just an accuser.

When Jesus met the demon-possessed man at the tombs near Gadara, the demons that inhabited that man identified themselves as legion. A Roman legion of the first century was comprised of five thousand soldiers. The demons were acknowledging themselves by their most dominant trait and were soon cast out and entered into two thousand pigs that were nearby. If you stop and think about it a moment, every one of those demons once had a name in Heaven and Jesus would have known them all individually. When they fell with Satan, they were not only stripped of their ranks, as is the case in the military, they were stripped of their names and are now unrecognizable to the Lord.

When we see names being used to identify spirits such as Leviathan or Jezebel those descriptions are given to them to describe in a word picture, their characteristics, and function. These are not necessarily even ruling spirits; for that is determined by how entrenched their influence is over a population. Their identifying trait does not even necessarily mean that it is one entity; for there can be a whole host of demons operating in that symbolized function. The Jezebel spirit is nothing more than a spirit of idolatry and witchcraft seeking to exert its control through any form of vice. The historic Jezebel who introduced the worship of her gods through her marriage to King Ahab of Israel gives the defining traits of that spirit. Leviathan or the python spirit seeks to choke off the life of its victim through suffocation. It does this spiritually through demonic oppression that seeks to cut you off from God's presence and uses a different tactic in the natural realm. In the parable of the sower, Jesus describes a healthy plant being choked because it is surrounded by weeds. The lust for other things, the cares of this life and the deceitfulness of riches are used to describe how they suffocate a plant and make it unfruitful. The python spirit at its root is the drawing of the believer into the snare of separation from the Lord in oppression and constricting your life in God through oppression and worldliness.

We should be careful not to give these fallen devils rock star status and then look for them around every corner in the church. This kind of elevated imagery only makes for paranoia amongst the fearful and becomes a distortion of the truth.

Antichrist's Aplenty

Do I even go there and discuss eschatology? For those of you who may be asking, "What is eschatology?" it is the theology that relates final events of history known as "the end times." Since I probably have ruffled enough feathers already, I suppose I shall add some more ruffling. The discussion of the antichrist takes many believers' thoughts to a person of superhuman proportions and extreme evil power. He holds a major role and is a central figure in the last days to many who embrace certain end-time doctrines. But is that what the early church believed? Is that what John and the early apostolic fathers wrote about to the churches? These images come from some of the popular end-time doctrines, which create some confusion as to the degree of Christ's victory and the extent of Satan's rule and power.

The truth be known, there are only five references that are directly stated as the antichrist in the Bible. Listed below are those verses,

> *Children, it is the last hour; and just as you have heard that the **antichrist** is coming, so now **many antichrists** have appeared. This is how we know it is the last hour. They went out from us, but they did not belong to us. For if they had belonged to us, they would have remained with us. But their departure made it clear that none of them belonged to us. You, however, have an anointing from the Holy One, and all of you know the truth. I have not written you because you lack knowledge of the truth, but because you have it, and because no lie comes from the truth. Who is the liar, if it is not the one who denies that Jesus is the Christ? This is the **antichrist**, who denies the Father and the Son. No one who denies the Son can have the Father; whoever confesses the Son has the Father as well* (1 John 2:18-23).

> *For many deceivers have gone out into the world, refusing to confess the coming of Jesus Christ in the flesh. Any such person is the deceiver and the **antichrist*** (2 John 1:7).

> *By this you will know the Spirit of God: Every spirit that confesses that Jesus Christ has come in the flesh is from God, and every spirit that does not confess Jesus is not from God. This is the **spirit of the antichrist**, which you have heard is coming, and is already in the world at this time* (1 John 4:2, 3).

You will notice that two of John's references draw attention to a person or leader with the inference that many leaders are the antichrist on the earth. A third reference that John makes implies that anyone who denies the Father and Jesus is an antichrist. The fourth reference has John implying that anyone who denies the Lord's physical appearing on the earth is an antichrist. Lastly, John speaks of a spirit of the antichrist that is already at work in the world.

Five references, all written by John, all with a plurality of meaning attached to them. What John was stating was that anything that opposes the deity and Lordship of Jesus Christ is by its very nature; antichrist. This means leaders and their governments, religions or any person who opposes and denies the Lordship of Jesus was deemed in John's writing as the antichrist. John also highlighted those who denied that Jesus came in the flesh, as antichrists. This was written to confront the doctrinal heresy of Gnosticism that was sweeping through the early church. A key component of that heresy was a denial that Jesus came in a physical body and was a spirit being; therefore He did not die physically. This falsehood and the teachings by others that Christians should return to the Law of Moses were the two extreme doctrines attacking the early church at that time.

The apostle John coined the phrase "antichrist," and he defined the meaning of this in his writings. Polycarp of Smyrna (69-158 AD) who was one of the foremost fathers of the next generation of leadership in the body of Christ also communicated John's words on the antichrist spirit.

> For every one who shall not confess that Jesus
> Christ is come in
> the flesh, is **antichrist**: and whosoever shall
> not confess the
> testimony of the Cross, is of the devil; and
> whosoever shall pervert
> the oracles of the Lord to his own lusts and
> say that there is
> neither resurrection nor judgment, that man
> is the firstborn of
> Satan (Polycarp 7:1).

Polycarp had no sooner passed than new doctrines arose across Christendom that pointed to one, diabolical individual as the antichrist, with many pointing to an evil regime of their day. The fact is, they were all correct as that evil spirit was and is at work in every generation. We don't have to wonder about when antichrist will come because that spirit is always at work on the earth.

All of John's references are still true in our day, for we see an ever-increasing hostility against the Lord Jesus from governments, rulers, religions, and individuals trying to silence the gospel. This demonic spirit has and will continue to war with the church in violence and deceit to whatever level people will come under its influence and act on its behalf. The past genocides of recorded history should serve as reminders that every generation can be prone to a new wave of violence against the people of God. In fact, The Center for the Study of Global Christianity, an academic research center that monitors worldwide demographic trends in Christianity, estimates that between the years 2005 and 2015, more than 900,000 Christians were martyred. We are not awaiting a battle; we are in the midst of battle.

Final thoughts on Eschatology

Lastly, as Christians, we need to examine very closely any doctrine that puts off the victory that Jesus achieved through the blood of His cross to some future day. This takes the "now' of faith and reduces it to the "tomorrow" of hope. These interpretations unwittingly disarm the authority of prayer to an uncertainty of which "day" or "age" they are in. Think about that for a moment; if you are uncertain about what has been completed for you in Christ, how do you act as it relates to the "kingdom now" and the "kingdom not yet"? Be certain of this, the kingdom of God is in you for the purpose of affecting the world — right now!

EPILOGUE – SUMMARY

Throughout this book, I have tried to limit the discussion of personal experiences in spiritual warfare and kept it within a scriptural framework. I have done this because many of the current teachings on this subject reflect a writer's viewpoint or experience, with some books offering limited scriptural backing or context for their statements. Often, a single verse or passage is turned into a theology, which at best should make the reader proceed with caution. Personal experiences and their interpretations of those expressed experiences should flow out from the reality of the context of the New Covenant. So often, I read of Old Testament paradigms being used as if they are still in effect for the Christian in the New Covenant. It is as if the absolute devastation of the enemy did not happen on the cross. Be assured, it did.

The Current Spiritual Battlefield

When God subjected all things to him, He left nothing outside of his control. Yet at present we do not see everything subject to him. But we see Jesus, who was made a little lower than the angels, now crowned with glory and honor because He suffered death, so that by the grace of God He might taste death for everyone.

In bringing many sons to glory, it was fitting for God, for whom and through whom all things exist, to make the pioneer of their salvation perfect through suffering. (Hebrews 2:8-10)

The act of spiritual warfare in our day is to bring into our everyday realm what Jesus accomplished in ushering in the New Covenant. We are to reveal what His victory has made available to mankind and enforce the Lord's victory to every principality and power. What has been completed in the spiritual realm must now be made manifest to the natural realm, through His church to our world.

The power and authority of Satan's kingdom were cast down when he lost legal right to hold mankind under judgment. Any judicial authority Satan held as accuser was cast down with him when Jesus took upon Himself the sins of the world. No longer can the enemy use the written code against man; this truth has disarmed him. His time is short, and he can only consolidate any rule through lies and vice to hold captive the lost and wage war against the church.

Most people have never heard the true gospel of Jesus and are unaware that a great victory was won on their behalf. It is like a poor man who had a wealthy relative who passed and had left that poor man a colossal inheritance. Unfortunately, he is completely unaware of it because he has not received the communiqué. That poor man needs to be told what has been freely given to him.

Satan can only hang on to rule through mankind in those who have rejected Christ and through those he can keep bound by his propaganda of lies. Those who have not yet understood that all of the rights lost by Adam have been restored to them in Christ. People need to hear this good news; this is the inheritance of Christ that is ours in Him. He who died left the inheritance to the one who would rise again, and we, through His resurrection are made partakers of the divine inheritance in Him.

Summary of the New Covenant Age

The victory of our Lord Jesus brought forth the advent of a new age that was and still is offered to any who would receive Him. Every gain the enemy achieved in the spiritual realm over the first four thousand years of biblical history was destroyed. His attempt to ascend into the heavens with his kingdom is now a tattered ruin. Jesus stripped Satan of all legal rights against mankind and has returned that birthright to all those who stand in the covenant that was cut with His blood. The Lord's victory re-established the birthright to those who believe in Him and they are as follows:

1. ALL power in heaven and earth is now bestowed on Jesus.

2. Spiritual death has ceased for those who have been made new creations in Him.

3. You have been made a joint-heir with Christ.

4. Intimacy and friendship with God are restored.

5. The birthright of salvation is restored to mankind.

6. Eternal Life — a provision of salvation

7. Deliverance from the rule of the god of this world — a

provision of salvation

8. Preservation, His safekeeping for you and your family — a provision of salvation

9. Welfare, His care and wellbeing for you and your family — a provision of salvation

10. Deliverance from every affliction of the soul — a provision of salvation

11. Healing for every affliction of the body — a provision of salvation

12. Prosperity, the supply for your every need — a provision of salvation

13. Jesus endows His church with the authority of His name.

14. Jesus releases His power through the Holy Spirit in and through us.

15. Holy Spirit is sent to be our help and comfort.

16. Holy Spirit is sent to be our teacher and guide.

17. Holy Spirit is sent to reveal the will of God for our lives.

18. Holy Spirit is sent to continue the works of Jesus through us.

19. You are a citizen of the kingdom of God with the right to an open heaven.

20. You are honored with the distinction of being a king, priest, ambassador, and son.

These are just some of the things that are now your privilege as a joint-heir with Christ. Each one of these listed gifts from His grace offers so much more when they are investigated with prayer and study of His Word. As with everything in the kingdom of God, they are accessed by faith. The same open heaven that existed for Jesus has been made possible for you, the believer through Christ. A portal to heaven is over your life and is switched on by the prayer of faith. Paul encouraged the Thessalonians to pray without ceasing and so by keeping your life in an atmosphere of prayer, it is like keeping the portal switch, always set to "on."

The War is about the Gospel, the Battleground is Always Belief

The battleground for mankind is the battle for belief in Christ. The battleground for the Christian is still an ongoing battle over belief; only now it is about believing that His words are true for you.

It can be said of spiritual warfare that at its essence, it is a propaganda war that is waged over the belief of mankind. The kingdom of God's airwaves are filled with truth, while the prince of the power of the air broadcasts their lies, presenting them as truth. Everything in this warfare always comes down to those words that are believed.

It was pointed out earlier that Jesus told His disciples to ask and receive that their joy would be made full. The Lord stated that without pre-condition, but we know He taught them throughout His ministry that those results are released through believing prayer.

In the morning, as Jesus was returning to the city, He was hungry. Seeing a fig tree along the road, He went up to it but found nothing on it except leaves. "May you never bear fruit again!" He said. And immediately the tree withered.

When the disciples saw this, they marveled and asked, "How did the fig tree wither so quickly?"

*"Truly I tell you," Jesus replied, "if you have faith and do not doubt, not only will you do what was done to the fig tree, but even if you say to this mountain, 'Be lifted up and thrown into the sea,' it will happen. **If you believe, you will receive whatever you ask in prayer"*** (Matthew 21:18-22).

Last Thoughts

I consider that our present sufferings are not comparable to the glory that will be revealed in us. The creation waits in eager expectation for the revelation of the sons of God. For the creation was subjected to futility, not by its own will, but because of the One who subjected it, in hope that the creation itself will be set free from its bondage to decay and brought into the glorious freedom of the children of God. (Romans 8:18-21).

The earth is in travail, and deep in your spirit (whether you are aware of it, or not) you too are crying out for God's manifest presence on the earth. We long to see the fulfillment and consummation of all things and it will surely come. That move of God that we are all crying out for will come, although it may come in ways that we are not expecting. But one thing is for certain; it starts by simply loving our neighbors by telling them the truth about Jesus. And who is my neighbor? Anyone and everyone in need is the definition that Jesus gave, and everyone needs Jesus.

In reading this book I trust that we have agreed with the scriptures that Jesus holds all things together by the word of His power. We can then conclude that the unseen Quantum realm, which science holds that this invisible atomic world is responsible for everything that comprises the visible world. Having said that, we also believe the scriptures that teach us that all things were created by the powerful words spoken by Jesus. He spoke and creation came into being and everything is held together to this day by His faith filled words. The authority enveloping His words were endorsed by and through the power of God and the universe came into being.

This awesome authority and power has been placed upon us His church and it is initiated by hope, operates through love and completes its assignment by faith. This is part of your inheritance in Christ Jesus; this is part of your birthright. You can speak by faith to any circumstance, physical, spiritual, emotional or financial and your words will go to work. They will summon the atomic realm to come together to create what your words endorsed by God are decreeing into the natural realm. In my minds eye I picture it like atoms coming together with every prayer and decree that is made is made by faith. The Holy Spirit has been sent by the Lord to indwell us and be the catalyst for God's mighty power to be released on your behalf to bring those words to reality.

Jesus said, *"all things are possible to Him that believes to Him who believes"* (Mark 9:23) and our Lord never exaggerates or speaks an idle word. This is truth for anyone who would grasp onto it and believe it without doubting that God will answer his or her spoken prayer of faith. As this relates to the subject of spiritual warfare we need to be releasing words as a decree in agreement with the Father's heart over our cities. Declarations of God's favor and blessing over our cities will make the environment ripe for a move of God. Spoken words of blessing and not cursing, life and not death, will create an atmosphere of faith to release the miraculous power of the gospel of grace. That is the horizontal attack plan. The vertical warfare is in binding the principalities and powers that seek to hold the people's hearts in spiritual blindness and darkness. Release those creative words into the spiritual realm and then watch as the fortresses of evil hemorrhage and give up the lost that they have held captive for far too long. The message in Isaiah 61 as found in those first two verses was the Lords' mandate and it is now our mandate as His commissioned disciples.

There is an awakening that is about to be released in the earth, rise to its morning and herald its good news. Blessing to all who love the Lord Jesus and read the words of this book.

Then Jesus came to them and said, "All authority in heaven and on earth has been given to Me. Therefore go and make disciples of all nations, baptizing them in the name of the Father, and of the Son, and of the Holy Spirit, and teaching them to obey all that I have commanded you. And surely I am with you always, to the very end of the age" (Matthew 28:18-20)

About the Author

T M Leszko has spent over 30 years in combined ministry and the corporate world. His current business interests are on three continents but his focus is shifting to writing and ministry.

He also serves as a director of the Noiva Foundation. The organization's chief purpose is to work towards a non-political solution for reconciliation between Israel and its neighboring Arab nations. In working with governments and the private sector, Noiva has found a willingness in those from both sides of the political and cultural spectrum to work towards peace in the Middle East. Noiva also shares a vibrant vision of ministry that provides aid to the poor in the Middle East and Africa. For more information, please visit our website at *www.noiva.ch*

For more information about this book or other offerings by T M Leszko please visit our website at, www.mergingstreamsmedia.com

www.ingramcontent.com/pod-product-compliance
Lightning Source LLC
Chambersburg PA
CBHW031218120726
47905CB00002B/376

9 780099 595202 7